Once the hot tide of passion began to simmer down to a warm, liquid glow, Marcel filled her hands with Naomi's dark curly hair and kissed her.

"Tell me again why we bother putting on pajamas," Marcel said with an exhausted, sleepy voice.

Naomi kissed her sweetly on the lips before rolling over beside her.

"Because coaxing you out of your clothes is some of the only exercise I get all day."

Marcel chuckled and put her arm around her spoon-fashion. Her nipples felt good pressing against Naomi's back.

"So will you go on vacation with me?" Naomi whispered sleepily into the darkness.

"After what just happened I'd go anywhere with you."

D1114249

Visit

Bella Books

at

BellaBooks.com

or call our toll-free number

1-800-729-4992

All That Glitters

Peggy J. Herring

Bella
BOOKS

2007

Copyright© 2007 by Peggy J. Herring

Bella Books, Inc.
P.O. Box 10543
Tallahassee, FL 32302

All rights reserved. No part of this book may be reproduced or transmitted in any form or by any means, electronic or mechanical, including photocopying, without permission in writing from the publisher.

Printed in the United States of America on acid-free paper

First Edition

Editor: Cindy Cresap
Cover designer: Stephanie Solomon-Lopez

ISBN-10: 1-59493-107-0
ISBN-13: 978-1-59493-107-9

For Stormy

Acknowledgments

Thanks to Frankie J. Jones, always my first reader. Your suggestions are invaluable and right on target.

Thanks to Martha Cabrera for the brainstorming sessions that help me stay focused. The more outrageous the ideas get . . . the better time we always have.

A special thanks to Freida and Abel Russell for sharing the adventures of Fireball. It was a moment I'll never forget.

With loving thanks to Laverne Bell. You have a way of goosing the muse right out of me. I need that more than you realize.

About the Author

Peggy J. Herring lives on seven acres in south Texas with her cockatiel, hermit crabs, two wooden cats and several chickens. When she isn't writing Peggy enjoys traveling. She is a recipient of the Alice B Award and the author of *Once More With Feeling, Love's Harvest, Hot Check, A Moment's Indiscretion, Those Who Wait, To Have and to Hold, Calm Before the Storm, The Comfort of Strangers, Beyond All Reason, Distant Thunder, White Lace and Promises, Midnight Rain* and *Shelter from the Storm*. Peggy is currently working on a romance titled *Forsaking All Others* to be released in 2008 by Bella Books. You can contact Peggy through Bella Books at Bellabooks.com or directly at FishstickRancher@aol.com.

Chapter One

"I never thought I'd hate the sight of a Hamburger Helper box," Cricket whispered to Marcel as she took a few things out of the refrigerator to make a salad.

"It's not as traumatic for me now that I'm older," Marcel whispered back, "but I know what you mean."

"What are you two talking about over there?" Roslin asked. She set the box on the kitchen counter and reached for a measuring cup in the cabinet.

"We're discussing the condition of some of these vegetables," Marcel said, holding up a tomato for closer inspection.

"I'd prefer there not be anything questionable in the salad if we can help it," Roslin said. "Will Naomi be joining us?"

"She's hosting the gay and lesbian teachers' meeting this evening," Marcel said. "After dinner I'll be going to her place to spend the night."

Marcel could see the relief and a silent "thank you" in Cricket's eyes. Neither of them liked the Hamburger Helper dinners that Roslin insisted on preparing after a streak of bad luck on a gambling trip. No one ever knew what to say to her the first night back if there weren't any winnings to talk about. Over the years Roslin's daughter, Marcel, had handled scores of evenings like this. Cricket, Roslin's lover, had mentioned several times that having her there for Hamburger Helper night made things much better for everyone. The three of them had been through a lot together over the last few years with Marcel retiring from the army and getting her antique shop up and running. Lately they had all settled into a quiet routine that involved food and friends.

Roslin Robicheaux had spent the last forty-five years of her life as a professional gambler. She was good at it and had made a nice living for her and Marcel. Cricket and Marcel had been best friends since the seventh grade, so the Hamburger Helper meals weren't new to either of them. Roslin always made the concoction each time she returned from an unsuccessful business trip. No one dared ask her how much she had lost while she was away. That particular information was never revealed, but now that they would have to endure a meal that came out of a box, it was obvious that things hadn't gone well with the cards. Marcel had explained to Cricket once that this was her mother's way of reminding herself how bad things could get when the cards weren't dealt her way. It didn't matter what they had in the freezer or the pantry when Roslin returned after a bad run of cards. Her first meal home from a losing streak had to be Hamburger Helper. Once they got this meal over with, things would be back to normal again in a day or two.

"What else do we have to go with this?" Roslin asked. She opened the pantry door and tied an apron around her waist that had "Life is too short to drink cheap wine" printed on the front of it.

Cricket washed her hands in the sink and dried them off on a paper towel, leaving Marcel in charge of the salad. She slipped up behind Roslin and put her arms around her. "I missed you," Cricket said.

Roslin leaned back against her and tilted her head so Cricket could kiss her neck.

"I missed you, too. So what goes good with Hamburger Helper?"

Marcel knew Cricket was refraining from saying what she thought at that particular moment since in her opinion there wasn't anything that could save this meal. Going along with Roslin's desire to fix a simple economical dinner seemed like a good idea to both of them at the time. Giving Roslin a hug, Cricket said, "We could pretend it's filet mignon and nuke some baked potatoes in the microwave or something."

Roslin nuzzled Cricket's hair and then nibbled on her ear. "Can you call them baked potatoes if they're nuked?"

"Sure you can," Cricket said. She kissed her lover and gave Roslin's butt a slow rub. "Nuked potatoes don't sound as appetizing as baked potatoes, but it's sure a lot faster."

Marcel cleared her throat loudly on the other side of the kitchen to remind them that she was still in the area. "We'll never get dinner ready if you two don't cut that out."

"Who invited her?" Cricket asked as she kissed Roslin's neck again.

"You did," Roslin and Marcel said at the same time.

"Oh, yeah," came the reply above their laughter. "That's right. I guess I did."

It always surprised them when they ended up enjoying a Hamburger Helper meal. It didn't seem right that something coming out of a box and looking totally unappealing at first sight could actually taste so good. Marcel reasoned that another positive thing about having such a meal was being with her mother again. Each time she went away for a gambling tournament, any type of homecoming was an event to celebrate whether Roslin had won or lost on the road. At least now they were all together again.

The other interesting thing for Marcel was seeing how her mother slowly transformed into her old self again once they had finished the meal. It was evident that for Roslin the hamburger preparation was nothing more than a ritual and some sort of bizarre punishment for coming home without much more than the original bankroll she had started with. Roslin was a superstitious woman and insisted on keeping up with her routine. In her eyes, luck was extremely temperamental and any deviation from the norm could only be viewed as tempting fate.

Marcel poured the last of the wine into her mother's glass and offered to clear the table and do the dishes before she left.

"You don't need to do that," her mother said.

Cricket laughed. "Sure she does! It'll give us more time to be alone."

Marcel looked briefly over her shoulder and said, "You two go into the living room and finish your wine. I'll take care of the dishes and be out of here in no time."

The three of them shared the six bedroom, four bath house that Roslin had acquired several years ago in a local high stakes poker game. The house was nestled in one of the oldest and most prestigious neighborhoods in San Antonio. There was plenty of room for everyone and they all respected each other's privacy. Naomi Shapiro, Marcel's lover, had her own home on the other side of town, but Marcel and Naomi spent nearly every evening together at either one place or the other. Naomi had chosen not to move in with Marcel since it didn't seem like a good idea for her and Cricket to have the same address being as they taught at the same school. While at work Naomi and Cricket went to great lengths to give the impression that teaching was the only thing they had in common. Keeping their personal lives under wraps was working well for them so far. All four women got along and were good friends. Even though Naomi didn't officially live there, she was considered an intricate member of the household.

The 1919 Tudor mansion sitting on two acres of prime real estate near Trinity University was one of the many assets Roslin had acquired over the years through gambling. This was her home and it was paid for. Everything else she owned was used to sustain her lifestyle and keep her gambling bankroll where she needed it to be in order to stay competitive in the world of poker. The house and surrounding property she owned in Key West had been lost, won again, and exchanged for so many other pieces of real estate or expensive jewelry that it was known throughout Roslin's gambling circle of friends as the Florida Shuffle. Occasionally, instead of money, she would come home with a new piece of property from somewhere around the world to add to her collection. Along with the Key West real estate, she owned condos in Las Vegas, Manhattan, Honolulu and Berchesgaden, Germany. The Tuscan villa, the beach house in Tahiti and the condo in Vancouver were holdings she seldom visited and had very little emotional investment in owning, so they were used more often to settle gambling debts when she needed something extra to negotiate with. Since she had acquired them that way in the first place, it seemed fitting to continue using those holdings for the same purpose if the cards weren't kind to her.

Marcel unloaded the dishwasher, put away the clean dishes and then filled it up again. On her way out of the kitchen she made plenty of noise in the dining room by pushing all the chairs in against the table, making sure her mother and Cricket knew she was still in the house. She disliked catching them engaged in some form of intimacy. After all, Roslin *was* her mother.

"Okay, you two," Marcel called from the foyer as she collected her overnight bag and car keys. "I'm leaving now. I'll call you tomorrow, Mom."

"Come and give your mother a hug," Roslin said.

Marcel set everything down again and went to the living room where she found her mother and Cricket sitting next to each other on the sofa holding hands. She leaned over and gave her mother a hug.

"Will I see Naomi tomorrow?" Roslin asked.

"I'm sure you will."

"Enjoy your evening, baby."

"See you both tomorrow," Marcel said. On her way back to the foyer she felt such a huge sense of relief to be leaving. She was no longer the one who had to help see her mother through a patch of bad luck. That had become Cricket's responsibility now. There was no guilt associated with leaving for the night, and Marcel was just glad to know that her mother had someone who loved her and would be there to nurture her back from the complicated highs and lows of a gambling loss. It certainly made Marcel's life less complicated having Cricket there.

Chapter Two

Marcel parked in the driveway behind Naomi's car and saw Juanito's truck in front of the house. That meant there were still a few stragglers left from the meeting. Opening the front door, she set her overnight bag down near the potted fern by the bay window. Marcel could hear Reba's laughter in the kitchen.

"There you are," Naomi said. She took Marcel into her arms and kissed her sweetly on the lips. "Steak or hamburger tonight?"

"Hamburger," Marcel said.

"Oh, I'm sorry, darling. How's she doing?"

Marcel shrugged. "Mom's okay. Not saying much yet. I'm sure Cricket will get it out of her and tell me more tomorrow."

They went into the kitchen holding hands and found Reba and Juanito, two retired gay teachers, putting away leftover snacks from the meeting.

"Marcel!" Juanito said. "Good to see you!"

"How was the meeting?" Marcel asked.

"Two new people came," Reba said. "That's always encouraging."

"Are they keepers?" Marcel asked. That was usually the first question she asked after a new gay or lesbian teacher came to a meeting. As with any organization, some members of the group were more trouble than they were worth, while others joined for the right reasons.

Juanito nodded. "So far so good. Two more lesbians. One a P.E. teacher. Imagine that. A lesbian gym teacher."

After the chuckles died down, Reba said, "He's just waiting for the perfect male Home Economics teacher to stroll into one of these meetings."

Juanito laughed. "Oh, puleeze. Where are the gay male coaches? Or the handsome Driver's Ed instructors who would admire my parallel parking skills?"

They sat down on stools at the breakfast bar. Reba and Juanito were on one side and Marcel and Naomi were across from them.

"I almost failed Driver's Ed in high school because the Sex Education class always had the car," Marcel said. She reached over and took a handful of peanuts from a dish on the counter. Naomi leaned against her in a rare fit of giggles.

"I ran over a scarecrow in my mom's garden once trying to stop my father's old pickup," Reba said. "I had nightmares about fleeing scarecrows for months after that. We didn't have anything like Driver's Ed when I was younger. That's what older relatives were for."

"Or Sex Ed either, for that matter," Juanito added. "If we had depended on parents for *that* kind of info back then, we would've been in really bad shape."

"I think kids tend to learn about sex from each other," Reba surmised. "I know I would've been horrified if either of my parents had tried to discuss such a thing with me."

"Same here," Naomi said. "All I ever got from my parents was 'you'll find a nice Jewish boy some day'." Her exaggerated New York accent made them all laugh.

"I guess I was lucky," Marcel said. "My mother was very informative and helpful when I had questions about anything—including sex. I felt comfortable asking her all sorts of things."

"But you don't have an average parent," Naomi said.

"Oh, don't I know it." She moved the dish of peanuts closer to Juanito. "How many male teachers are in the group now?"

"Three," he said with a frown.

"We'll get more gay male teachers in this group," Naomi said. "I promise we'll step up the recruiting efforts."

"He just hates being the only one who can open a pickle jar once everyone gets here," Reba said, teasing him.

"Eventually there will come a time when I won't be able to get one of those jars open," Juanito said, "and it would be nice to be able to hand it over to another guy instead of the closest lesbian P. E. teacher."

Marcel and Naomi walked out to the truck with Reba and Juanito where they continued chatting for another twenty minutes. Finally, they waved and Reba and Juanito drove off. Marcel and Naomi went back in the house and began winding down for the evening.

"Those two are something else," Naomi said. "They've been very helpful whenever the group needs something done."

"Reba's a big help at the shop, too," Marcel said. "Carmen loves having her there."

Carmen Morales was Marcel's business partner at the Antique Villa. They specialized in selling and restoring antique furniture. Carmen and Reba were lovers who shared a home with Juanito. The three of them were avid yard sale, garage sale and estate sale fanatics. Reba, Carmen and Juanito had so many things in common that it was rumored their neighbors kept wondering if perhaps Juanito had started his own harem.

"So the meeting went well?" Marcel asked as she locked the front door.

"We had about fifteen people including the two new ones," Naomi said. "We're working on outreach and helping the all-gay high school in Dallas. We've raised some money, and it's a cause we all support."

They stopped in the hallway just outside Naomi's bedroom door. Marcel put her arms around Naomi's neck and kissed her.

"I'm very proud of you," Marcel said. Naomi's passion for teaching was reflected in everything she did. It was one of many things she loved about her. Marcel had held that sort of devotion and commitment for the military once. She knew how wonderful it was to enjoy one's work.

"Thank you, my love," Naomi said. "I'm proud of you, too."

Marcel looked forward to their quiet evenings alone at Naomi's house. The pace was slower and the atmosphere was more conducive to intimacy and relaxation. When Naomi stayed over at Marcel's place, there was always a bit of a slumber party feeling in the air. Roslin liked to stay up late and talk over a few glasses of wine. That was the way she and Cricket preferred to unwind and reconnect in the evenings, whereas Marcel and Naomi usually liked talking over dinner and watching television or reading. Sometimes it was just nice to be alone. Marcel assumed her mother and Cricket felt the same way about the evenings Marcel spent with Naomi at her house.

While Naomi took a quick shower, Marcel unpacked her overnight bag and switched the TV on to watch the Nine O'clock News. Since Naomi had come into her life five years ago, Marcel no longer had to go through unusual sleeping rituals before going to bed. Having spent the majority of her adult life suffering from insomnia, it was a relief to be back in the Land of Zzzzz's as her mother called it.

After they had been together several months, Naomi wanted Marcel to go with her to pick out a new mattress. They went from store to store trying them out until they found one that was just right.

"I feel like Goldilocks," Naomi said as she wiggled around to get comfortable on the display bed. "They're either too hard or too soft, but this one's just right. How's it feel to you?"

"All this bed-hopping is wearing me out," Marcel said, "so they're all starting to feel pretty good."

"I like it."

"Me, too."

"I'll take this one," Naomi told the salesman. She reached over and gave Marcel's arm a pat. "You stay right here and nap while I take care of all the paperwork."

Marcel looked at the bed now and smiled. They had made many good memories on that mattress!

The bathroom door opened and Naomi came out wearing new pajamas. She smelled delightfully of soap and Passion perfume. Marcel reached for her small bag of toiletries before heading for the bathroom.

"Will I need pajamas?" she asked with a wink.

Naomi smiled. "Yes, you will. I like taking them off of you."

"Oh, my. Hold that thought and I'll be right back."

Marcel loved Naomi's playfulness and overall good nature. Their lives were filled with laughter, and they enjoyed many of the same things. They were in love and felt fortunate to have found each other at this stage in their lives. In addition, the living arrangements suited them nicely. Marcel liked having her space, and Naomi's need for the same was just one more thing to love about her.

Marcel was in and out of the shower quickly and felt refreshed and rejuvenated as she patted herself dry. The ends of her hair were damp as she ran a brush through it and slipped on her pajamas.

"The weatherman says possible thunderstorms tonight," Naomi said. She was sitting up in bed with two pillows propped behind her. The mere mention of thunderstorms brought a sense of anticipation and excitement to the air. South Texas had been in a drought for several months, so any sign of rain was a huge bit of breaking news.

"They're showing the Doppler radar now," Naomi said. She turned up the volume on the TV. "Wow. Looks like the Hill Country is getting hammered."

"With our luck, it'll go right around us," Marcel said. Sleeping to the sound of rain on the roof was something to look forward to.

Naomi turned off the TV and the lamp on her side of the bed. The bathroom door was open and the soft glow of a night-light near the vanity gave the room a romantic Thomas Kincade feeling. Marcel took off her slippers and got into bed. The clean sheets felt soft and inviting.

"Was your mom depressed or just subdued at dinner tonight?" Naomi asked.

"More distracted than anything else," Marcel said. She fit easily into Naomi's arms and took in the sweet, clean scent of her. "She asked about you."

"I'm sure Cricket will help get her back on track again."

"I was thinking about that earlier," Marcel said. It felt wonderful to be in Naomi's arms. "Whoever thought I'd be happy that my best friend was sleeping with my mother?"

Naomi chuckled and kissed Marcel's brow.

"But it was such a relief to have Cricket there to deal with all of this tonight," Marcel said. "You should've seen Cricket on the way to the airport to pick Mom up. You would think she'd been gone for a year instead of a week." Marcel sighed. "Whatever initial reservations I had about those two being together are gone each time I see that side of Cricket."

Naomi gave her a warm hug. "To love someone as long as Cricket's loved your mother and then to finally have those feelings returned . . . well . . . it's a remarkable thing. Cricket's very lucky. They're both lucky."

Marcel kissed Naomi's cheek. "So, Ms. Shapiro," she whispered. "Are you feeling particularly lucky tonight?"

"Every minute I'm with you I feel lucky," Naomi said.

Marcel slipped her hand under Naomi's pajama top and slowly caressed a nipple. "There's a big difference between feeling lucky and getting lucky, you know."

Naomi's light laughter was the response Marcel was looking for. They undressed each other and took their slow, sweet time making love. Marcel adored this woman and everything Naomi had brought into her life. She couldn't remember ever being happier and for Marcel, that meant more than anything else.

Chapter Three

The thunderstorm woke them up a little after two, but Marcel turned over and snuggled closer to Naomi before falling back to sleep again. When the alarm went off hours later, they both got up right away. Marcel made them a quick breakfast of coffee and toasted bagels with cream cheese. They watched a local morning news program on TV while Naomi nibbled at her breakfast and got ready for work.

"Wet streets will make traffic a nightmare," Naomi said. "I should probably leave a little earlier."

"Are we interested in dinner with Cricket and my mom this evening?"

"Sure," Naomi said as she put a stack of papers in her brief-case. "I'll come by the shop after work. We can fine-tune our plans then."

Marcel poured the rest of Naomi's coffee in the travel mug

she took with her every morning. With a quick kiss at the front door, Naomi was off to work. As Marcel stood on the porch in a robe and slippers, she breathed in the fresh, earthy scent of a spring morning after a rain. The grass and trees were as appreciative of nature's cleansing as Marcel was.

She tidied things up, made the bed and took a shower. While her hair dried, Marcel finished her coffee and watched another news program on TV. The Antique Villa didn't open until nine, so her mornings were a leisurely launch into each new day. Even though she had a business that consumed a good portion of her time, Marcel still thought of herself as retired. Having left a satisfying but exhausting twenty-year army career behind, she was finally doing things she really liked to do. Being around antique furniture, shopping for old pieces, finding something truly exquisite and giving it to Carmen for her to nurture back to life had never seemed like work to her. It was more like a hobby—a fairly lucrative hobby at that. Marcel reasoned that as soon as the Antique Villa and everything that was involved with its operation started to feel like work, then it would be time to give it all up. But for now she was satisfied to be semi-retired and somewhat of an expert in fine old furniture.

She pulled on a pair of tan cotton slacks and a brown tunic sweater made of soft cotton flake yarns. She ran a brush through her hair and checked her reflection in the bathroom mirror. The gray in her hair was getting more noticeable, but she wasn't willing to do anything about it yet. *Time to go*, she thought and locked up Naomi's house before driving home to see how her mother was doing. She hoped the Hamburger Helper meal and a night alone with her lover had put Roslin in a better frame of mind.

Marcel turned into the winding driveway and parked in front of the house. She got her overnight bag out of the backseat and followed the sidewalk to the front porch. She pushed open the huge, ornately carved wooden door. The house was quiet.

"Hello. Anyone home?"

"In the kitchen," Roslin called.

Marcel set her bag down in the laundry room on her way to the kitchen where she found her mother dressed in a robe drinking coffee and reading the newspaper.

"Have you had breakfast?" Roslin asked.

"I did. How are you today?"

"Well, let me just say this. That little friend of yours is something else."

Marcel always laughed when her mother referred to Cricket as "that little friend of yours." Roslin only said it when they were alone and Cricket couldn't hear them.

"You mean my stepmother?" Marcel asked.

"Oh, lord, don't call her that!"

Marcel could tell that her mother was feeling better. Whatever financial losses she had incurred while she was gone were neatly tucked away in the past. At least they had gotten over that disappointing hump already.

"Are you going to work today?" Roslin asked. "You look very nice this morning."

"Thanks. That's my next stop. I thought I'd drop by and see how you were doing before I headed over to the shop."

"How about I bring lunch for you and Carmen later?"

"That'll be great." Marcel leaned over to give her a kiss on the cheek. "I'll see you then."

At eight forty-five, Marcel parked in her usual spot in front of the Antique Villa. The marigolds she had planted along the sidewalk were full of color and life after the rain. Carmen hadn't arrived yet. Since moving in with Reba and Juanito, she wasn't as close to work as she used to be. Before the big move, Carmen had always been the first one to arrive each morning.

16

Marcel got out of her car and picked up a wet gum wrapper on the sidewalk before unlocking the front door. She loved the way the shop smelled when she first came in. The mixture of lemon oil and lavender never failed to make her smile. She kept lavender sachets in all the drawers to help alleviate some of that musty, antique furniture smell. To Marcel, the shop had a quaint museum scent to it, which was just the ambiance she was looking for. Old furniture didn't need to smell old to be authentic, but she imagined that a certain amount of mustiness was also good for business.

She put her keys in a desk drawer in her office and switched on the coffee pot. The front door jingled open and Carmen called out a cheery, "Good morning!"

Marcel stuck her head out the office door. "Good morning."

"Steak or hamburger last night?"

Marcel frowned. "Hamburger."

"Ah. Sorry to hear that. How is she?"

"I saw her briefly a few minutes ago and she was fine. Cricket did her usual magic last night."

Carmen wore a dark green pocket tee, starched jeans and brown work boots. Her short black hair had streaks of silver that helped give away her age. She and Marcel had served in the Army together. Marcel retired with the rank of colonel after twenty years, while Carmen had stayed in for thirty with the rank of command sergeant major. Their experiences as lesbians in the military helped seal a friendship that would last them a lifetime.

"I hope we sell something big today," Carmen said. "I have other pieces finished in the back that we don't have room for out here."

Marcel looked around the showroom and had to agree. There wasn't much space left to bring anything else up front. They needed room where customers could walk around and shop. Neither of them wanted the space to be cluttered.

"I'll do my best to sell it all," Marcel promised.

Carmen's laughter filled the showroom. "You say that every morning."

"The coffee's not ready yet. I'll bring you some when it is."

Carmen nodded. "I guess that's my cue to get to work."

At ten thirty, Cricket called. She was between classes. Marcel could hear kids chattering in the background as if Cricket were standing in a busy hallway.

"I just talked to your mom," Cricket said. "She mentioned you dropped by the house this morning. How was she when you saw her?"

"She was fine. Even offered to bring us lunch today. Why?"

"Remember how weird she always gets around tax time?" Cricket asked.

It was still March. They had a few more weeks to go before the tax crunch would be upon them.

"Yeah," Marcel answered hesitantly. "I remember."

"Well, something tax-related happened on this last trip. She started to tell me about it then clammed up. So our goal this week—notice I said *our* goal?"

"Yes. I heard that."

"Our goal this week is to get that info out of her."

"If she doesn't want to talk about it," Marcel said, "you won't get anything out of her."

"I know, but sometimes she tells you things she won't tell me."

"That's true."

"And it really pisses me off when that happens," Cricket said. "I'm her lover. She should be telling me everything."

"Have you been reading those cheesy romance novels again?"

"I'm serious, Marcel! We shouldn't be keeping secrets from each other. I've told her enough stuff about me to fill the

Smithsonian. It gets me all whacked out when she doesn't do the same."

"It's not fair to blame my mother for you being whacked out, as you call it. You've been whacked out ever since I've known you."

"Why do I bother with either of you?"

"Why?" Marcel repeated. "Because you adore the Robicheaux women. We're irresistible, and if we make you all whacked out, then so be it."

There was silence on the other end of the phone. Finally, Cricket said, "Oh, you think you're so smart." Then she began to laugh. "But you're right, and you know how much I hate that, too."

"What? Me being right?" Marcel teased.

"Yes. You being right. Hey, I have to go. Just remember what I said. She's stewing over something to do with taxes. See what you can get out of her."

Marcel closed her cell phone and shook her head. Being stuck in the middle of communication problems between them wasn't where Marcel wanted to be, but if her mother was experiencing the usual upcoming April 15 income tax anxiety, perhaps there was something she could do to help.

Marcel went to fix Ralph, the mailman, some coffee as soon as she saw his truck pull into the parking lot. The Antique Villa was one of his daily bathroom stops. He was a cousin of Carmen's and used his daily unofficial break to catch up on family gossip when they all had time to chat.

"Wasn't that rain great last night?" Ralph asked. The door jingled closed behind him.

"It certainly was," Marcel said. She stuck her head in the workshop to let Carmen know he was there.

"That first clap of thunder brought four shaking dogs on my

bed," he said. "My wife and I didn't get much sleep after that."

Carmen came in from the back with protective eyewear perched on top of her head and traces of sawdust in her hair. Marcel shuffled through the mail while the cousins talked about an older relative who had just purchased a motorcycle.

"He wants to ride it to Atlanta!" Ralph said incredulously. "I asked him if he meant Atlanta *Street* or the real Atlanta."

Marcel chuckled at hearing their hearty laughter. "How old is he?" she asked.

"Eighty-three," Carmen said. "Still in great shape, too."

"He's going for his license today," Ralph added.

"Well, good for him," Marcel said. "I'm sure it's great having something like that to plan for and look forward to."

"I'll tell you what he can look forward to," Ralph said. He poked a finger up and began to count. "Broken bones. Getting lost. Bugs in his teeth—"

"He can just take his teeth out, wipe 'em off with one hand and pop 'em back in and keep on riding," Carmen said. As she ran a hand through her hair, she found the safety goggles perched on top of her head. "Well, damn. I've been looking for these."

Marcel opened an envelope containing the electric bill.

"When I'm his age," Ralph said, "all I wanna worry about is getting up every morning."

"That's it?" Marcel asked. "Waking up to see if you're still with us?"

"At eighty-three I imagine that'll be a major accomplishment on its own," he said.

"This motorcycle might just be what he needs to keep him going ten or twenty more years," Marcel reminded them.

Ralph held up his fingers again. "Broken bones. Getting lost. Bugs in his teeth—"

"All I know is," Carmen said, "when he's out riding that thing, someone better call and tell me where he's going so I'm not anywhere near that particular part of town."

Ralph and Carmen enjoyed another laugh together.

"You two should be proud of him for having enough energy to do something he wants to do. None of us are going to live forever. We should all be making the most of whatever time we have left here. I admire this man for what he's doing."

Ralph sipped his coffee. "You're probably right, but a motorcycle? At eighty-three? Why not take up canasta or gardening?"

"Maybe he won't pass the test," Carmen said hopefully.

"As stubborn as he is, he'll keep taking it until he passes," Ralph said. "Or ride without a license. Some of his kids and grandkids think it's great."

"So do I," Marcel added.

"My cousin Laverne even rides with him sometimes," Carmen said. "She went with him to buy his bike."

"Laverne?" Marcel repeated. "Our tax attorney Laverne?"

"That's the one!" Carmen said.

"Wow. She rides a motorcycle?"

"She's got one that's bigger than some battleships I've seen," Carmen said. "When those two get together that's all they talk about now."

"Maybe he won't pass the test," Ralph said.

Marcel opened another envelope and slowly took out the water bill. "When he passes this test—"

"Did you hear that?" Carmen asked her cousin. "She said *when* he passes the test. Not *if* he passes the test. *Ay carrumba.*"

"He'll pass it," Ralph said.

"*When* he passes the test," Marcel continued, "someone should throw him a little party and wish him well."

Carmen and Ralph looked at her for a moment to see if she was serious. Finally, Carmen grunted and mumbled, "*Ay carrumba,*" again under her breath.

Chapter Four

Several hours later the door jingled open and Marcel looked up from the check she was writing. Her mother had arrived with lunch for them as promised.

"How's business today?" Roslin asked. She set two large white paper bags down on the counter. Marcel got a brief whiff of something nice and oniony.

"We sold a small table and a bookcase already," Marcel said. "So far so good."

"What are you doing?"

"Paying bills." Marcel finished writing the check for the shop's electric bill and stuck it in the envelope.

"You can do that online, you know," Roslin said. "It's easier and cheaper. No postage."

Marcel looked at her mother with a flicker of surprise. "I know, but I prefer doing it this way."

Roslin opened the door to the workshop to tell Carmen lunch had arrived. Rummaging through the small refrigerator in Marcel's office, she came back with three cans of soda.

"What are we having?" Marcel asked. "It smells wonderful."

Carmen sniffed a few times on her way to the bathroom to wash her hands. "Cheese enchiladas."

Roslin cleared a place on the counter and pulled up two more stools. "We're having tortilla soup and cheese enchilada plates," she announced.

"See?" Carmen said as she dried her hands on a paper towel. "You can't slip enchiladas past this Mexican."

After they all got settled, Marcel wrote one more check for the shop's water bill. Roslin popped the lids off three containers of tortilla soup and passed out plastic spoons and napkins.

"How do you pay bills?" Roslin asked Carmen. "Writing checks or online?"

"Online," Carmen said. "It's easier and cheaper. I hear stamps are going up again soon. Can you believe that?"

"How do you know so much about doing anything online?" Marcel asked her mother. "I've never even seen you on a computer."

"Cricket's teaching me," Roslin said proudly. "She pays all our household bills online." She got the three large Styrofoam containers out of the other bag and passed them around. "So what's up with this check-writing thing? It's not like you to be so traditional about stuff like this."

"What?" Carmen said. "Did you just hear yourself?" She nodded toward Marcel. "Little Miss West Point graduate here? Not traditional?"

With a slightly puzzled expression Roslin said, "You're right. What was I thinking?"

"Cut it out, you two," Marcel said. "All these virtual money dealings just don't appeal to me. I like holding the checkbook and writing a check. It feels like I have more control of my money this way."

"They'd probably even let you go to the bank and visit all your money if you asked them nicely," Roslin said with a wink.

Marcel arched a brow at their boisterous laughter and chose not to engage in more of this discussion. After a while, Carmen asked when Marcel was going on another buying spree.

"We're getting low on inventory in the back," Carmen said. "I'll be needing more pieces to work on soon."

"I'll look around and see if any out-of-town auctions are coming up."

"I might like to go with you," Roslin said. "It's such a hoot watching you wheel, deal and finagle with those people."

Carmen nodded. "I know what you mean. I've seen her in action, too."

"I'll need the truck," Marcel reminded her, "so if we sell something big while I'm gone, you'll have to make other arrangements to get it delivered." Going on a buying trip with her mother would be fun, she decided. It had been quite awhile since they had done it.

"Naomi's bringing the steaks," Cricket said as she set the grocery bag down on the kitchen table. "Hey, check out these cute little vegetables I found for the grill."

Marcel emptied the dishwasher while her mother wiped the dust off a wine bottle she had just retrieved from the wine cellar.

"I've been saving this one for a special occasion," Roslin said.

"What's the occasion?" Marcel asked.

"We're all having a nice dinner together. That's special enough for me."

Marcel didn't bother reminding her that they had dinner together nearly every evening.

"Look at these!" Cricket said. She pulled a package crammed full of small zucchini, yellow squash, asparagus and mushrooms from the grocery bag. "I got some corn on the cob too, but those are regular size." Handing the package of tiny vegetables and the corn to Marcel, Cricket said, "I'll get the fire going while you figure out a way to keep these smaller things from falling through the grill when we cook them."

"Great," Marcel muttered. Cricket's fleeting moment of genius and vegetable-buying luck had suddenly become Marcel's cooking problem to solve.

"I saw that look," Cricket said. "Just make a little boat out of aluminum foil and put some butter in it. I swear, Marcel. Didn't the army teach you anything?"

"I think you're confusing the United States Army with a Girl Scout merit badge project," Marcel said dryly. She reached in the cabinet for the foil and tore off a large piece. Cricket had the tiny vegetables out of their package and was washing them in the sink.

"Do you know the difference between the army and the Girl Scouts?" Cricket asked no one in particular. "With the Girl Scouts you have adult leadership," she said before the other two could answer.

Marcel ignored their laughter and made what she thought looked like a nice square boat just right for the miniature vegetables. Naomi came into the kitchen with grocery bags of her own. She gave Marcel a quick kiss on the lips and had a hug for Roslin.

"Good to have you home again," Naomi said as she set the bags on the counter.

"It's good to be here," Roslin said. "Let's see those steaks. Oh! And you bought garlic bread. This is already turning into a fine meal."

After dinner Marcel and Naomi were alone in the kitchen doing the dishes. "Those little veggies were quite tasty," Naomi said.

"Must've been that aluminum boat they were sizzling in."

Marcel put the last dirty plate in the dishwasher and got it going. She poured two cups of fresh decaf coffee and followed Naomi out of the kitchen and into the living room where Roslin and Cricket were relaxing with what was left of the wine.

"This is always my favorite part of the day," Roslin said. "Chillin' with the girls." She took a sip from her wineglass. "Marcel and I will be going on a buying trip soon. Did she tell you?"

"Really?" Cricket said. "When?"

"I'm not sure," Roslin said. "When are we leaving?"

"In a few days," Marcel said. "I have some calls to make first. I've got friends in Fort Worth and Dallas who know what I'm looking for. They can have some nice pieces for us to select from if I give them enough notice."

"Did you sell anything today?" Naomi asked.

"We had a good day, actually," Marcel said. "A woman and her young granddaughter came in just before we were ready to close. The little girl was really cute." Marcel started to laugh. She looked directly at her mother and said, "She had an imaginary friend. The grandmother was quite amused by the whole thing."

Roslin held her wineglass and smiled. "Fireball," she said quietly.

"Yes. It reminded me of Fireball."

For a moment they were both lost in thought. Finally, Cricket asked, "What or who is Fireball?"

Marcel met her mother's gaze again and gave her a slight nod as if acknowledging permission to relay the story. Roslin cleared her throat and began to speak quietly.

"Fireball was a little dragon and just happened to be my daughter's best friend." She looked up at Marcel. "How old were you when Fireball first appeared? Four? Five?"

"About four, I guess."

"He could fly and he breathed fire," Roslin said. "The whole bit. He went everywhere with us."

Cricket and Naomi were now looking at Marcel expectantly, as if more details were needed.

"Why haven't I ever heard about Fireball?" Cricket asked. "I thought I knew all there was to know about you."

"Apparently not," Marcel said. It was nice knowing there was still *some* mystery left about her.

"I remember one time . . . " Roslin said.

"Okay, here we go," Marcel mumbled with a playful eye roll. The other three chuckled.

"I remember one time," Roslin said again, sipping her wine. "Now keep in mind that Fireball was with us twenty-four seven. He was there when Marcel went to sleep at night and he was there when she woke up every morning. She talked to him all day long and felt comforted by his presence. He became part of our lives."

"How big was he?" Naomi asked, fascinated.

"Did he have his own plate at the table?" Cricket asked.

"He was a small dragon," Marcel explained.

"I remember feeling like such a failure as a mother," Roslin said. "Then I did some research on it. I read a lot about raising kids in those days. Having an imaginary friend is quite normal. Lots of kids do that sort of thing." Roslin took another sip of wine. "But I remember one time we were in a hurry. There was a local poker game with some high stakes involved. I had gone to the store and picked up a few things and we were on our way back home, when all of a sudden, Marcel decides that Fireball is missing. Apparently we'd left him behind at the store."

By now everyone was laughing.

"I've got milk and ice cream in the car," Roslin said, "and we're about three blocks from home. I still needed to get dressed and Marcel is crying. 'We left Fireball at the store!' At first I pretended not to hear her, but that wasn't working. You can imagine my frustration."

"Oh, my," Naomi said. She reached over and took Marcel's hand.

"I remember saying, 'Are you sure? He's gotta be in the car somewhere.' But did that line of reasoning work? Noooo! She kept crying and saying, 'We left Fireball at the store!'" Roslin leaned forward a little. "I then tried using some dragon logic on her. She's a kid. I'm the adult. I think I'm smarter than her. So I said, 'He's got wings, right? He's probably waiting for us at home already.'"

"Oh, that was good," Cricket said.

"Did it work?" Naomi asked.

"Hell no, it didn't work! She cried even harder then. 'He's got little wings! He can't fly that far!'" Roslin wailed, making them all laugh again.

"Was that the end of Fireball?" Cricket asked. "He's still flying around in a Kroger's somewhere forty years later?"

"Not at all," Marcel said. An unexpected sense of pride, love and admiration filled her heart as she looked at her mother. "She turned the car around and drove back to the store."

"You did?" Cricket asked, surprised. More laughter filled the room.

"Well, I'm impressed," Naomi said. "What happened when you got there?"

"As soon as I turned around, she stopped crying," Roslin said. "Let me just interject here that Marcel was not a whiny child. Between the two of us I was always the whiny one, so if leaving Fireball behind was enough to make her cry, I knew it was serious, no matter what else I had to do or where I needed to be. So anyway, I pull up in front of the store and Marcel is craning her neck looking for him. I said, 'Do you see him anywhere?' and I'm thinking *if I have to park this car and go inside that store . . .*"

Once again the laughter got the best of them. Roslin took another sip of wine and continued.

"Finally, she says, 'There he is!' and I'm letting out a giant sigh of relief." Roslin bent her head and studied her hands.

"Then she told me to open the car door," Marcel said. "I was just so happy to see him."

"*See* him?" Cricket said with a raised brow.

Roslin chuckled. "Once the door was open I remember saying, 'Fireball, *get* in this car!' Then after a moment the door closed. I asked her if he was in and she said yes, so back home we went."

"What a great story," Naomi said.

"What a little weirdo you were," Cricket said to Marcel.

"Did I ever thank you for going back for him?" Marcel asked her mother.

"I don't remember. You stopped crying. That was the important thing."

"So whatever happened to Fireball?" Naomi asked.

Suddenly, all eyes were on Marcel. With a little shrug she said, "One day he told me there was another little girl who needed him more."

"Mind you, he could fly to another kid's house, but his wings were too small to fly home from the store," Roslin said with a playfully stern look at Marcel.

"Fireball knew you didn't need him anymore," Naomi said. "What an adorable story."

"How old were you when Fireball finally flew the coop?" Cricket asked.

"I don't think I'll be discussing Fireball with *you* any longer," Marcel said to her.

"Those were interesting times," Roslin said. "That kid of mine taught me a lot." She finished the last of her wine and gave Cricket's knee a friendly pat. "You about ready for bed, my sweet?"

"I am," Cricket said. She finished her wine and set the empty glass on the coffee table. They said goodnight to the other two and left the room holding hands.

"Are you sleepy yet?" Marcel asked her lover.

"Not really," Naomi said. "I have some papers to grade if you have something else to do."

They went to Marcel's study where her computer was and both worked until they were tired. Much later, on their way up the stairs, Naomi asked, "Did Fireball walk or just fly?"

"He could walk."

"What do you think prompted there to be a Fireball in the first place?"

"I don't know. I never really thought about it before." Once they were at the top of the stairs Marcel opened their bedroom door. "But after Fireball first appeared, my mom began spending more time with me. I mean quality time. We would play games together and she would read to me. I think she was a little jealous of Fireball."

"I can understand why," Naomi said. She closed the door and took off her shoes. "You had a new best friend. I wouldn't have liked that either." She put her arms around Marcel's neck and kissed her. "Every day I learn something new about you," she whispered. "I like that."

Marcel kissed her again and knew how incredibly lucky she was.

Chapter Five

A few days later Cricket dropped off Marcel and Roslin at the Antique Villa on her way to work. Marcel was pleased to see that Carmen and Reba were already there. Reba enjoyed working with Carmen whenever they needed extra help at the shop.

"You two all packed?" Carmen asked. She was holding a cup of coffee and standing inside the doorway to her work area. Her pocket tee and jeans had their usual starched, military creases.

"We're ready," Roslin said. "Good to see you both again. How's your garden coming along, Reba?"

Marcel stood in the middle of the showroom looking around with both hands on her hips. It was obvious that this buying trip was happening just in time. "Do we have anything else back there that's ready?" she asked Carmen with a nod toward the workshop.

"A bookcase, an end table and a small desk," Carmen said.

"I'll have another piece ready by tomorrow, and Juanito is bringing in a few things today, so hurry back with some good stuff."

"Then let's move whatever you have ready up here. We can't sell it if they can't see it."

They moved the furniture pieces to the showroom while Reba and Roslin continued chatting and drinking coffee. Marcel was eager to get going. She had decided to stay off the interstate driving up to Dallas so they could hit the flea markets in the smaller towns along the way.

"I put gas in the truck for you," Carmen said.

Marcel smiled. "You're too good to me."

"I know how you hate starting out on empty."

"You ready to go, Mom?" Marcel asked. "Got your shoppin' shoes on?"

Roslin tugged on a pant leg and held up a foot showing off her new white sneakers.

"Then let's get going."

Before they even got out of town they stopped at a huge flea market just off the highway where Marcel found five furniture pieces that interested her. To save room in the truck, she paid for them and then called the shop to arrange for Juanito to pick them up later that day.

"That way you'll have something to do while I'm gone," Marcel told Carmen on the phone.

"Gee, thanks."

As she and her mother got back in the truck, Roslin said, "That was more like a junkyard than a flea market."

"Now there's a thin line if I ever saw one."

"Got my new sneakers dirty!" Roslin said as she held up her foot. "I saw an old trumpet that had no doubt been in a fire, mixed in with a pile of gunky costume jewelry. The end of the horn was all black, and he wanted twenty bucks for it! Junk, I tell you. Piles and piles of junk."

"Some junk pays well if you know what you're looking for."

"Well, the only thing I got out of it was a dirty shoe."

An hour later they were in Blanco, Texas, at another flea market Marcel was familiar with. Down the road from there they found a yard sale that had a nice hutch sitting on the sidewalk. It took two big men to get it into the truck for them. Each time she went on one of these buying sprees Marcel secretly thanked Carmen for insisting they pay extra for a truck with a lift on the back.

"Hurry up and get out of here," Roslin said as she climbed in and closed the door. "We're practically stealing that hutch from these people."

Marcel started up the truck. "It's best not to appear too eager to leave."

"It's like someone somewhere is waving a giant furniture wand over you," Roslin said, fastening her seat belt. "You were made for this business."

"Good karma goes a long way." Marcel reached over and turned the radio on low. "I haven't heard you say much about your last trip. Everything go okay?"

"Not really. I prefer winning."

"Other than that, do you still like doing it?"

"You mean playing and traveling?"

"Yeah. The tournaments. Winning and losing. Packing and unpacking. All of it. Do you still like it?"

"I love it," Roslin said. "It's even better now that I have a family to come home to. When you were in Korea, Saudi and Germany all those years, it was hard coming back to an empty house after a difficult loss. Hamburger Helper just isn't the same if there's no one to share it with."

When Marcel was in the army and had assignments overseas,

her mother came to visit quite often, but they never lived together then. It wasn't until Marcel's last assignment in San Antonio that they were able to share a home again.

"So you haven't given any thought to slowing down the tournament play and just taking it easy?" Marcel asked.

"No. Why should I?"

"I was just wondering. I'm retired and I love it."

"The only part of you that's retired is the military part," Roslin said. "We wouldn't be here now in this truck schlepping old furniture if you were really retired."

Marcel frowned, but reluctantly had to agree. "You know what I mean. I'm doing what I love to do. This isn't like work to me."

"And beating a bunch of rich old men at poker is what I love to do. That doesn't seem like work either most of the time."

"I know."

"When I get tired of it, I'll think about cutting back. How's that?"

"Tell me about the last tournament," Marcel said. Cricket had made her promise to ask about whatever happened when Roslin had been in Montreal. Cricket was certain something involving taxes had come up, and she wanted more details. At least Marcel could go back home and report that she had tried to broach the subject. Marcel would never break her mother's confidence, but if she could tell Cricket enough to get her off the subject, she hoped everyone would be at lot happier.

"Montreal was great," Roslin said. "The weather was cold and my flights were all on time."

"Who hosted the event?"

"A minister and his wife," Roslin said. "An older couple with thousands in their flock. I think they call them mega-churches or something. Like a Super Wal-Mart with pews. These two were monumental hypocrites, but avid poker players and filthy rich."

"Who else was there? Anyone I would know?"

"My friend Skippy was there."

"Senator Skippy?" Marcel asked. They both laughed. Senator Harlow Wainwright had been a gambling friend of Roslin's for over twenty-five years. He had endorsed Marcel's appointment to West Point after she graduated from high school. Roslin was one of the few people who could get away with calling him Skippy.

"Who else was there?" Marcel asked.

"A car dealer from Toronto," Roslin said. "All big car dealers have a lot of money, so it's customary to invite the local ones if they like the game. The minister didn't want the car dealer from Montreal there since he's a member of the flock. Bad for business. Oh, and some coach from the New York Giants baseball team."

"Football," Marcel corrected. "Not baseball."

"Whatever. I did better than he did, but we both lost. I guess the change in weather was the best part of that trip after all."

"Had you ever met the coach before?"

"Once in Boston," Roslin said. "He's not a good card player. I think that's why they keep inviting him to these things. His eyes light up when he has what he thinks is a good hand, so we're all watching him when he draws his cards." She laughed. "We can read him like a book."

"Which hand was the turning point for you?"

Roslin sighed. "I had a full house. Jacks over nines. The boys started folding right and left. All but the minister's wife. She had four deuces and raked in the pot. I kept my confidence through the next few hands, but the cards weren't coming my way. Then the coach started talking about the IRS."

Marcel felt a huge sigh of relief leave her body. This was the subject Cricket had been after her about.

"What did he say?" Marcel casually asked.

"Apparently the coach has a gambling problem," Roslin said. "Cards, horses, sporting events. When he wins, he talks. That's never a good thing in this business. He's also made some enemies—pissed off a few people in New York. According to him, someone turned him in to the IRS for not claiming his winnings, and you know me and talk about the IRS. I lost my concentration and let the game get away from me." Roslin looked out the window as the brushy Texas landscape passed by. "I think all of us got a little edgy after that. I was the only one who does this for a living, but no one but Skippy knew that."

Marcel could tell that her mother was still upset by the IRS conversation. She felt bad for encouraging her to talk about it, but knowing what had happened seemed important.

"I'll never understand why Americans put up with it," Roslin said. "Making us pay a tax on money that we earn," she said slowly. "Money that we worked hard for. Money that belongs to us. Why does our government think any of that should go to them? Why?"

Marcel shifted in the seat. This was not a new conversation for them. They'd had this discussion numerous times over the years.

"Freedom has a price," Marcel said simply. "We pay that price with our wallets and with the lives and blood of our sons and daughters. It's who we are as Americans."

Roslin nodded. "My little patriot. I admire your convictions and I respect your point of view. But the government isn't getting one red cent of my money if I can help it."

Marcel chuckled and continued driving through the Texas Hill Country in search of flea markets and yard sales. There were several issues they would never agree on.

Marcel backed the truck up as close to the motel room door as she could get it. They had arrived in Fort Worth early enough to get some rest and a shower before dinner with friends of Marcel's. They had found several excellent buys on the way up, so Marcel was already happy with what they had.

"How can I need a nap when all I've been doing is riding in a truck all day?" Roslin asked while easing down on the bed closest to the bathroom. "Watching you drive and haggle over prices must've worn me out."

"Don't forget we've got dinner plans," Marcel said.

"Maybe you should go without me."

"You'll feel better after a nap. Besides, we're having dinner with two gay men. You'll love it." Marcel switched on the air conditioner and locked the door before taking off her shoes and stretching out on the bed.

"What are gay boys doing in a cow town like this?"

"Fort Worth has a large gay population," Marcel said. "These guys do very well in their auction business. If you're ever in the market for nude male statues, this is the place to be."

Roslin's sleepy giggle made Marcel smile. "I don't think I'll ever be in the market for something like that, but thanks for the info."

Marcel received a call on her cell phone. "We're here, honey," Don Rice said.

Marcel and Roslin were ready and hungry. Marcel locked the door to their room and then checked the lock on the back of the truck again.

"A new Lexus," Roslin said as both men got out and opened the back doors of the new car for them. "Very nice."

Marcel introduced her mother to them and noticed that "new car smell" immediately when she got in the backseat. She had explained to her mother earlier that the Rice brothers weren't really brothers, but a successful gay couple with a passion for antique furniture. They pretended to be brothers for several reasons. Their business was called Rice Brothers' Auction House, and it was just easier to do business in town that way. Don had legally changed his last name to Rice several years ago, but anyone who knew them well was aware of their real relationship.

"Steak or seafood?" Jeff asked as he put the car in gear.

"Either one sounds good to me," Marcel said.

"Same here," Roslin said. "I'm starving. My daughter didn't stop for lunch today."

"I'm voting for steak," Don said.

"Then steak it is."

Marcel and Roslin both had wine with dinner since neither was driving. The restaurant was quiet, expensive, and the food was excellent.

"We have some great things for you, Marcel," Don said. He was in his mid-thirties, a tall thin man with wavy red hair. "As soon as I got your e-mail I started looking through the warehouse."

"Business must be good in San Antonio," Jeff said. "It hasn't been that long since you were here last."

"The housing market is booming," Marcel said. "It helps that yuppies like antiques."

"And that's one of the reasons we like yuppies," Roslin said before cutting into her steak.

"Since I have an idea what you like, furniture-wise," Jeff said, "we could put things aside for you when they come in and let you know when we have enough to justify you making another trip."

Don smiled at him. "He hates the fact that you leave here and go to Dallas to shop around."

Marcel studied Jeff for a moment and could see the embarrassment and displeasure in his expression. He gave his lover one of those "I can't believe you said that" looks.

"I'll tell you what," she said. "If we can fill up my truck with furniture in the morning, we'll just go home with treasures from the Rice brothers. I won't need to go to Dallas."

"Maybe we could work something out where we'd be your main source for antiques," Don said.

"We also do repairs on damaged furniture," Marcel said. "The pieces don't have to be in perfect condition."

"We'll give you a fair price," Jeff said. "It's just that I hate those homophobic jerks in Dallas. Yeah, they might occasionally have a better variety, but we've got more heart and personality than that cold fish Raymond Palmer."

Marcel reached over and touched his hand. "Jeff, I never knew you felt this way. I wish you had said something sooner. I'd be more than happy to do all my business with like-minded people." She took a sip from her wineglass and met Jeff's wounded look. "I don't really know Raymond Palmer that well," she said, feeling the need to defend her reason for buying anything from someone the Rice brothers so adamantly disliked. "I never got the impression I was being treated any differently because I'm a lesbian, though."

"Marcel honey," Don said with an exaggerated limp wave. "Only your girlfriend and your mother know you're gay." He leaned toward her and stage-whispered out of the side of his mouth, "Your mother *does* know you're gay, right?"

The other three tossed their heads back and laughed.

"Everyone at our house has a girlfriend," Roslin said with pride. "We're all gay there."

Don held his glass of tea up in a mini-toast. The four clinked glasses.

"What Mr. Palmer-the-homophobe doesn't realize is how much business he's losing by hanging on to such an attitude," Don said. "He's driven all the gay antique hunters in this part of the state our way, and everyone knows how much a queen likes to brag about her antiques."

"All the queens I know aren't talking about furniture when they mention their antiques," Jeff said.

"Be that as it may," Don continued, "on the weekends we see a steady stream of family from the Metroplex down this way looking for something different. The distance they have to travel doesn't seem to bother them."

"I wish you had told me about Palmer before," Marcel said. "Can you fill my truck up tomorrow with furniture I'll like?"

Jeff looked at her and smiled. "We'll certainly do our best, Ms. Robicheaux."

Before the evening was over, Marcel and the Rice brothers worked out a deal where they would try to keep furniture pieces they thought she would like, and when they had enough to give her a nice variety, they would give her a call.

"We'll take care of you," Don assured her.

"I know you will," Marcel said.

Chapter Six

The next morning Marcel and Roslin met the Rice brothers for breakfast.

"That wine last night put me right to sleep," Roslin said as she picked up her menu.

"Then you should be plenty rested for the drive home later," Marcel remarked, teasing her since her mother tended to fall asleep if they weren't getting in and out of the truck very much.

"That reminds me," Roslin said. "My daughter never wants to stop to eat. I'd better get something that'll last me the rest of the day."

Their orders were taken and a round of coffee was set in front of them. When the waiter was gone, Jeff asked if there were any good clubs in San Antonio.

"I take it that's not a golf question," Roslin said with a wink.

"No, Mom. That wasn't a golf question." Marcel said to Jeff,

"I'm really not up on the local bar scene, but I could check into it for you."

"We're not really bar people either," Don said. "It's just nice to get away sometimes."

"I did the Alamo, missions and River Walk with the family as a kid," Jeff said, "so the tourist aspect of your fine city doesn't interest me."

"Come to San Antonio and stay with us," Roslin said. "We've got plenty of room and we can find something to do." She poured creamer into her coffee and stirred it slowly. "Do we even have gay bars in San Antonio?"

"Sure we do," Marcel said.

"Why haven't I ever been to one?"

"Why? I don't know why," Marcel said. "That's a good question to ask your girlfriend since your lesbian education is her responsibility."

"Well, listen to you," Roslin said. "Don't sass your mother, by the way. Not all of us were born gay, you know."

"I'd have to agree with Marcel on that one," Don said. "One time my mother started asking me questions, and all I could think of to do was find a number for PFLAG and have her call someone."

"Couldn't handle it, eh?" Jeff said with a laugh.

"Staying in the closet has its advantages," Don said. "I'd rather be in there hiding behind a faded prom dress than discuss anything gay-related with one of my parents."

"It also keeps the local homophobes from burning our warehouse down," Jeff said. "When did you come out to your mother?" he asked Marcel.

"Oh, I had her trained at an early age to tell me everything," Roslin said proudly.

Marcel smiled and nodded toward her mother. "She still believes that, too."

"You told me all about Cricket, remember?" Roslin said. "So

once again, off to the library I went. I read up on teenage crushes until I had those chapters practically memorized." She took a cautious sip of her coffee. "All the literature I found on the subject said you would grow out of it. What a bunch of bunk."

Everyone laughed.

"I will tell you this much, though," Roslin said. "There's one thing that has to be worse than coming out to a parent, and that's being a parent and coming out to a child. That was a tough one."

"My first girlfriend is now my mother's girlfriend," Marcel said with a nod in Roslin's direction.

"Oh, my," Jeff said delightedly. "Do tell!"

"Cricket was always such a cute, silly little thing," Roslin said with fondness in her voice and a special light in her eyes.

"How long were you together, Marcel?" Don asked.

"Through high school," she said. "After that I was at West Point, and Cricket stayed in Texas to go to college. We didn't officially break up until I received my commission after graduation. The long distance thing was just too hard."

Roslin set her coffee cup down. "I went along with my daughter's lesbian phase because I didn't have to worry about her getting pregnant or any of that. And all the books said she would grow out of it. I'm still waiting for that part to happen."

"It's a little late for that, I'm afraid," Don said.

With a truck full of furniture, Marcel and Roslin waved to the Rice brothers and headed back home again. It was still early and the traffic was light.

"Remember, Marcel. If you see something you really like on the way back, just keep driving," Roslin said. "There's no room for anything else."

"We've got enough to keep Carmen busy for the next three months." Marcel was happy with what they had. It had been a successful buying trip.

"You want to hear something interesting?" Roslin asked. Without giving Marcel a chance to answer, she said, "I'm glad we're going back early. I like being away and I like coming back home again. It's more fun when I'm not gone as long."

"That's probably because you have more of a reason to want to be home now."

"You were always the best reason to be home," Roslin said with a touch of emotion in her voice.

"Now you have me, Cricket and Naomi. Let me tell you something interesting," Marcel said. "It was kind of strange to hear you say that everyone at our house was gay. Is that how you see yourself now? When you and Cricket first got together you never wanted to talk about it."

"I think I was embarrassed back then," Roslin admitted.

"Embarrassed about what?"

"I'm too old to be confused about my sexuality. That's something an eighteen-year-old struggles with."

"You're never too old to fall in love, Mom. That's just human nature. And we really have no control over who we fall in love with."

"It doesn't sound so bad when you say it that way."

"So do you consider yourself to be a lesbian now?" Marcel asked. She continued to watch the road as she drove, but occasionally caught a glimpse of her mother.

"That's still some of the confusing part," Roslin said. "I don't see attractive women in a sexual way, but I never did that with men either. I loved your father. In many ways I'm still in love with him. He's the only man I've ever been with. When he died, I lost more than a husband and the father of my child. I lost the love of my life and my best friend." She looked out the window for a moment and then turned to look straight ahead. "If it hadn't been for you—an infant needing my full, unwavering attention—I'm not sure what would've become of me. I put all of my energy into you. I realized that I wasn't the only one who had lost something. My darling little baby didn't have a father. Each time I would lean toward depression, you would make a noise and pull me out. You were like a little guide leading me back to the land of the living. After we lost your father, sex was a foreign word to me. It was something I'd forgotten about and never expected to experience again. I wasn't interested in it, and my focus became providing a life for us. I was a gambler when I met your father. That's what I did best, so that's how I made my living. I was very fortunate to have a child who gave me absolutely no trouble. Except for that little phase where you thought you were a lesbian."

They laughed together for a moment. "I'm expected to grow out of that anytime now," Marcel said.

"Oh, and Fireball," Roslin added. "Let's not forget Fireball." She took a deep breath and shook her head. "Did I answer your question?"

"I don't think so," Marcel said. She loved having these kinds of talks with her mother. It had been one of the things she had missed the most when they were separated during Marcel's time away in the army.

"I already forgot the question," Roslin said.

"The question was whether or not you consider yourself to be a lesbian."

"It's kind of hip to be gay," Roslin said. "I really like that part of it. Another thing that's helped me is meeting other women my age who are gay—like Carmen and Reba, even though I've robbed the cradle and they haven't."

"Robbed the cradle?" Marcel said. "You mean Cricket? Forty-seven is hardly cradle material."

"She's the same age as my daughter, so that's pretty close to cradle-robbing for me."

"You still haven't answered the question," Marcel said. "Do you consider yourself to be a lesbian?"

Roslin shrugged. "I think of lesbians as people who notice

and identify with women instead of men. If a handsome man walks into a room, a lesbian doesn't give him the time of day. But if a woman walks into a room, the newcomer will get adequately checked out. Am I right?"

"Maybe," Marcel said. "I think you have lesbians confused with men in general."

"I guess what I'm saying is, if a handsome man walks into the room I don't care what he does for a living or if he's any good in bed," Roslin said. "I'm more likely to wonder if he's any good at poker."

That made Marcel laugh. "And if an attractive woman walked into the room?"

"I'm more than likely wondering the same thing," Roslin said. "How good is she at poker? Can she bluff? Is she lucky? Until Cricket came along and kissed me that first time, it never occurred to me that I could be with anyone else other than your father, much less a woman. But you know what? Cricket just jams up my circuits. That's the best way I can describe it. She's wonderful. I can't imagine my life without her. Did I answer your question?"

"No," Marcel said with a smile, "but that's okay."

Chapter Seven

Marcel had called ahead to let Carmen know they were just coming into the edge of town. Once they arrived at the Antique Villa, she parked the truck behind the shop and tapped the horn to let Carmen know they were there.

"Let me guess," Roslin said. "Now we have to unload everything."

"You don't have to help, of course," Marcel told her mother, "but an extra pair of hands would sure be nice."

"You know how grouchy I'll be if I break a nail."

Marcel heard the electronic hum of an overhead door opening. Carmen's brown boots appeared at the bottom as the door slowly rose from the ground.

Ducking beneath it, Carmen asked, "Good trip?"

"I'll let you be the judge of that." Marcel unlocked the back of the truck, and with a little push, the door rumbled up and out of sight. Furniture was piled so high that Marcel was impressed all over again with how much the Rice brothers had been able to pack inside.

"Ohhh!" Carmen cooed. "Will you look at that? I bet you couldn't squeeze a toothpick in there." She handed Marcel a pair of heavy gloves. "Who's in for the spider count?"

"I'm in," Roslin said. "I saw where some of this stuff came from. I bet a few of those flea markets started out as trading posts. Uh . . . I guess I'll go with six."

Whenever they got a large load of furniture like this in, they enjoyed playing a "Guess How Many Spiders We'll Find" game. The person picking closest to the correct number of spiders without going over got a home-cooked meal prepared by the person with the next to the highest number correct.

"I'll go with four," Carmen said.

Marcel and Carmen worked together to get down a few of the smaller pieces closest to the front. "Five for me then," Marcel said.

"I'll write down the wagers," Roslin announced with a little wave. "It's like swatting flies in a poop factory out here. Too much work for me. You can find me inside with Reba if you need anything."

"Don't break a nail while you're in there," Marcel called after her. "We wouldn't want you getting all grouchy or anything."

"Oh, just listen to my funny, funny daughter."

"Juanito should be here soon to help us," Carmen said. "I gave him a call when I heard you were back in town already."

"See if Juanito and Reba want in on the spider count," Marcel told her mother before she got too far away. "Those two cook pretty good. I'd like it if one of them lost."

As they worked at getting the lighter pieces down and wiping off the first layer of dust, they were constantly looking for spiders and watching for splinters. There was no telling where

48

some of these pieces had been before the Rice brothers or a flea market had obtained them. In addition to finally being able to see each piece in the daylight and inspect it at a more leisurely pace, Marcel also enjoyed listening to the sighs and murmurs of appreciation whenever Carmen saw something she really liked. This part of the trip—where they were able to take their time unloading the truck and checking everything over for individual flaws or unexpected magnificence—was just one more reason Marcel loved what she was doing. Old furniture was like a window to the past for her. She often wondered whom each piece had originally belonged to and who had made it. How many people had owned it? Where had it been in the house? Occasionally Carmen was able to touch a piece of furniture and get a sense of where it had been. Even though Marcel found that fascinating whenever it happened, she had never pressed Carmen for more information. They had an unspoken under-standing about such things where words would have gotten in the way. Sometimes Carmen just had to smile or place her hand on a furniture piece, and that was all it took for Marcel to know that something special had happened. Marcel often thought that some day when they had more time she and Carmen would talk about things like that and what it all meant, but there was always too much to do and there never seemed to be the right opportu-nity to bring it up.

"Here we go," Carmen said while slowly tipping a small table back on two legs. They both bent over to see under the table better. Marcel spotted the black widow spider, full of attitude and poison, crouching in a corner.

"There you are," Marcel said quietly with a bit of awe in her voice. "Waiting there so patiently. Protecting your space."

Carmen found a sharpened pencil perched behind her ear. She and Marcel both looked up to see Juanito pull into the park-ing lot in his pickup.

"You in for the spider count?" Marcel asked him when he got

out of the truck.

"I am," he said. "Phoned my guess in a few minutes ago. Why? Have I lost already?"

"We just found our first one," Carmen said. She carefully moved the pencil in closer toward the spider. The red dot on its back was like nature's version of a stop sign—the Goddess's way of warning something not to go any further.

Carmen took a deep breath and slowly moved the pencil point in closer. "I don't like having to do this," she said to the spider, "but I can't have you and your black widow friends hanging around in my shop." She flicked the spider on the ground and planted her boot on top of it before announcing, "That's one."

Marcel and Juanito got another small table down from the back of the truck. "How many are you in for?" Marcel asked him.

Juanito wore a white cap with the word "Antique" on the front of it. She and Naomi had gotten him the cap for his birthday last month. It made Marcel smile to see him wearing it.

"Seven," he said. "This is quite a haul you've got here. The spiders are all probably moving to the back and having a union meeting even as I speak."

"They can unionize all they want to," Carmen said, "but there won't be any spiders in my workshop if I can help it."

Now that there was more room to work in, Juanito climbed up into the back of the truck and carefully moved other furniture pieces closer to the edge.

"Why can't I find a boyfriend as butch as you?" he jokingly asked Carmen.

"Because all you do is hang out with lesbians," Carmen replied.

"Speaking of hanging out with lesbians," Marcel said, "do we have any good gay bars in this town?"

"Depends on what you consider good," Carmen said. "You

50

wanna get laid? Meet friends for a drink? Dance your butt off? Just depends."

"All those options are available?" Marcel asked with a raised brow. She climbed up into the truck to help Juanito move a small desk onto the lift. "A friend of mine in Fort Worth was asking about the club scene here, and I didn't have a clue what to say. I felt like a bad San Antonian."

"Was this friend a he or a she?" Juanito asked.

"A he."

"Single?"

"No. He has a partner."

"Oh." He picked up his end of the desk, and they easily moved it on to the lift. "Everyone has a husband but me."

"And me," Marcel said.

"And me," Carmen added.

"You two *are* somebody's husband."

"Excuse me?" Marcel said.

Carmen pushed the button on the lift and lowered the desk to the ground. Juanito rode down with it and helped her move it off to the side.

"Trust me," Carmen said. "I'm nobody's husband either. When was the last time you had a partner?" she asked him. "You ever lived with a guy before?"

"Fifteen years ago," Juanito said. "I lived with someone for three years before I moved in with Reba."

"There has to be somebody we can fix you up with," Marcel said, reaching for one of the six captain chairs stacked and stuffed on top of everything else.

"I have a gay nephew," Carmen said, "but he's too young for you."

"What's he look like?" Juanito asked.

"Young," Carmen said over Marcel's chuckle.

"I don't want someone I'll have to train," he said. "Or write a note for when he skips school."

51

"How long has it been since you had a date?" Carmen asked. She looked at a small table carefully before setting it to the side with the others.

"Too long ago to remember," Juanito said as he pushed the button on the lift to take him back up again.

"Maybe you're being too picky," Marcel suggested.

"Picky? There're only two things I insist on."

"What are they?" Carmen asked.

"Employed and breathing," Juanito answered.

"Ohmigod," Marcel exclaimed with a hoot. "That's it? Employed and breathing?"

"Hey, I just added the employed part recently."

They set two small desks on the lift and Juanito pushed the button to let them down.

"It shouldn't be that hard to find a gay man to fit that description," Marcel said. "Employed and breathing," she mumbled under her breath.

"Ya think?"

"Got another one," Carmen said from the ground.

Seconds later Marcel heard a stomping boot. "That's two."

After an hour and a half, the truck was empty and all of the furniture had been inspected twice, dusted and moved into the workshop. The three of them took off their gloves and joined Reba and Roslin in the showroom where it was a lot cooler.

"How many spiders were there?" Reba asked.

"Five," Carmen said. "So who won?"

Marcel smiled and nodded. "I picked five. I won!" Craning her neck to get a look at the paper with the wagers on it, she asked, "Who has to cook for me?"

"Cricket," Roslin announced.

Marcel crinkled her nose and said, "Cricket? The worst cook in the group? Instead of winning, now I feel like I'm being punished!"

Roslin and Reba snickered at Marcel's expense. Finally, Roslin said, "I'm teasing you. Carmen actually lost, so she'll be cooking for you."

Juanito took his cap off and wiped his brow. "How is it that the person with the big spider-squishing boot lost at this game? Such honesty is commendable."

"Where's the fun if you cheat?" Carmen reasoned.

"I personally think it's kind of creepy knowing there were five of those spiders all in one place," Reba said with a shiver. "How many just crawled off and stayed in the truck?"

"Having a union meeting?" Juanito said. "They're probably marching with little picket signs in there somewhere."

"What?" Roslin asked. "Picket signs?"

"Never mind," he said over Carmen's and Marcel's chuckles. "Got any bug spray? I'll go spray the back of the truck for you."

Marcel went into her office and came out with two cans of insect spray. "Here you go. I'm sure they'll love seeing you show up with these at their spider union meeting."

Roslin looked at all four of them as if no one had any oars in the water. "If those spiders are smart enough to hold a meeting, then they're all probably wearing little oxygen masks, too. So you might as well just save the spray."

Chapter Eight

Marcel closed her cell phone and checked on the shark steaks that were grilling. Cricket came out on the patio with an aluminum foil boat full of vegetables.

"Where's Naomi?" Cricket asked. "I thought she would be here by now."

"Stuck in traffic. She just called."

Cricket opened the grill and set the foil packet down where Marcel had left a space for it. They sat on the cool, shaded patio in Adirondack chairs to wait for dinner to finish cooking.

"How was the buying trip?" Cricket asked.

"Good. We found a lot of interesting things."

"Did you and your mom talk?"

"We always talk." Marcel only felt a little guilty about taking such pleasure in reminding Cricket how close she and her mother were. There were times when she and Cricket went through phases where they didn't appear to like each other very much, and they seemed to be struggling through one of those phases now. As best friends, they had been through a lot over the years, but living under the same roof was getting to be more togetherness than Marcel cared for at times. These episodes never lasted that long, but in the meantime she found Cricket to be mildly annoying.

"Did anything come up about the IRS?" Cricket asked.

"One of the guys at the last event has been audited because of his gambling habits," Marcel said. "Any talk about the IRS sets Mom off, and she's still a little uneasy about it. That's basically what happened."

Cricket sighed heavily. "Okay. If you're sure that's all there is to it." She picked up her wineglass setting on the small table between them. "She worries me sometimes."

"Why?"

"She travels with so much money, and some of the people she gambles with are almost strangers." Cricket took a sip of wine. "I wish she would give it all up. I don't like her being gone so much."

"We talked a little about that, too," Marcel said.

Cricket's eyes beamed with interest. "Really? I've been trying to find a way to bring it up again with her, but she's pretty good at dodging the topics that don't interest her. Tell me what she said."

"She's not ready to retire," Marcel said simply.

"Did she give you any indication when she *would* be ready?"

"No."

"I've been thinking about some of the things she could do instead of traveling and gambling. She knows this business better than anyone. Suppose she started promoting these events or even held a few of them here?"

"Here where?"

"*Here* here. At the house."

"You just said the people she plays with are strangers. Why would we want them in our house?" Marcel asked incredulously.

"If the gambling takes place here, then she's home right after it's over."

"No, no, no," Marcel said. "The only illegal thing I want going on in our house is lesbian sex. No gambling."

"Okay. If not here then somewhere else in San Antonio maybe."

Marcel looked at Cricket for a moment to try to gauge her sincerity. When she finally determined that Cricket had indeed given all of this some serious thought, Marcel just shook her head in disbelief.

"What?" Cricket asked. "What's that look for?"

"Do you even know my mother at all?"

"In some ways I know her a hell of a lot better than you ever will."

"Not in the ways that really count," Marcel said dryly.

"You don't think I know what counts?"

Marcel looked away from her. "Not really. You're much too focused on your own needs to care about what anyone else wants."

"Because I'd like to spend more time with my lover?"

Marcel went over to the grill to check on the shark steaks again. "Gambling isn't just something she does, Cricket. It's who she is. All you see is someone who flies all over the world just to play cards. There's so much more to it for her than that. It's the main thread of her existence."

"I know that," Cricket said in a meek, tiny voice.

"Do you?" Marcel carefully turned the shark steaks and closed the grill. "Have you ever watched her pack for a trip? Or gone to the bank with her before she leaves? Have you ever seen her count and recount her bankroll to make sure she has what she needs?" Marcel sat down again and leaned back in the chair. "Have you ever seen the little ritual she goes through at the airport before she gets on—"

"Yes, I know," Cricket said impatiently. "Your mom always says it's bad luck to be superstitious, but she still goes through her little rituals. I see your point. It's not just getting on a plane to go play cards somewhere."

"Your lips are moving, but you don't get what I'm saying."

"So I'm a selfish person," Cricket said. "I want her to retire so I won't miss her so much. Is that a crime?"

Marcel could hear the emotion in Cricket's voice. It surprised her a little. "No, it's not a crime, but you can't keep harping on this. You'll just make yourself nuts. Well, let's just say even *more* nuts than you already are."

"Oh, aren't you the funny one."

They both got quiet when Roslin came outside. "The salad's done and the table is set."

"We're waiting on Naomi and the sharks," Marcel said. "I heard the vegetable boat sizzling on the grill earlier, so those should be done soon."

Roslin sat down in another Adirondack chair across from them and stretched out her legs. "I wonder where I left my wine."

Cricket handed her glass to Roslin who took a sip and gave it back.

"Spring break is in two weeks," Cricket said. "I wish we could all go away somewhere together."

"Like a vacation?" Roslin asked with a tinge of interest.

"Yeah, why not?" Cricket said. "Naomi's off too, and I'm sure Carmen and Reba can run the shop. Do you two have any plans?" she asked Marcel.

"Not that I know of," Marcel said. She went over to the grill to check on the shark steaks again. "These are ready. Let me go get a plate."

On her way back into the house, she met Naomi coming in the front door. "There you are," Marcel said. "The shark is

57

ready."

"Are we talking about a card shark or a real shark?" Naomi asked with a peck on Marcel's cheek.

"A real shark. Oh, good. You brought dessert." They both went into the kitchen. "Got any plans for spring break?"

"Not really. Maybe working out in the yard. You know. Planting flowers and trimming shrubs. Domestic things. Why?"

"Cricket's hatching a plot for all of us to go on vacation together, so if that's not something we're interested in, then get to thinking of a way to get us out of it."

Marcel kept her mind on her food and let the others carry on with the vacation chatter. She knew that eventually one of them would notice her lack of enthusiasm for a group vacation and hoped her silence would speak for itself. She was reluctant to encourage them, but not yet willing to voice her disapproval for the idea of getting away for a few days. In the meantime, Marcel filled wineglasses and enjoyed the shark steak that she had so carefully labored over.

"Plane tickets this late will be astronomical," Naomi said.

"Maybe not," Cricket said. "After dinner I'll get online and see what's available, but first we need to decide what we want to do and where we want to go."

We, we, we, Marcel thought as she speared a chunk of roasted potato on her plate. *Maybe I don't want to ask Reba to work at the shop for a week. Did anyone think about that?*

"A cruise maybe?" Cricket said. "A Vegas package? Those vacation options are usually cheap."

"Vegas?" Roslin said with a laugh. "I thought this was supposed to be a vacation from work."

"Okay, maybe not Vegas," Cricket said with a shrug.

"I do have all those places I've won in poker games," Roslin said. "When was the last time we were in Key West, Marcel?"

Hearing her name brought Marcel out of her reverie. "What?"

"Key West," Roslin said. "Oh, wait. Do I even own that Key West place anymore?"

Everyone at the table laughed.

"I'll have to check in my briefcase upstairs," Roslin said. "I keep all the deeds in there. We could make one of those places our vacation getaway if you like. It might even be fun to check them out. A few of them I've never even been to."

After dinner Marcel volunteered to do the dishes and clean up the kitchen while the other three picked out a place to spend their vacation. Once she finished with the dishes and the usual sprucing, she no longer had an excuse not to be out there with them. Marcel made a pot of decaf coffee and got the dessert ready to serve. By the time she went out to the living room, there were papers spread all over the coffee table and Naomi was on her laptop searching for cheap airline tickets.

"We've narrowed it down to three places," Cricket said when Marcel took a seat on the sofa. "Vancouver, Key West, which your mom still owns by the way, and Sedona, Arizona."

Marcel glanced over at Naomi who was typing away on the laptop. *Looks like we're going on vacation*, Marcel thought with a sigh. *Things sure happen quickly around here.*

Naomi closed their bedroom door and slipped off her shoes. "You've been kind of quiet tonight."

"I guess I'm just tired," Marcel said. "We unloaded a full truck today. That's a lot more physical work than I'm used to."

"Who won the spider count?"

Marcel smiled. "I did." Naomi stepped into her arms for a hug. "What would you like for Carmen to cook for us?"

Naomi kissed the side of Marcel's neck. "Her chicken and rice soup is my favorite. What's yours?"

"Mmm," Marcel said dreamily. "Whatever it is you're doing right now is my favorite."

"I want a shower," Naomi said. "Can you hold that thought for a few minutes?"

Marcel stretched out on the bed and contemplated going on vacation for a week. The plans had become more of a reality once her mother announced that she had enough frequent flyer miles to get each of them around the world and back at least five times. Then with the added surprise that Roslin had a list of romantic places she either owned or could get from the owner for a week, Marcel had to resign herself to the fact that there would be a vacation in her immediate future.

Hearing the shower turn off, she got up to find her pajamas. *At least I'll start off in pajamas*, she thought with a smile.

When Marcel came out of the bathroom she found Naomi propped up in bed reading. Naomi's dark, naturally curly hair was damp on the ends. She wore her glasses for reading, and to Marcel she was the most beautiful woman she had ever seen.

Naomi closed the book and set her glasses on the nightstand. "How are you feeling about this vacation idea?"

"If the truth were to be known," Marcel said as she slipped into bed, "a vacation for me would involve quiet time alone with you. It wouldn't include Cricket or my mother, even though I love them both dearly."

"I see."

"I'm going through one of those periods where I'd like to spend less and less time with Cricket, I guess. I've reached my Cricket limit for this quarter."

Naomi leaned over and switched the lamp off. She turned toward Marcel and propped her head up with her hand. "What if I promise we'll have time alone and we'll do things on our own wherever we go?"

Marcel smiled at the warm, sweet scent of her. "You could arrange that?"

"I can and I will."

Suddenly, going away for a week sounded a lot more appealing.

Naomi moved closer and touched Marcel's lips with her own. Slowly, she lay down beside her and pressed her body against Marcel's. Naomi looked her over with longing and passion in her eyes, making their next kiss feel like a whisper in its softness. She gently covered Marcel's mouth with slow, drugging kisses, and Marcel felt something intense flare inside of her just as her heart jolted and her pulse quickened. Her body ached for Naomi's touch. Every day her love for this woman seemed to deepen and intensify. Marcel found her heart swelling in the comfort of her nearness before the spark of excitement gradually turned into a raging need to touch her.

Their hands were busy fumbling with buttons until finally Marcel felt Naomi's soft breasts against hers. The caress of her lips on Marcel's mouth and along her body sent a velvety warmth spreading through her veins. Shivers of delight gradually became currents of desire as Naomi's hand moved over Marcel's belly and gently tugged on the waistband of her pajamas. The kissing never stopped as they both struggled to free themselves of their clothing. The cool brush of Naomi's fingers on her skin brought another ripple of excitement and a melting sweetness inside of her. Marcel welcomed Naomi's hand as it moved downward, skimming either side of her body to her thighs. Needing to feel their closeness, Marcel pulled Naomi on top of her. Their breasts touched in a moment of divine ecstasy. Naomi snuggled against her as their legs entwined. Fire spread to Marcel's heart, while her entire body became flooded with desire.

As her warm lips grazed Marcel's ear, Naomi whispered, "You

feel so good."

Marcel wrapped her legs around her, and within seconds their bodies were in exquisite harmony with one another. The feeling was much more than sexual desire as they moved and rocked together in a raw act of possession and heat. The turbulence of their passion swirled around her. Marcel felt Naomi's mouth kissing the soft curve of her shoulder as a gust of desire shook her before they came together in a wild flash of uncontrollable joy.

Once the hot tide of passion began to simmer down to a warm, liquid glow, Marcel filled her hands with Naomi's hair and kissed her.

"Tell me again why we bother putting on pajamas," Marcel said with an exhausted, sleepy voice.

Naomi kissed her sweetly on the lips before rolling over beside her.

"Because coaxing you out of your clothes is some of the only exercise I get all day."

Marcel chuckled and put her arm around her, spoon-fashion. Her nipples felt good pressing against Naomi's back.

"So will you go on vacation with me?" Naomi whispered sleepily into the darkness.

"After what just happened, I'd go anywhere with you."

Chapter Nine

The following evening while Marcel grilled chicken and vegetables out on the patio, the other three stayed in the kitchen to discuss where they would spend their week's vacation. Marcel didn't really care where they went, but offered an occasional comment whenever she was in the house.

"Oh, by the way," Marcel said a while later when she entered the kitchen in search of another fork to turn the chicken. "Carmen found two more spiders today, so I didn't win the spider count after all."

"Then who did?" Cricket asked. She was busy scrubbing four large potatoes.

"Reba won," Marcel said, "and Mom has to cook for her."

"Does Reba like Hamburger Helper?" Naomi queried to a kitchen filled with laughter.

Defending herself, Roslin said, "I can cook other things."

"Not when you lose," Cricket reminded her.

"I have a question about this spider count game," Roslin said. "When is the game actually over? Once the truck is unloaded? Or not until the last spider shows up? How do we know the spiders she found today had anything to do with the most recent furniture we hauled in?"

"Now that's a good question," Cricket said.

"Does anyone ever officially declare the game over?" Roslin asked. "There's a lot at stake here. Heaven forbid someone should get stuck eating an entire meal Cricket had to prepare."

"Amen to that," Marcel agreed.

Just as Cricket put on her pouty face, Roslin gave her cheek a tweak and said, "I'm just teasing, my sweet. You can cook for me anytime."

Marcel got a fork out of the silverware drawer. "Did we decide where we're going on vacation yet?" she asked.

"Either Sedona or Key West," Cricket said. "Vancouver is a little more complicated to get to, and we only have a week. We're saving that for later in the summer. We'll talk more about it over dinner."

Marcel left the kitchen and went back outside to tend to the chicken. *Sedona or Key West*, she thought. *I guess I can live with either one of those.*

"Did I get an answer to my spider game question?" Roslin asked as she passed the salad bowl to Naomi.

"What was the question again?" Marcel asked. She was hungry and the chicken smelled delicious.

"When is the game over?" Roslin wondered. "I thought we added up the spiders as the truck was being unloaded." She shook her chemically-enhanced-auburn-colored head. "It's not like me to play a game I don't know anything about. Where are the rules? What are the odds?"

"It's just a game, Mom. It's something to keep us aware of what we're doing, and it helps pass the time while we're lifting, tugging on and moving dusty old furniture."

"Well, she's right about the rules," Cricket said. "There don't seem to be any."

Marcel made a mental note to not include these two in any spider count games in the future.

"So," Naomi said in a valiant attempt to change the subject. "Where are we going on vacation?"

"Since my beautiful lover will be supplying the tickets and the accommodations," Cricket said proudly, "I think she should decide."

"Good idea," Naomi said.

All three of them looked at Roslin, who was busy buttering her nuked potato. Finally noticing she was the center of attention, she said, "I don't care where we go as long as we're all together."

"Aww, what a nice thing to say," Cricket said. "Then I'm voting for Key West. The beach was made for spring break."

Naomi looked at Marcel. "Where would you like to go?"

"Key West is fine with me, too," Marcel said. "You still own it, right?" she asked her mother.

"Oh, listen to my funny, funny daughter." Roslin blew on a piece of potato and looked directly at Marcel. "I checked on that already, remember?"

"This is going to be so much fun!" Cricket said.

Marcel met Naomi's eyes across the table and saw an unspoken promise there. Marcel was counting on having some much-needed alone time with her.

Ralph, the mailman, had just left and Marcel was washing out the coffeepot when she heard the front door ding open. She stuck her head out of her office to greet the customer when she saw about a dozen people come in.

"Hello," she said. Setting the coffeepot down, Marcel dried her hands on a paper towel.

Several customers returned the greeting. Other than their grand opening, Marcel had never seen so many people in the showroom at one time. She glanced out the huge display window and saw a tour bus in the parking lot, but not everyone on the bus came inside. There were several men on the sidewalk smoking.

"Excuse me," one of the male tourists said to Marcel in heavily accented English. "Do you ship to Mexico?"

"Yes," she said with a smile. "We can ship to almost anywhere in the world."

The man turned to the group and said something in Spanish. Marcel was fluent in French and German, but spoke only passable Spanish. The cadence of his words was much too fast for her to feel comfortable attempting to join in with the conversation, but she could understand enough to tell that these were serious shoppers.

She went to the workshop and got Carmen's attention. As it turned out, one of Carmen's nephews was the bus driver and had recommended the Antique Villa for some specialized shopping. Once Carmen came up front, the noise level increased dramatically as the Spanish buzzed all through the room. It wasn't long until almost everything in the showroom was sold. After a while, Carmen took a few shoppers back to the workshop area so they could see what else was available that hadn't been moved up front yet.

As Marcel ran credit cards, she gained more confidence in her conversational Spanish skills. Her efforts to communicate were appreciated by the tourists, and Marcel's Spanish was actually much better than she realized. Getting each sold furniture piece tagged and labeled correctly for the right customer was her biggest concern. Once she got that taken care of, her focus turned to estimating the shipping cost.

After a while, the door dinged open again and one of the men who had been smoking on the sidewalk came in and said something to the group, making several of the shoppers laugh. Marcel understood enough to realize he was asking his wife if he had any money left. Between their limited English and Marcel's Spanish, successful negotiations went on to everyone's satisfaction. One couple bought several items to help furnish a ranch house south of Mexico City. Marcel also learned that a few of the tourists were doctors with lots of money to spend. She and Carmen were more than happy to help them with that.

Marcel and Carmen plopped down on stools after the bus pulled away. Overall, they had sold several thousand dollars' worth of antiques in less than forty-five minutes.

"This is our best day since we opened," Carmen said, still recovering from the rush. "I sold things back there that I didn't even realize we had."

Marcel went into her office and came back with something cold for them to drink. "I think your nephew deserves a commission for bringing them to us," she said. Glancing around the room at the little "Sold" signs on everything, she added, "With some of these pieces, the shipping cost will be more than what we paid for the item to begin with."

Carmen touched her soda can to Marcel's and chuckled. "I love this business."

"Yeah, me too," Marcel said. "And here we are sitting on our butts like we don't have anything to do."

Marcel spent the rest of the day making arrangements to have most of the furniture packed up and shipped out. Some pieces still needed Carmen's attention before shipping was possible. Marcel didn't like the way the showroom looked once things were loaded on the truck. An empty showroom wasn't good, so she made a note to give the Rice brothers a call soon to see if they had anything else for her. She would need to find a few local estate sales soon and then make another buying trip when she got back from her Key West excursion.

Vacation, she thought. *This is the absolute worst time for me to be going anywhere.*

Marcel went back to the workshop area and saw the sea of old furniture needing attention. The pieces that were closest to the front of Carmen's immediate work area were the ones that needed to be taken care of first and then shipped to Mexico.

"Is there anything I can do to help?" Marcel asked.

"You can stop stressing over this," Carmen said. "I can see it in your eyes."

"We've got orders to get out, and all I'm doing is dusting up front. I even cleaned the display window, and you know how much I dislike doing windows."

"I explained it all very carefully to the people who bought stuff from back here," Carmen said. She had sawdust in her hair and safety goggles on top of her head. "They know I have things to do to each piece, and they were willing to wait for it."

Marcel took a deep breath and shrugged. "I know." She pointed over her shoulder toward the front of the shop. "Empty showroom. I hate that."

Carmen laughed. "I know you do, but think of it this way. We work hard at this . . . from finding each piece, all the way to restoring it. Others appreciate what we do, and that's why there's an empty showroom. I'll get more things in there as soon as I finish with all of this."

"Nothing I can do to help?" Marcel offered again.

"Just chill out and let me take care of this part of the business. If there's something I need help with, I'll let you know."

"In other words," Marcel said, "get the hell out so you can work, right?"

"You have such a way with words, my friend."

Carmen made it very easy for Marcel to leave the shop and go on vacation. Marcel wanted to make sure she gave Carmen the same opportunity to get away at some point in the future.

Friday evening when she got home from work, Marcel found her mother on the patio feeling no pain with a frozen margarita in one hand and a paper fan in the other.

"Where is everybody?" Marcel asked. She leaned over and kissed her mother on the cheek.

"Naomi's taking a shower and Cricket is upstairs repacking again."

Marcel glanced over at the grill at the edge of the patio. Smoke was coming out of it, so someone had already made dinner arrangements.

"What are we having?" Marcel asked as she raised the lid and waved the smoke away.

"American cuisine. Hamburgers and hot dogs."

"Blackened hamburgers and hot dogs?" Marcel commented while staring at the four charred silver-dollar-sized hamburger patties. The wieners looked like black sticks. "Who put these on?" Marcel casually asked.

"Cricket."

"Did she leave you in charge of watching them?"

"No. Why? Was I supposed to?"

Marcel closed the lid and turned off the grill. "It might be a good night for pizza." She went back in the house and started upstairs to her room to find Naomi. She met Cricket coming down the stairs with an armload of dirty laundry.

"Could you check on the stuff on the grill for me?" Cricket asked.

"You mean the hamburgers that look like little black coasters?"

"What?" Cricket hurried down the stairs and dropped the

laundry in a pile on the floor.

Marcel knocked softly on the door to her room so she wouldn't startle her lover and waited for Naomi's voice. Dressed in shorts and a T-shirt, Naomi's curly hair was wet, and the smile on her lovely face when she saw Marcel was as nice as a cool breeze on a scorching hot day.

Naomi pulled her into the room and put her arms around Marcel's neck. The kiss was warm and lingering. Marcel could feel all the irritation and anxiety that had accumulated during her first five minutes home begin to slip slowly away as Naomi held her.

"What's the matter, darling?" Naomi asked with a light kiss on the neck.

"Can I take you somewhere for dinner?" Marcel asked. "Just the two of us?"

"I thought we were having hamburgers and hot dogs with Cricket and your mom."

"That was the original plan, but when Cricket's in charge of anything to do with food, there had better be more than one plan."

Naomi gave her another kiss. "You really have reached your Cricket limit."

"Like you wouldn't believe. So can I take you to dinner?"

"I'd love to have dinner with you."

Marcel took off her shoes. "Are you all packed for the trip?"

"Yes. I have my luggage in the car ready to go."

"Then I have a favor to ask."

Naomi's good-natured smile made Marcel feel one hundred percent better. They both sat on the edge of the bed.

"I'd like to take a shower," Marcel said, "finish some last-minute packing, and take you to dinner."

"So what's the favor?" Naomi asked.

Marcel unbuttoned her shirt. "After dinner I'd like for us to spend the night at your place and meet Cricket and my mother at the airport in the morning."

"That's the favor? Staying at my place for the night?"

"If we're spending a week cooped up with them, I'll need this evening to mentally prepare myself for it," Marcel said with a chuckle. She could hear how lame and whiny she sounded, but at the moment she didn't care. These were desperate times. *One should not be dreading a vacation*, she thought. *It defeats the whole purpose of going.*

"We can do whatever makes you feel better," Naomi said. "But I also have a favor to ask."

"What's that?"

"You have to be the one to tell your mom we won't be here tonight."

The restaurant they chose wasn't fancy, but they got a table right away. It was just such a relief for Marcel to be out of the house and dining alone with her lover. They ordered, and Marcel even had time to finalize the arrangements for Carmen to pick them up in the morning and take them to the airport.

"Did you see how much luggage Cricket plans to take?" Naomi asked.

"At least one suitcase for shoes," Marcel said. She really didn't want to talk about Cricket.

"How many times have you been to Key West?" Naomi asked.

"Just once. I came home on leave for thirty days when I was in Korea. Mom had just won it back in a poker game in San Diego."

"Did you spend all of your leave there?"

"We did and it was a lot of fun."

"What's the house like?" Naomi asked.

The waiter arrived with an appetizer and tea and water refills.

"It's not fancy or anything," Marcel said, "but it's about thirty yards from the beach and has its own pier. Nice distance from the neighbors on each side. It's the location that makes it so valuable. I can't believe how little respect it gets in Mom's gambling circle. At one point it had changed hands four different times in the same year."

"How big is this place?"

"Three bedrooms and two baths, a nice kitchen area and living room area. It has a pool table and a really nice screened-in porch facing the water." Marcel picked up a deep-fried cheese stick and dunked it into some Ranch dressing. The more she talked about the Key West beach house, the more relaxed she began to feel. Marcel remembered having a really nice time with her mother there. "Have you ever been fishing?"

Naomi smiled. "I used to love it when I was a kid. One of my uncles had a boat and he liked to take it to Oyster Bay Harbor on Long Island. We would load up the whole family and make a day of it."

"Well, this beach house has a pier, and there's a nice place to clean fish there near the carport area at the house."

Naomi held her hands up. "I wouldn't know the first thing about cleaning a fish."

"Ahh," Marcel said. "You're one of those."

"Those what? I had three brothers. That would've been something they were in charge of."

"I didn't learn anything about fishing until I was in the army and went a few times with some friends."

"Ever cleaned a fish?" Naomi asked.

"I have," Marcel said.

"Then let's go fishing while we're there."

Fishing, Marcel thought. *Maybe this really will be a fun vacation.*

Chapter Ten

Carmen arrived early enough for Marcel and Naomi to take her to breakfast before they had to be at the airport. Dressed in her usual starched jeans and pocket tee, she heaved one of Naomi's suitcases into the back of the truck. "How are the other two getting there?" Carmen asked.

"My mom has a friend who owns a limo service," Marcel said. "They'll arrive in style."

"Well, whoop-de-do," Carmen said. "If your mother keeps spoiling her that way, you won't be the only one reaching a Cricket limit."

"All of you take Cricket way too seriously," Naomi said. She got in the backseat of the truck and dug around until she found both ends of the seat belt.

Marcel and Carmen were in the front seat. Carmen looked in the rearview mirror to see Naomi better so she wouldn't have to turn around.

"That might be easy for you to say since Cricket isn't sleeping with *your* mother," Carmen noted.

"Oh, goodness," Naomi said. "I can't even begin to comprehend such a thing. You're right. You're absolutely right."

"It's not even that," Marcel said. "It's just Cricket being Cricket. The sleeping with my mother part is secondary to that. Even if Cricket weren't sleeping with anyone, she would still be irritating the crap out of me right now. It'll run its course. It always does. This too shall pass."

"Let's just forget about it for now," Carmen said. "We'll have a nice breakfast and send you off with smiles, a full tummy and a few warm fuzzies."

"Does this place you're taking us to have breakfast margaritas, by chance?" Marcel asked.

Carmen backed out of Naomi's driveway in a pickup filled with laughter.

"Here you go," Carmen said as she parked in front of the airline they would be taking. She jumped out of the truck and had their luggage on the curb quickly. "Thanks for breakfast."

"Thank *you* for the ride," Marcel said.

"Make sure she has some fun, okay?" Carmen said to Naomi as she gave her a hug.

"I promise."

With waves in between carry-on juggling, they got into line for the Sky Cap service. Once they were inside, the airport was bustling with businessmen, tourists and military personnel all trying to get somewhere. The lines were long, but they were there in plenty of time.

"Look at all these people," Marcel said glancing at her watch and then back at the security line.

"Spring break," Naomi said. "Now I remember why I always

stay home."

"Hey, only one of us at a time is allowed to get bitchy."

Naomi nodded and inched closer to the man in front of her in line. "Do you think the other two are at the gate already?"

Marcel noticed how her mother and Cricket were now being referred to as "the other two." *Perhaps I'm not the only one a little irritated by what's going on*, she thought.

Naomi glanced at her watch. "Or should we be concerned about them even being awake and moving around yet?"

"My mother's very meticulous about her travel plans. I'm sure she's had Cricket up and going for awhile now."

The security line moved quickly, and by the time they reached the gate they still had an hour before boarding.

"See?" Marcel said as she waved to her mother. "There they are."

Weaving their way through rows of seats, carry-ons and out-stretched legs, she and Naomi got as close to Roslin as they could.

"Where's Cricket?" Naomi asked.

"Getting some coffee."

Marcel sat down and picked up a copy of the *USA Today* that was in the seat next to her and had obviously been read and abandoned several times already. She could hear Naomi and Roslin talking, but didn't pay much attention to them. Mentally, Marcel was hoping to be able to get herself in a positive frame of mind so she could relax and enjoy herself over the next few days. She was determined to keep her issues with Cricket to herself whenever possible. Taking her time reading the paper, she hadn't even noticed that Cricket was back with coffee. Feeling restless and eager to get on the plane, Marcel decided to go buy either a book or a magazine at one of the newsstands nearby. She told Naomi where she was going and asked her to watch her things.

A magazine, Marcel thought. *Most books take too long to get into. I won't feel as bad about losing a magazine.*

As she stood looking at the multitude of covers with celebrity headlines she was momentarily torn between Hollywood gossip and the top world news stories. *Maybe I'll try some crossword puzzles and word jumbles*, she thought.

"You got a minute?"

Marcel turned to find her mother standing beside her.

Reaching for a crossword puzzle book, Marcel said, "Sure. What's up?"

"I remembered to call ahead and have the utilities turned on at the beach house."

"They let you do it that way now?" Marcel asked. The first time they were there it took them hours to find out where to go and what to do in order to have electricity and running water. The place wasn't used often enough to keep them on all the time.

"The utility companies probably think Skippy still owns it," Roslin said. "Senators get instant service no matter what they need. All it took was me giving them the address, and I had their attention." She reached for a copy of *Good Housekeeping* and thumbed through it. "You've been acting weird lately. Is everything okay between you and Naomi?"

"We're fine, Mom."

"Well, something's wrong. It's like you're avoiding me."

"It has nothing to do with you." Marcel selected a *Time* magazine and decided to keep on top of world events. It might also put her to sleep after reading a few articles.

"Is it Cricket?"

Marcel didn't answer.

"Okay," Roslin said. "What did she do?"

"She didn't do anything. I really don't want to talk about this."

Roslin selected a *Cosmopolitan* magazine and stood behind Marcel in line.

"Anything I can do to help?" Roslin asked.

"Maybe," Marcel said. "One meal a day together. The four of us. The rest of the time we're on our own. That would make me a very happy person."

Roslin smiled. "Too much togetherness for you lately?"

"At times like this, just the sound of her voice is like a fingernail scraping against a chalkboard."

Roslin's hearty laughter was a relief to hear. At least her mother wasn't upset by her honesty.

"I'm sure seeing that crispy dinner last night didn't help," Roslin said.

"None of this is new," Marcel said. She paid for her magazine and stepped out of the way. "And don't take any of it personally."

"I expect that we can all be in the same place and have fun anyway. After all, this is a vacation."

They walked back to the gate in silence. Marcel was glad they had gotten that out in the open. Her vision of what kind of vacation they would have still wasn't in focus, but no matter how it turned out, at least she was getting away for a few days and they would all know whether or not other trips of this nature would be possible in the future.

"Why are we getting two rental cars?" Cricket asked. "That's silly. We're all going to the same place."

Marcel ignored her and got in line to pick up her rental car at the Key West airport. Her mother got in another line, both deciding to let Naomi deal with Cricket and her endless string of questions.

After thinking about it last night, Marcel had gone online and made reservations for her and Naomi to have their own transportation while they were in Key West. Being stuck sharing one car wasn't something she wanted to do. This way they could really be free to do whatever they wanted.

Marcel was finished first and went over to where Naomi and

Cricket were standing. Cricket seemed to be agitated about the wait.

"Two cars?" Cricket said. "What's up with that?"

"Do the math," Marcel said. "Four adults, each with at least two pieces of luggage. Where would we put everything in one car?"

"I didn't even think of that," Naomi said as she looked around on the floor at all of their luggage. "Here I was explaining our need to be alone during this trip."

"There's that, too," Marcel said.

"How much was it?" Naomi asked. "I want to pay for half."

"We'll settle up when we bring it back," Marcel said. At the mention of Naomi wanting to split the bill, Marcel watched as Cricket walked over to Roslin who was still at the counter. Marcel had noticed before that Cricket hardly ever paid for anything if she and Roslin were out together. It was very unlikely that Cricket would offer to pay for half of the other rental car either.

"I don't think you're the only one who's maxed out on togetherness," Naomi said. "Cricket is really ticked off at us for getting our own car."

"She'll get over it."

"What have we gotten ourselves into?" Naomi mumbled.

The drive along the coast was beautiful, and Marcel was glad to be there. Once they got going, she was amazed at how different everything seemed. Following her mother's car, Marcel didn't see much that she recognized. Roslin turned right at the next street, and then everyone began looking at addresses on the houses. Marcel reached over and turned the radio down.

"Can you see better without the radio blaring?" Naomi asked, teasing her.

"I believe so."

Still, nothing looked familiar, and Marcel was suddenly relieved that her mother was leading this convoy. They drove a few more blocks before Roslin's signal light went on. She turned down an oyster-shell driveway and pulled into the carport.

The grass was high and all the shrubs around the house were overgrown. Roslin got out of the car and marched through the calf-high grass directly to the house next door.

"Which place is it?" Naomi asked.

"This one," Marcel said.

"Then where is your mother going?"

"Probably to chew someone's ass," Marcel said simply. "The guy next door is supposed to watch the house and keep the grass and bushes trimmed in exchange for using our pier when no one is here."

"Ahh. I see."

Marcel, Naomi and Cricket got out and could hear the loud exchange. Before Roslin could wade through the tall grass on her way back to the carport, the neighbor had his lawnmower started and seemed to be more than ready to keep up his end of the bargain.

"It's not like he's got to mow the Ponderosa," Roslin said when she returned to the car. "They make postage stamps bigger than this yard."

"Did he have an excuse?" Cricket asked.

Everyone started taking luggage out of the cars.

"He mentioned that his back had been out," Roslin said. "I bet his back was well enough to use my pier! And not only that, but *his* yard looks pretty good!"

There were several steps to climb to reach the door. The other three carried luggage while Roslin looked for the key.

"You have one, right?" Marcel asked.

"Oh, listen to my funny, funny daughter," Roslin said as she pulled tissues, gum packets and a wallet out of her purse. "Yes, I have one. I just don't happen to remember offhand where I put it."

"I don't see any water," Cricket commented as she looked around.

"It's in the backyard," Marcel said.

That made her mother laugh. "She's right," Roslin said. "We have the Gulf of Mexico in our backyard." She pulled a set of keys out of her purse and held them up triumphantly for all to see. "Here they are! Let's get this vacation started."

Chapter Eleven

Once they were inside Marcel felt a little queasiness in her stomach. It was almost as if they were in someone else's house. The furniture was arranged differently, and whoever had stayed there last hadn't cleaned up after themselves. The place was a mess.

"Will you look at this?" Roslin said. "I see the screw-up fairy has visited us again."

Marcel flipped on the light switch in the kitchen to find empty beer cans all over the counter. She walked over to the sink, turned the faucet on and was relieved to see that they actually had running water.

Roslin opened the empty refrigerator and then closed it again. "Skippy's grandson was here last. That little pig and his friends left it this way. Will you look at this?" she said again. "They didn't even take out the trash!"

Marcel was furious at the condition the house had been left

in. There were paper plates and plastic cups everywhere. Sand was all over the floor, and towels were piled up in several places around the pool table in the living room. Coming from a military background, Marcel liked neatness and order to her surroundings. What she was witnessing now showed a total lack of respect for everything.

"We have two choices," Roslin said. She opened the door that led out to the large screened-in porch. The others followed her, and they all stood side by side gazing at the beach and the water.

This is why we're here, Marcel thought. She reached for Naomi's hand as all four of them watched the waves rush toward the beach.

"We can spend a few hours cleaning this place up and making it ours again," Roslin said, "or we can see if any of the hotels have rooms."

"It's spring break," Cricket reminded her. "There's probably not a room available anywhere between here and Baltimore."

"I'm okay with cleaning," Marcel said. "It's been years since I was involved in a GI party of this magnitude."

"Looks like a bunch of GI's already had a party," Cricket said while glancing over her shoulder.

Marcel unlocked the back door and took Naomi by the hand again. They stood out on the deck and let the salty Gulf breeze introduce itself to them. Marcel could feel all the tension and angst leave her body as the sound of the water and the cry of seagulls overhead helped get her centered again. Whatever problems she had recently been experiencing with Cricket, or just life in general, were slowly beginning to slip away. Being here by the sea with those she loved was exactly what Marcel had needed.

Since Roslin knew her way around better than anyone else, she volunteered to go get cleaning supplies. Marcel made a list for her while the others checked the place out to see exactly what they would need.

"Those little pigs were at least practicing safe sex," Roslin called from one of the bedrooms.

"Laundry detergent for the bed linens," Marcel mumbled as she wrote.

"Is that a condom on the floor?" Cricket yelled, horrified. "Ohmigod! How disgusting!"

"We get the other bedroom," Marcel heard Naomi say from somewhere in the house.

"Skippy will be glad to know his grandson was being responsible in at least one area," Roslin said. "Just wait until I see him again."

As she collected all the beer cans and put them in one place on the counter, Marcel mumbled to herself, "The screw-up fairy wears condoms. That's good to know."

"Well, I'm not touching any dried-up rubbers," Cricket declared.

"Ice tongs," Marcel said while scribbling something else on the list.

"Speak up, Cricket," Naomi said. "The neighbors on the other side didn't hear you."

Roslin came into the kitchen where Marcel was and said, "I've got an idea what we need. I'll be back soon, then we can get our ducks in a huddle."

Marcel handed her the list and decided to go for a walk on the beach while her mother was gone. There was no sense in getting stressed over this. Marcel was determined to not let anything get in the way of her having a nice vacation.

She took her time on the boardwalk from the house to the beach. The native grass in what would be considered the backyard grew in clumps and stayed green year-round. Marcel walked out to the end of the pier and instantly became mesmerized by the water. As the salty wind caressed her face, she imagined how easy it would be to think that someone could sail right off the edge of the earth. She lost track of time and thought seriously about asking her mother to retire this piece of property from her cache of gambling assets. It was a place that meant more to her than Marcel had realized. The one and only other time she and her mother were there they'd had some of the best talks she could ever remember.

Eventually, it was the sun beating down on her that got Marcel's attention. Slowly she walked back to the house, psyching herself up for a few hours of intense cleaning. Getting away like this had been an excellent idea.

Marcel reached the deck and found Naomi and Cricket relaxing in the patio chairs that had been inside the screened-in area earlier.

"So what did you see out there?" Cricket asked.

"Water," Marcel said. "Serenity." She sat down beside Naomi.

"Are there any sharks in this area?" Cricket asked.

"If people knew what they were out there swimming with," Naomi said, "there would be no one in the water."

"So that's a yes on the sharks?"

"Oh, yes." Naomi pointed toward the water. "That's where sharks live."

A while later they heard Roslin arrive. She had bags of supplies and groceries. "There's more in the car," she said.

Cricket and Marcel went out the back door and down the steps to the car. Admiring how nice the yard looked now that the grass had been cut, Cricket said, "Do you think if your mom yelled at the neighbor again he'd come over and clean the inside, too?"

Marcel smiled and could almost see such a thing happening.

Cleaning was actually more fun than Marcel thought it would be. They all got serious about it and a few hours later had four loads of towels and bed linens done, three garbage bags full of trash, and the floors swept and mopped in an orderly fashion.

"Look what I made," Cricket said at one point. "I swept up our own little sand dune right here in the living room."

"You bought exactly what we needed, too," Naomi said to Roslin.

"That's because I gave her a list," Marcel said.

Beds were made as soon as sheets and pillowcases came out of the dryer, and room deodorizers were plugged into all outlets that weren't being used for something else. Before long, the place was spotless and smelling sweetly of citrus. Afterward, they were all too tired to do anything other than sit on the deck and enjoy the view.

Later that evening, after a light dinner that consisted of ham and cheese sandwiches and chips, they were sitting back out on the deck enjoying the moonlight reflecting off the water. Feeling tired and peaceful, Marcel listened to the sound of the waves rolling on shore and marveled at the soothing reminder of how the simplest things could bring such pleasure.

"I have a confession to make," Cricket said quietly.

"What did you do now?" Roslin asked.

"After I picked up those used condoms with the ice tongs, I threw them away."

Teasing her, Roslin asked, "You threw the condoms away or the ice tongs away?"

"Now why would I keep those nasty condoms and just throw away the ice tongs? I threw everything away. Tongs and all."

Chuckles went around the deck.

"I couldn't help it. Men are just so gross. I'll probably never be able to use tongs again."

"I would've done the same thing," Naomi said. "All I found were a few popcorn kernels in the bed in our room, so thanks for claiming the one with its own bathroom right away. I'll take a popcorn kernel over a used condom any day."

"How about we don't mention the words 'used condom' anymore?" Roslin said while cringing.

"Good idea," Marcel agreed with a nod.

"I can't believe you didn't get any wine while you were gone," Cricket said.

"Blame Marcel," Roslin said. "It wasn't on the list."

"Neither were the chips, bread and lunchmeat you brought back," Marcel reminded her, "so I can't see how that's really my fault. I had cleaning on my mind. Not eating and drinking."

"Then you don't get to make the list next time," Cricket said.

"Maybe we could try making a batch of margaritas one night," Naomi said. "I think I saw a blender in the kitchen."

"You know what I've always wanted to do?" Roslin said. "Find some of those Popsicle things and put a margarita in there and freeze it."

"And have margaritas on a stick?" Naomi said.

"We'll call them stick-a-ritas!" Roslin said.

"Now I could go for that," Marcel said.

After they settled down again, Naomi asked, "What are you two doing tomorrow?"

Marcel was glad to hear someone else mention that the four of them would have different agendas the next day.

"Going shopping for wine is first on my list," Cricket said.

"What about you two?" Roslin asked.

"In the morning I want to see what kind of fishing tackle has been left here," Marcel said. "Then we're going to get our fishing license."

"Do you need a license to fish off a private pier?" Roslin asked.

"I would think that fishing is fishing no matter where you're standing or sitting while you're doing it," Marcel said.

"Sounds like a rip-off to me," Cricket commented. "Those fish belong to the ocean. Not the state of Florida. You should be able to do whatever you want with them."

"Be that as it may," Marcel said, "we're getting a fishing license, and we're doing some fishing while we're here."

"So what else is on our list for tomorrow besides buying wine?" Roslin asked her lover.

"Baggin' some rays on the beach and watching Marcel fish, I guess," Cricket said. "After I sleep in, of course."

"There's no sleeping in on vacation," Roslin said. "You can do that at home."

Cricket laughed. "Some of us work when we're home."

"There's a place up the road where we can rent Jet Skis," Roslin said. "That might be fun."

"I'd get up early for that," Cricket said.

Roslin and Cricket went for a walk on the beach while Marcel and Naomi stayed on the deck talking and listening to the sound of the ocean.

"I always forget how much I like being close to the water," Naomi said. "I could get used to this quite easily."

"That futon on the screened-in porch is really comfortable," Marcel said. "Would you like to sleep there tonight so we can hear the water?"

"Excellent idea. You know, Cricket was telling me earlier that this summer she wants to visit all the places Roslin has."

"That'll make for a busy summer."

"Cricket thinks that if she keeps her busy traveling, Roslin won't have the need to gamble as much."

Marcel tilted her head in a nod. "What Cricket doesn't real-ize is how much it'll cost to do that kind of traveling. Even with the accommodations already taken care of and the frequent flyer miles kicked in, my mother will probably do a few gambling gigs to make sure she's got the money to go on vacation. She likes to have a good time, and she'll want to make sure she can afford it."

Naomi laughed. "Well, that's something Cricket certainly hasn't thought of. She just wants to go, go, go."

"On someone else's dollar."

"Cricket makes good money," Naomi said. "I've never known her to hang onto it so tightly before."

Marcel watched the two figures walking together on the beach in the moonlight. "Cricket's finally living part of her fantasy," she said softly.

"Which fantasy is that?"

"Being kept by my mother."

Chapter Twelve

They stripped the bed in their room and made up the futon out on the porch. After showering and then putting on pajamas, Naomi suggested a game of pool before they turned in for the evening. They racked the balls and selected pool sticks. The last time Marcel was there, she and her mother had played several games when they had been forced to stay inside while it rained.

"I'm not very good at this," Naomi said as she lined up the cue ball to break. She sent the white ball soaring toward the triangle-shaped ball cluster at the other end of the table, only to have four balls in the triangle barely move. "See? What did I tell you?"

Marcel had played a lot of pool while in the army and felt comfortable with her shot selection and the ball setup Naomi had left her with. She easily won two games and spent the last one giving her lover a few pointers on how to improve her game.

"You ready to try out that futon?" Naomi asked.

"I am."

They put everything back the way they had found it and went out on the screened-in porch. Clouds had covered the moon, but it was still light enough to see. Marcel kicked off her slippers and stretched out on the futon. She was tired, and it felt good to be lying down.

Naomi lay beside her and asked, "How do you think day number one went?"

"Very well despite having to clean. We all could've done without that."

"It's to be expected," Naomi said. "The place has been closed up for months." She snuggled into Marcel's arms, and they both listened to the intoxicating sounds of a Key West night. Somewhere out in the yard the low croak of a bullfrog was synchronized with the tide hugging and releasing the shore. With the faint scent of strawberry in Naomi's hair and a myriad of soothing elements in place to lull her to sleep, Marcel felt relaxed enough to let go and begin to doze.

As she slowly slipped into a peaceful sleep, Marcel heard a low moan as if it were off in the distance somewhere. She moved her head and felt Naomi lightly kiss the side of her face. Seconds later she heard another moan drifting from a place much closer.

"Is that you?" Marcel mumbled from the shallow well of sleep.

"No," Naomi said. With a tinge of impatience in her voice, she added, "It's coming from the other side of the wall. In their bedroom."

Suddenly Marcel was wide-awake and listening. "Are you sure?" she whispered just seconds before another moan seeped through the wall again. "Oh, for cryin' out loud." Marcel sat up and put her hands over her ears. "That's Cricket!" she hissed.

Naomi sat up too and struggled to find her shoes on the floor.

"Cricket," she said. "Great. Just great. I'd nearly forgotten the reason you would know which one of them it was."

They were both scrambling around looking for shoes now. Marcel didn't want to think about what was causing Cricket to make that kind of sound, but it certainly didn't stop her brain from forming a conclusion. *She's having sex with my mother!*

By the time Marcel got her house shoes on, Naomi was already out on the deck sitting in one of the chairs. Marcel joined her and chose the chair that was the farthest away from the moaning wall.

"I'm sorry," Naomi said quietly. "It's not that often I'm reminded of the fact that you and Cricket were once lovers."

"It's okay," Marcel said with a sigh. "It's not that often I'm reminded of the fact that my mother has sex with Cricket on a regular basis."

Despite Marcel sounding depressed and defeated, they both managed to find a snippet of humor in the situation.

"I guess the walls at home are pretty thick," Marcel said. "I've never heard anything like that there."

Naomi reached for her hand and held it in the darkness. "You're a remarkable woman. I'm not sure I could do what you're having to do. Seldom do I think of Roslin as your mother. I think of her as Cricket's lover, and I think of her as a friend. This morning when Carmen put it all in perspective, it was a real eye-opener. I can't even comprehend the scenario where my mother and my first lover would even be in the same room together, much less in the same bed. It's just so . . . so . . . I can't even put it into words." Naomi gave Marcel's hand a squeeze before letting go. "I don't know how you do it."

"On the futon a few minutes ago wasn't one of my finer moments."

"Well, I think you're amazing. I'll try to be more supportive in the future," Naomi said, "and less jealous of Cricket and your teenybopper relationship with her."

"Why don't we go to our room and make a few moaning noises of our own?" Marcel suggested.

"Might as well. Neither one of us is sleepy anymore."

When they got up the next morning, the coffee was already made and there was a bag of bagels on the kitchen counter. Marcel opened the refrigerator and saw that they now had wine, lox, cream cheese and enough food to get them through a few days.

"Wow. What time is it?" Marcel asked. "They must've been up and about for a while already. I didn't hear a thing."

"It's nine thirty," Naomi said. "I can't remember the last time I slept this late."

"They left us breakfast," Marcel said as she set the lox container on the kitchen counter then poured them each a cup of coffee.

"Maybe this is their breakfast."

"Well, it's ours now."

"You're certainly in a good mood."

"I like the idea of waking up and having them gone already," Marcel said. "I need to put some time and distance between us before I'll be able to look my mother in the eye again anytime soon."

"Everything will be fine." Naomi spread cream cheese on her bagel and cut it in half. "Tell me about you and Cricket when you were younger."

Marcel pulled one of the barstools around the other side of the counter so they could have breakfast across from each other.

"We first met in the seventh grade," Marcel said. "Cricket was cute and funny. Very popular. I'd had a growth spurt that summer which resulted in me being about six inches taller than everyone else, including the boys. I felt geeky and awkward. Cricket had a huge crush on me, but we didn't have any classes together. We'd see each other in the hallway, and she would actually turn around and walk backward so she could watch me." Marcel smiled at the memory and took a small bite of her bagel. "She was bold and fearless. She managed to get herself transferred into my homeroom, and after that we became friends."

"So Cricket pursued you," Naomi said.

"Like a cheetah running down a limping gazelle."

"A limping gazelle," Naomi repeated before taking another bite of her bagel. With an amused expression she said, "I can easily visualize Cricket as a pouncing cheetah out on the Serengeti, but you as a limping gazelle? Helpless? Waiting for the inevitable end?"

"I was a babe in the woods," Marcel said. "I wasn't comfortable with the feelings I'd been having about other girls my age. Somehow Cricket sensed that about me and went in for the kill."

"You fought her off, of course."

Marcel laughed. "I was a willing participant and felt like the luckiest person in the world. Cricket Lomax liked me. Life was good."

"To know that you were gay at such an early age must've been a blessing," Naomi said.

"When I look back on it now, I know it was, but at the time it was a heavy burden for any thirteen-year-old to have to deal with. Cricket helped me work through several things, and together we survived puberty without too many bumps and bruises. I was also fortunate to have a mother who would go to the library and look things up if she ran across something she wasn't sure how to handle. We spent a lot of time at the library. I probably had a library card before I got my first tooth."

"Things would've made more sense to me when I was growing up if I had known about lesbians," Naomi said. "You were lucky in a lot of ways."

Marcel heard footsteps on the stairs. It was Cricket and Roslin.

"Are we eating your breakfast?" Naomi asked as soon as they both came in.

"What if I said yes?" Roslin raised an eyebrow while glancing at their paper plates and what was left of the two bagels.

"Then we would apologize and offer to share," Marcel said.

Roslin gave Marcel a hug and said, "Actually, I brought you breakfast because I knew we'd need a favor later."

"Must there always be a catch to kindness?" Marcel asked Naomi.

"Can you drop us off at the Jet Ski place?" Roslin asked. "We're renting them for the week and didn't want to leave our rental car there at the marina."

"Sure," Marcel said. "We'll be out and about getting our fishing license anyway."

"This is the best vacation ever," Cricket said. She put her arms around Roslin's neck and kissed her.

Marcel remembered the previous night where the moaning on the other side of the wall had forced her to think about things that she didn't want to think about. She glanced up to see Naomi looking at her. They finished their breakfast in silence, but Marcel felt a mixture of angst and uncertainty as her mother and Cricket held hands and left the kitchen practically skipping to their bedroom.

Chapter Thirteen

All the fishing gear was right where Marcel had seen it the last time she was there. *It's nice to know the screw-up fairy doesn't like to fish*, she thought. After a quick inventory of what they had in the fish-cleaning area off the carport, Marcel climbed the back steps in hopes of finding one of the showers empty by now. She and Naomi would do some exploring while they were out. Since there was just one main road going to and from the Keys, there was only a slim possibility that they would get lost enough to not be able to find their way back again.

Marcel and Naomi were ready to leave long before the other two were. Finally, Roslin came out on the back porch wearing white sneakers and a flowery tangerine-colored blouse with matching shorts.

"Big discussion going on," Roslin said. "What does one wear while operating a Jet Ski?"

Marcel nodded. "Can't have an FFP on a Jet Ski."

"What's an FFP?" Naomi asked.

"Fashion faux pas," Marcel replied.

Their laughter brought Cricket out in a huff.

"Well, I'm wearing a swimsuit," Cricket said. "I need to work on my tan while I'm here." Her bright pink bikini covered next to nothing. She wore a shirt over it with the buttons undone, which made her look casual, younger and even less like the tourist she actually was. She put on a cap with the San Antonio Spurs logo and tucked some of her hair under it.

"Jet Ski etiquette," Marcel said. "I'm not sure such a thing exists."

"We can ask around once we get there," Roslin said.

"I'm not asking anyone anything!" Cricket said.

Marcel and Naomi couldn't hide their amusement over this ridiculous discussion. *Why care about what you wear on vacation?* Marcel wondered. *Who are these two trying to impress anyway?*

"I have an idea," Naomi said. "How about we drive over to the Jet Ski place and see what other people are wearing? If either one of you are about to commit an FFP, we'll bring you back to change clothes."

"Now you're talkin'," Cricket said. "You happy with that?" she asked Roslin.

"Yeah, I guess so, but I'm not changing clothes no matter what everyone else is wearing. If a Jet Ski won't operate because I'm in shorts and sneakers, then I don't want to rent one anyway."

Marcel smiled at her mother's sense of self, her determination and confidence to be her own person. No FFP was going to rule how she did things or what she wanted to wear while doing them.

"Whose dumb ass idea was it to rent Jet Skis anyway?" Roslin asked.

"Yours," the other three said at the same time.

"Well, remind me to stop thinking out loud so much."

"I see wet suits, bathing suits, shorts and jeans," Naomi said as she craned her neck to check out the Jet Ski customers in line.

"Then let's go before they rent them all," Roslin said.

Marcel stopped the car and Roslin opened the door and got out before sticking her head back in to thank them for the ride. "We'll see you for dinner tonight," she said.

As they watched them get in line Marcel said, "I think we should wait until they scoot off into the sunset on those things. They might change their mind and need a ride back."

"Then let's find a place to park and walk around a little," Naomi said. "It's really beautiful here."

Marcel enjoyed being at the marina. It was a buzz of activity and had a little bit of everything. She could see a few people parasailing over the water off in the distance, a crowded tour boat on its way back in with chattering onlookers, signs for snorkeling guides, fishing tours and big-wheeled paddleboats for rent by the hour.

After parking, they got out of the car and glanced around at all the people there. Marcel also noticed how everyone was dressed—it looked like any other place during spring break—shorts, jeans, sweats, sundresses, sandals, boots, sneakers. "The Keys want our money," she decided. "They don't care what we're wearing when they take it."

"It's nothing like Oyster Bay," Naomi said. "I'm glad we're here."

They walked over toward the Jet Ski rental and saw Roslin getting some instructions from a teenage boy with green spiked hair and a golden tan. Marcel spotted Cricket in her pink bikini with her red hair still tucked up into the Spurs cap. She no longer had the shirt on over her swimsuit.

"I hope they have sunscreen," Naomi said. "This sun will make them a pair of crispy critters in no time."

They watched Roslin and Cricket take off slowly and then pick up speed as they gained confidence in their Jet Skiing abilities. Once they were out of sight, Marcel suggested she and Naomi go on one of the boat tours to see the area.

"My treat," she added.

"It's been years since I've been on a boat," Naomi said. "What a great idea. That sounds like fun."

It was over an hour's wait before the next tour. They found a place to get their fishing license then walked around the marina and occasionally saw Roslin and Cricket laughing and racing side by side across the water.

"Do you have any desire to ride one of those?" Marcel asked.

Naomi shook her head. "Not when I think about what's out there. Big, hungry fish looking for a meal."

Cricket and Roslin seemed to be having so much fun it made Marcel wonder what it would be like to ride one. "What if we were on a lake instead of the ocean?" Marcel asked. "There aren't any fish that would eat you in a lake."

"A lot of lakes have alligators."

"Alligators?"

After a moment, Naomi began to laugh. "I'm teasing you. Would you like to rent some Jet Skis?"

"I'm not dressed right for that sort of thing," Marcel said looking down at her khaki shorts and T-shirt with humor in her eyes.

"That excuse won't fly in these parts. I imagine the closest thing to an FFP around here would be the total absence of clothing on a Jet Ski."

"Let's see how they do today," Marcel suggested. "If they make it sound as much fun as it looks, then maybe it'll be something we can do."

Occasionally they got a glimpse of Roslin or Cricket zooming along on the water with several other Jet Skiers all attempting to get their sea legs in the immediate area. *Noisy and annoying*, Marcel thought while watching them send waves up to the dock, keeping all the boats in the marina rocking back and forth.

"I've always admired people who want to try new things," Naomi said. "Seeking adventure was never something that interested me. I would've made a lousy pilgrim." She cupped her hands over her mouth as if calling to passengers on the *Mayflower*. In a strong Brooklyn accent she said, "When you get to that Plymouth Rock place, write me a letter and tell me all about your trip. I might come to visit in the summer."

Marcel's laughter and genuine delight in Naomi's presence as well as her sense of humor kept them both in good spirits. They walked over to a fishing guide boat that had just docked. Other tourists were there too waiting to see what they had caught. One pale, shaky fisherman got off the boat, fell to his knees and kissed the pavement in front of the crowd.

"Now that can't be very good for business," Marcel said.

A boy about ten was by the man's side saying, "Dad, get up. You're embarrassing me."

Marcel and Naomi moved on to give the seasick fisherman and his son some privacy even though the rest of the crowd didn't practice that type of thoughtfulness. There were others coming off the fishing boat with a lot less energy than the pavement-kissing man had, but everyone seemed to be very happy to be on land again.

Having decided to get to know more about their surroundings, they were close to the front of the line when the tour boat captain finally began taking tickets to let everyone on board. Marcel and Naomi got seats up front in the air-conditioned section of the boat. They were pleasantly surprised at how many gay couples there were at the marina as well as on the tour.

"We've found our people," Naomi said.

"Our people keep this place in business, I bet. We'll have to check out the gay district soon. My mother might like that better than the Jet Skis."

The tour took them to interesting places and showed them things they couldn't have seen or learned about on their own. Key West was a truly beautiful national treasure in its own right, full of history and quaint businesses sure to pique almost anyone's interest. By the time the tour was over and they were back at the marina again, Marcel and Naomi were ready to do some exploring on their own in the car.

"Let's make a pact," Marcel said as she unlocked the car doors. "If we get lost, we never tell anyone about it. Deal?"

Naomi laughed. "Deal."

Chapter Fourteen

They shopped for a while and then had a late lunch at a restaurant on the water at another marina. Everywhere they went they saw gay couples holding hands and enjoying the freedom to do so. Marcel felt more comfortable there than anywhere else she had ever been with a lover. It was a miracle that after having spent over half of her life in the military under such rigorous homophobic oppression, none of that had scarred her for life. She had served her country well and now it was time to do the things that meant the most to her. It was very invigorating to be so free, and she and Naomi took full advantage of this opportunity by holding hands, going from shop to shop and standing closer than they normally would when they were out in public anywhere else.

After purchasing some postcards and a T-shirt for Carmen, Marcel said, "I think I'm ready for a nap."

"Depending on whether or not we can find our way back to

the house, that sounds like a great idea."

Once they were in the car with all their purchases, getting to the beach house was easy. Marcel found it as if she had lived there all her life. Lugging their bags up the steps from the carport, Marcel heard voices inside the house. They opened the door to the kitchen in time to see Roslin and Cricket making sandwiches.

"There you are," Roslin said. "We were starving and needed a bathroom break."

From the living room Marcel peered through the opened door that led to the screened-in porch where she could see the two Jet Skis parked on the beach. *Here I was all worried about finding this place in a car, and these two ride in on Jet Skis from an entirely new direction*, she thought. *Okay. I'm impressed.*

"I *love* Jet Skis," Cricket said. "I'd spend every weekend on the lake if I had one of my own."

"Alligators," Marcel said on her way to the bedroom with her bag of souvenirs. By the time she got back to the kitchen the other two were finished with lunch.

"We're headed out again," Cricket announced.

"We'll be back in time for dinner," Roslin said.

"About what time would that be?" Marcel asked. "We found a great restaurant we want to take you both to."

"Around five," Roslin said.

"Put some sunscreen on," Naomi warned. "You're both starting to turn pink already."

Cricket waved a tube of something over her head as they hurried across the boardwalk toward the beach and the Jet Skis.

"Those two worry me sometimes," Naomi said.

"Nothing we can do about that. Let's go take a nap."

By the time they got up from a nice long nap, took showers and got dressed again, it was four o'clock.

"Fishing tomorrow for sure," Naomi promised. "This day has

just completely gotten away from us."

"That's what vacations are for, I think. It's great not having anything to do for a change."

They played a few games of pool while waiting for Cricket and Roslin to return, but there was no sign of them at five, six or six thirty.

"So where are they?" Marcel asked, looking at her watch again for what had to be the thirtieth time already. Her initial annoyance was now beginning to turn into worry.

"They probably lost track of time."

"I'll give 'em another thirty minutes, then I'm going back to the marina to see if anyone has seen them." Marcel sat down in one of the deck chairs, her eyes focused on the beach hoping to see her mother and Cricket arrive. She tilted her head in order to hear better, but the distant hum of Jet Skis never materialized.

At seven o'clock sharp, Marcel got up and kissed Naomi on top of the head. "I'm going to the marina. I'll have my cell phone on. If you see them, call me."

"You do the same, please."

Marcel walked down the back steps to her rental car with a mixture of anger and fear. The possibility that something had happened to them was weighing heavily on her mind. She took a deep breath, and as calmly as she could, drove to the marina where thankfully they hadn't closed for the day. Marcel didn't bother looking for a parking place. She just stopped the car in front of the Jet Ski rental building and got out. Spotting the young teenager with the green spiked hair, she asked him if he had seen any sign of Cricket and her mother.

"Pop!" the young man called. "Someone's here to see you!"

At that point Marcel wasn't sure if she should be even more upset than she already was. She certainly got the feeling something was up.

"Yes, ma'am. Can I help you?" The man was an older version of the teenager, with tattoos covering both arms and a crew cut instead of green spikes on his head, but the family resemblance was obvious.

"Two women rented Jet Skis from you this morning," Marcel said, "and they should've been back several hours ago. Have you seen them?"

"We've got reports from other customers that two women are stranded out there," he said.

Stranded, Marcel thought with relief. *That sounds much better than missing.*

"They probably ran out of gas," he added. "I have someone out looking for them now."

"How long have they been looking?"

"About an hour."

Marcel's cell phone rang. She snatched it out of her pocket.

"It's me," Naomi said. "They're here. A boat followed them in."

"Thanks. I'll be right there." She closed her phone feeling a huge sense of relief. Marcel looked at the man and said, "They're back safely. Thank you for your help."

"Yes, ma'am. This kind of thing happens all the time."

On her way back to the beach house Marcel took the time to calm down again and tuck her anger away. *They're safe,* she reminded herself. *That's the important thing now.*

Minutes later when she pulled into the oyster shell driveway, Marcel noticed that all the lights in the house were on. Naomi met her at the back door and urged her to sit on the steps so she could fill her in on what she knew so far.

"They aren't speaking," Naomi whispered, "and Cricket has such a bad sunburn I think she needs to go to the hospital."

"So much for your little sunscreen reminder," Marcel said. "Why aren't they talking to each other?"

"Both Jet Skis ran out of gas while they were a long way out from the shore. From what I gathered, it was Cricket's fault they were put in that position."

"That doesn't surprise me. Where are they now?"

"Cricket's in the living room sitting in the recliner staring at the TV. She's about the color of a cooked lobster."

"And my mother?"

"Roslin stormed off to take a shower."

Marcel nodded and made a decision. "I'll go see if either one of them wants to go to dinner with us. If not, then you're stuck with me for the evening. We're not getting sucked up in their little drama."

"Is it bad of me to hope they both want to stay here?"

Marcel laughed and stood up. "I'm hoping the same thing, but we should invite them anyway. That was the original plan."

They went into the house, where the TV was on showing a commercial for a local sailboat company. Marcel walked over to Cricket and was immediately shocked at how sunburned she was.

"Hey," Marcel said.

Cricket slowly reached up and took off her San Antonio Spurs cap. Her red hair tumbled down and was an interesting contrast to her new skin color.

"You got a little sunburn there, kiddo."

"No shit," Cricket said.

"You want to go to the hospital?"

"So they can do what? Tell me I've managed to roast myself? I put sunscreen on all day! How could this happen?"

"Jet Skiing in a bikini wasn't the wisest move you've made in a while," Marcel said. Seeing the large tube of sunscreen on the floor, she bent down and picked it up. "Is this what you were using?"

Cricket moved her eyes, but kept her head still. "Yes."

"It expired in June 2003," Marcel said. "Five-year-old expired sunscreen. You might as well have been rubbing sea water on yourself."

"Sunscreen expires?"

"Everything expires eventually. So you want us to take you to the emergency room?"

"No. Just leave me alone."

"We're going out to dinner then," Marcel said. "Can we bring you something?"

"I'm fine. Thanks."

"Okay. Let us know if you need anything." Marcel went to the kitchen to see if Naomi had seen any sign of Roslin yet.

"You were a little hard on her there," Naomi said.

"Even though she's a college graduate, she's not the sharpest tool in the shed," Marcel said. "I have very little patience for stupid behavior. I'm going to see if my mom wants to go to dinner with us."

Once again she reined in her anger and refused to let Cricket's juvenile actions get the best of her. Marcel was determined to have a nice vacation no matter what. She knocked on her mother's bedroom door.

"It's open," Roslin said. She was in a robe and her hair was wet from a shower, but neatly combed already.

"Naomi and I are going out for dinner. Are you up for that?"

"I've got other plans," Roslin said. "Thanks. Can you take me to the airport? I need to see if I can get a flight to Miami."

"Miami? Why? What's in Miami this time of night?"

"Everything. Besides, it's still early."

Marcel watched her mother fold some clothes into a small suitcase. "Why are you going to Miami?"

"I had a message from Skippy on my cell phone. He wants to get a poker game together. That's where we agreed to meet. He's setting things up."

"How long will you be gone?"

"A day or two."

"But we're on vacation. You can't work on vacation."

"Says who?"

Arguing with her mother never did much good, so she let it go. "Cricket's out there baked to a crisp," Marcel said. "Does she know you're leaving?"

"Ask her if she cares."

"Take her with you."

Roslin laughed. "No way. We need some time apart after today."

"What happened today?" Marcel asked. She lay across the bed and watched her mother continue packing. It was a ritual that dated back to Marcel's childhood—Roslin carefully folding clothes for a gambling trip, with Marcel on the bed talking and watching her.

"She never listens," Roslin said. "Gas gauges were registering low, but she didn't want to go in and take the time to fill up. The next thing I know, her Jet Ski is sputtering to a stop. She's out of gas. By the time I reached her mine did the same thing." Roslin folded a black silk blouse and placed it in the suitcase. "It's one thing to be riding on top of the water with the wind in your face. It's a totally different experience sitting there waiting for someone to come along and help you. I was so furious I couldn't even talk to her. Whose dumb ass idea was it to rent Jet Skis anyway?"

"Yours," Marcel said. She sat up on the edge of the bed. "You know how she is and you knew you needed gas. Why did you let her stay out there? I don't get it."

"I couldn't leave her and she wouldn't listen."

"Well, she's out there in the living room with a severe sunburn. I think she needs to go to the hospital."

"Did you tell her that?"

"Yes."

"And she won't go, right?"

"Right."

"Then let her snivel and whine. I'm going to Miami. I have work to do." She closed her suitcase just as her cell phone rang. "Skippy!" Roslin said. "Did you get things set up?"

Marcel sighed. *Great*, she thought. *Cricket's fried and now we're stuck with her.*

"What?" Roslin said into her phone. "No flights tonight? Oh! You can? Well, that's even better! Yes, Marcel can have me there by then."

Marcel arched a brow at the mention of her name.

"I'll see you later then. Thanks!" Roslin closed her phone and took off her robe. "That was Skippy. He's coming to get me. I need to be at the airport within the hour."

Marcel gave her a brief nod and walked away. "Well, we're ready when you are," she said. They weren't making it easy to stay calm and collected, and being stuck with a whiney, poached Cricket didn't sound like that much fun either.

Chapter Fifteen

After taking Roslin to the airport and having a nice dinner on the water, Marcel and Naomi were both tired. They made sure Cricket was as comfortable as possible in the recliner before they went to bed. The next morning when Marcel checked on her, Cricket was right where they had left her with the TV on. It didn't look like she had moved all night.

"Can you put me in a sitting position?" Cricket asked.

Marcel adjusted the recliner to an upright position.

"Ouch, ouch, ouch, ouch!"

"Sorry," Marcel said.

Cricket needed help getting out of the chair. She had to go to the bathroom. She held her arms out for Marcel to pull her up, and once she was in a standing position, she walked like a malfunctioning robot down the hall to the nearest bathroom. Apparently while she was in there, she couldn't get the bottom of her bikini off without screeching from the pain. Finally, Naomi and Marcel heard a pitiful cry of, "I need help," coming from the other side of the bathroom door.

"I'm not going in there," Naomi said emphatically while spreading butter on a piece of toast as if she were mad at it. "I know what she needs help with."

"I can't believe my mother left her with us this way."

"I need help," the tiny voice said again from the bathroom.

"You're going with me," Marcel told her lover.

"No way."

"Yes, you are."

"I like being the only one who's never seen Cricket naked," Naomi informed her.

"She's not naked."

"She will be if you go in there to help her."

The pitiful voice from down the hall said a little louder, "I need help."

"Fine," Marcel said as she got up from the kitchen counter and marched to the bathroom. She knocked on the door.

"Come in," Cricket said. "Thank goodness someone heard me."

Marcel went in and found her standing there as stiff as a statue.

"Where's Roslin?" Cricket asked. "I haven't seen her this morning."

"She went to Miami last night."

"Miami? Why is she in Miami?"

"What is it you need help with?" Marcel asked. Just looking at Cricket and the dark red color of her skin made Marcel momentarily forget their differences and tap into that part of her that held compassion for someone in pain. If Cricket's sunburn hurt only half as badly as it looked like it should, the pain would have to be excruciating.

"I need help getting my bikini bottoms off so I can pee,"

Cricket said. "I've held it as long as I can." She slowly looked down at her lower torso, which was a deep, painful red. "Can you get the bottoms off without touching my legs?"

Marcel looked at the bikini bottoms that fit her perfectly. There wasn't anything the least bit baggy as she reached over and tugged on the fabric. Marcel could feel the heat radiating from Cricket's skin.

"I don't think so," Marcel said. "There's not much give to the material."

"Then cut them off of me."

"If I do that then what will you wear?"

"Nothing."

"Well, *that's* not gonna happen," Marcel said. "You can't walk around here with just your top on."

"Sure I can. Hell, how much walking do you think I'll be doing anyway? I'm not leaving the house for a while. Just getting up out of the chair nearly killed me."

"Leaving the house," Marcel mumbled. "You can't even scratch your own butt right now."

"Go find something to cut them off with," Cricket insisted.

"Let me try one more thing," Marcel said moments before she reached over and yanked the bikini bottoms off. Cricket's eyes popped open and she sucked in a heavy breath in response to the pain. It happened so quickly that everything was nearly over with before Cricket even realized what Marcel had done.

"You bitch," Cricket whispered in a raspy, shocked tone of voice. Her bikini bottoms were around her ankles.

Marcel was even more stunned to see the contrasting skin colors from where the bikini bottoms had been. The part of her butt that had been covered and protected from the sun looked even whiter against the lobster-colored tone of the rest of her skin. The colors were so strikingly different that it almost looked like Cricket had on underwear.

"Go ahead and pee now," Marcel said. "I'll be back when

you're finished. We'll get those bottoms on you again the same way they came off."

"You bitch," Marcel heard her say breathlessly as she left to give Cricket some privacy.

Marcel and Naomi were both in agreement that Cricket needed to go to the hospital, but Cricket kept refusing to take that suggestion, so there wasn't much else they could do about it. Once that was settled, Naomi more or less stopped having anything to do with helping her.

"She needs to put lotion or something on the burn," Naomi said. "It'll help keep the skin moist and maybe she won't peel so badly."

Marcel thought that sounded like a good idea. She mentioned it to Cricket whose only answer was, "I can't bend to reach anything other than my arms and the tops of my thighs."

"Oh," Marcel said, which left her to lamely offer to help with applying the lotion. *Which should be my mother's job*, she reminded herself as she found the expired tube of sunscreen that had caused the problem in the first place. Having nothing else available, Marcel began putting the old sunscreen on Cricket's shoulders and back. Marcel could feel the heat of her burnt skin against the palm of her hand. Each time she touched her, Cricket would cry out.

"You want me to stop?" Marcel asked.

"No," Cricket said, constantly sniffing. "It sort of feels better after you get it on."

It wasn't until she was finished with the first coat that Marcel realized there was another problem. Glancing over at the kitchen counter, she caught Naomi glaring at them. Confused about Naomi's expression and her seeming lack of compassion for Cricket's condition, Marcel turned her attention back to applying more lotion on Cricket's arms.

"Are you hungry?" Marcel asked. "We've got all kinds of fresh fruit or I can make you some toast or something."

Cricket sniffed again and slowly leaned her head back. "Just shoot me."

Marcel smiled. "That's not an option." The tear scampering down Cricket's blazing cheek made Marcel want to help her even more.

"Why isn't she here?" Cricket whispered. "What's she doing in Miami? We've been having some animated discussions about her retiring, now this?"

"Animated?" Marcel repeated with a smile. "Was she speaking in capital letters?"

"You could say that."

"Make it easy on yourself and give that up. She's nowhere near being ready to retire." Marcel moved to the foot of the outstretched recliner and knelt down. Squeezing the last of the sunscreen into her hand, she started to put it on Cricket's ankles. "It's a good thing you had shoes on. Sunburned feet would've made things even worse."

"Right now I can't imagine things being any worse. The only difference in this place and being on the *Titanic* is that the *Titanic* at least had a band. I hate Jet Skis, by the way," Cricket said. Another tear rolled down her cheek.

Marcel finished applying the lotion and left her alone. Finally, Cricket fell asleep again. With her good deed for the day completed, Marcel set her sights on going fishing.

By the time Marcel changed clothes, she couldn't find Naomi anywhere. Shaking her head in exasperation, she got two fishing poles and a tackle box from the fish-cleaning area and headed toward the pier. On her way across the boardwalk in the backyard, she saw Naomi at the far end of the beach. Setting the fishing equipment down on the pier, she started walking toward her.

Staying just at the water's edge, Marcel took her time. She loved the sound and smell of the ocean, and being this close to it had a soothing affect on her. Whatever drama was taking place between her mother and Cricket could be nearly forgotten as long as there were waves rushing to shore and seagulls stating their opinion off in the distance. Even the things going on in her own life that weren't making any sense at the moment were taking a backseat as she enjoyed ambling along the beach. Finally, she caught up to Naomi and fell in step with her.

"You okay?" Marcel asked.

"Not really."

"What's the matter?"

Instead of answering, Naomi bent down to pick up a shell. Marcel waited a moment then said, "You were fine this morning when we got up, so this has to have something to do with Cricket."

Naomi stood up again and put the shell in her pocket. They started walking once more.

"I knew from the beginning that you and Cricket were lovers when you were younger," Naomi said quietly. The wind had scrambled her hair, which made her look adorable.

"That was over twenty-five years ago," Marcel said.

"I know."

"And?"

Naomi shrugged. "And it's starting to mess with my head all of a sudden. The other night when we heard the moaning—"

"Thanks for reminding me that my mother still has sex," Marcel said in an attempt to lighten the moment.

"This isn't about Roslin. It's about you and Cricket."

"What about me and Cricket?" Marcel asked. They had stopped walking again, and Marcel turned to look at her. "We've known each other since we were kids. She's my best friend."

"That's just one more thing to add to the list right now. I'm

114

your lover. I should be your best friend."

Uh oh, Marcel thought. *She's right. I walked into that one.*

"I keep remembering the moaning and how you knew which one was making that sound," Naomi said in a low voice filled with resentment. "I can't stop thinking about *why* you would know that sound. Then this morning with the lotion. You touching her that way."

"The lotion was your idea."

"Not for *you* to put it on her."

"Well, she certainly can't do it by herself in that condition and I didn't see *you* running over there to offer any help."

Naomi didn't say anything, and they started walking again.

"I don't understand why you're wasting time and energy thinking about two teenage girls groping each other during a sleepover."

"You must've been pretty good at it if you recognized that kind of moaning."

Marcel's groan signaled her frustration with this topic. "So are you telling me you're jealous of Cricket? The person who irritates me so much I didn't even want to make this trip?"

Naomi was quiet again.

"Are you nuts?" Marcel added. This whole conversation was overwhelmingly ridiculous to her. *Jealous of Cricket?* she thought. *How is that possible?*

"I'm glad you find my feelings so entertaining," Naomi said.

"I don't find any of this amusing. I'm in love with you. I don't understand this sudden fixation you have with my past and Cricket. If I remember correctly, Cricket spent several weeks trying to get in *your* bed before you and I ever met. You don't see me fretting over that, do you? It's over. It's history. Why dwell on any of it now? I don't get it. We should be past all of this."

"I can't help the way I feel," Naomi said.

"Okay. You're right. But in the meantime I'm going fishing, and it's your turn to tend to Cricket. When she wakes up again she'll need more lotion put on, and guess which one of us is doing it this time?"

"Not me!"

"Oh, yes. You. And you know why?" Marcel stopped and looked at her before saying simply, "Because I'm going fishing."

Chapter Sixteen

By the time it got too hot to stay out on the pier, Marcel had already caught a large flounder and several nice size trout. She carried everything back to the fish-cleaning area and started working on the fish right away. *More than enough for a meal this evening,* she thought. As she tried to decide the best way to keep it all fresh until time to be cooked, Marcel heard the back door to the kitchen open. Naomi called her name.

"I'm here," Marcel said as she stepped out of the carport. "Wait until you see what I caught."

"Roslin just called," Naomi said on her way down the steps.

"Is she winning?"

"She was calling from the police station in Miami."

Marcel stood very still and let her brain process that information. "The police station?" she repeated.

"That's what she said."

"Is she all right? What happened?"

"All she would tell me was that she and Senator Wainwright had been robbed and she would call us from the Key West airport when she arrives."

"Robbed," Marcel said quietly. She carried the cleaned fish up the steps and found some foil in the kitchen to wrap them in. All they could do now was wait for one of their cell phones to ring again.

A few hours later Naomi was putting lotion on Cricket's sunburned back when they got a call. All three cell phones had been charged and were lined up on the kitchen counter just waiting for the opportunity to serve. Marcel answered the one in the middle.

"I'm here," Roslin said.

Marcel could feel a lump forming in her throat at the sound of her mother's voice. "Are you okay? What happened?"

"Yeah, I'm okay. I'll tell you all about it when you get here."

"I'm on my way." Marcel closed the phone, slipped it in her pocket and picked up the keys that were on the counter. "She's at the airport. I'll be back soon."

"I'm going with you," Cricket said as she tried to get up from the recliner. "Ouch, ouch, ouch, ouch!"

"Me too," Naomi said.

"She might talk more if I'm alone with her," Marcel said. "You two stay here."

"Then get details," Cricket said. "You know how she is. She'll be tap dancing around your questions like her feet are on fire. Ouch, ouch, ouch, ouch!"

On her way down the stairs to the car, Marcel remembered how her mother had sounded on the phone. *Angry and tired. Not a good combination.*

118

Traffic was heavier than she thought it would be for that time of day. When Marcel got to the airport, she saw her mother waiting for her outside the terminal. Roslin tossed her bag in the backseat and got in the car.

"I'm starving," she said. "Do we still have things to eat at the house?"

"We'll find you something," Marcel said. "So what happened? I heard you got robbed and you were calling from the police station. Are you hurt?"

"Not physically," Roslin said, "but I know what it's like to have the bejabbers scared out of you. Ever heard someone say they saw their life flash before their eyes? Well, it's true. It happened to me."

"Start from the beginning," Marcel said. "Jesus, I'm so glad you're back," she said. "We dropped you off at the airport and Senator Wainwright picked you up in a private plane. What happened after that?"

"What a way to travel," Roslin said. Her tone was suddenly lighter and she seemed like her old self again as she talked about the flight to Miami. "Drinks, hors d'oeuvres, anything we wanted. I always enjoy my time with Skippy. He likes younger women for sex, so I've never had to worry about that. He's a perfect gentleman until we get at the card table. Then he's a fierce competitor."

"You got robbed?" Marcel asked, prodding her along.

Roslin shrugged. "Skippy had this game set up at the home of some Cuban mafia guy."

"Ohmigod."

"Now wait a minute. We didn't know at the beginning who he was. That's just how I'm describing him. If there *is* such a thing as the Cuban mafia, then this guy was the head honcho or close to it. You know what I mean?"

Marcel didn't like the sound of that at all.

"Let's just say we played cards with a Cuban Marlon Brando,

okay? That's what it felt like to me."

"Why would Senator Wainwright put himself and you in that kind of situation?"

"Skippy was in the area and he wanted a game," Roslin said. "He called me up to see if I was interested, and I just happened to be in the area too, so it was like a fate thing, you know? Meant to be. He set it up, got that football coach from the New York Mets to come down—"

"The Giants. Not the Mets."

"Whatever. There were two players from the Miami Heat—" She stopped and looked at Marcel. "Did I get that right? Is there a team by that name?"

Marcel smiled. "Yes, there's a team by that name. Who were the players? Someone I would know?"

"Tall, tall, tall black dudes. They didn't offer any names. Very nice and polite, though. Had a lot of money, too."

"Then what happened?"

"A limo picks us up at the airport and drives us to a gated mansion. Like something out of the movies, I tell you. Skippy's having a drink from the bar in the back of the limo and I'm thinking, 'Keep it up, buddy.' He gets sloppy with his cards when he's drinking. So anyway, we get there to the Cuban Marlon Brando's house and it's fabulous. This guy has some serious money. We walk into the house, and I hear that Latin music with the fast rhythm softly playing all through the place. We went from room to room and the music never changed or stopped. They probably sleep with it on. I never saw a stereo or any sound equipment, so it's being piped in from somewhere. It's been my experience that if they have a sound system like that, they also have video surveillance going on, too. I'm sure I was right about that."

Marcel waited for her mother to continue. When she didn't start talking right away on her own, Marcel said, "So everyone gets there and a poker game breaks out. Then what?"

"We're in this really nice room," Roslin continued. "The table is set up. The Cuban guy had a waiter and a bartender there. Kind of classy. The basketball players were impressed with the snacks while Skippy kept ordering from the bar. The Mets coach . . . oh . . . wait . . . the Giants coach, right? He was just impressed with himself. I kept looking around for the cameras and didn't see anything, but that could mean it's just a very good system he had installed. I make sure I keep my cards close and don't hold them up for the world behind me to see. I didn't like that hovering waiter, though. He wore too much cologne and it was a sweet, penetrating scent. There were just so many things wrong with that setup, but Skippy was getting looped on booze by then and wasn't in any shape to notice anything."

Confused, Marcel asked, "So where did you get robbed?"

"I'm getting to that part. The game goes on and I'm cleaning up. I'm not sure I had a really bad hand for three hours. The basketball players are out of the game early, but they hang around playing video games in another room. By now I've tuned all that music out and I'm focused on the cards. Skippy's still drinking and talking local politics with the Cuban guy. Skippy's sooo sloppy with his cards and doesn't really care about the game now. I need to talk to him about drinking at these events, but if I do that I might not be able to beat him as often." Roslin laughed. "Anyway, I cleaned them all out. I was winning right and left. I even drew into a gay waiter and that's usually a good sign for me."

Marcel laughed. She remembered the first time her mother had ever mentioned the term "gay waiter" as a poker hand. Marcel had been surprised to learn that it meant a pair of queens and a pair of threes—or treys. *Queens and treys*, she thought with a smile. *A gay waiter hand*. It was one of Roslin's favorites and she always bet heavily on it.

"The robbery," Marcel said. "You got robbed there at the mafia mansion?"

"No, of course not. After I won and raked in the last pot, Skippy and I thanked our host and off we went. I probably had a better time than the others did since I was the winner, but it had been an okay experience once I got used to the music. I also think I did better than everyone else because I played my cards as if someone were watching what I had each time. I don't trust anyone I don't know. The lengths some people will go to in order to win, but that's another story in itself. So anyway, I'm walking out of there with more money than I've won in a while. Skippy and I get in the limo and it takes us to some snazzy restaurant near South Beach. It's like two in the morning and the place is hopping. We get out of the limo, and before we can go inside the restaurant, two men bump into us and stick guns in our ribs. It took me a few seconds to realize what in the world was happening. After all, there are people everywhere! So anyway, one of them snarls, 'Gimme your money! All of it!' Well, I almost fainted right there. Just like in the movies, I tell you. Skippy was no help. He was too busy fumbling in his back pocket to get his wallet out. When I hesitated—mostly because I was about to pass out from fear—the guy jabs the gun in my ribs again. That got my attention for sure. He grabbed my purse and Skippy's wallet and off they ran.

"But you know what? I wasn't so woozy from fright that I couldn't recognize that sweet, penetrating cologne the waiter had been wearing earlier in the evening! They both had on long wigs and fake beards, and at least one of them had been at the Cuban's house. I told Skippy that the waiter from the poker game was one of the ones who mugged us. So while the owner of the restaurant called the police, who just happened to be right around the corner, Skippy got the Cuban guy on the phone. He gave Skippy the waiter's name and the cops caught them about ten minutes later."

"Ohmigod," Marcel whispered. "You must've been terrified. So you got your purse back?"

"I got my purse back, my winnings back and more." Roslin's light laughter made Marcel feel less uneasy about her mother's alarming experience.

"More? How did you get more?"

"For some reason, they had stuffed the rest of Skippy's money from his wallet in my purse while they were running away, but the police caught them before they could divide it all up and get rid of my purse. Why they kept it, I haven't a clue, unless they recognized fine Italian leather," Roslin said matter-of-factly. "So Skippy's money was mixed in with mine. He was just glad to have his wallet back. He didn't care about his money. Besides, I'd won most of it already anyway."

Marcel pulled into the oyster shell driveway and parked the car under the carport. They sat there together for a moment in silence before Marcel took the key out of the ignition. "You gave us a scare."

"This could've happened anywhere," Roslin said. "I think Skippy and I learned a few things this time, though."

"Like what?" Marcel asked as she opened the car door.

"Don't play with strangers."

Chapter Seventeen

Marcel let her mother go in first and set the pace for their arrival. Naomi met them at the door and gave Roslin a hug.

"Are you okay?" Naomi asked.

"I'm fine now. Thank you."

"Someone help me up!" Cricket yelled from the recliner. "Ouch, ouch, ouch, ouch!"

"What the hell?" Roslin said on her way to the living room. The moment she saw Cricket she said, "Look what you've done to yourself!"

"Where have you been?" Cricket demanded before starting to cry.

"I was robbed," Roslin wailed, now suddenly crying, too.

Feeling restless and irritable, Marcel glanced over at Naomi who was perched on a stool at the kitchen counter engrossed in the reunion. Marcel had seen enough. *Time to go fishing again.*

Marcel didn't have to be at the beach house to know what was going on. She had witnessed the crying scenes between her mother and Cricket often enough to know when it was time to be somewhere else. However, what had her really confused was Naomi's reaction to all the dyke drama they were suddenly surrounded by. Naomi seemed to be entertained by it with a lot of head shaking, smiling, wide-eyed incredulous stares and an occasional quiet chuckle.

Then there's that bout of jealousy my girlfriend had, Marcel thought. *Over Cricket, no less!* Just thinking of that made her laugh as she attached a shrimp lure on the end of her line then made her first cast of the evening. The sun was beginning to set and the sky was a wonderful blend of orange and lavender. A few minutes later she had a redfish big enough to bend her fishing pole. Marcel reeled it in and made sure it was a keeper. She put it on the stringer and lowered it back down into the water. Standing up again, she saw Naomi at the other end of the pier with a fishing pole in her hand.

"It was getting too deep in there for me," she said. "Roslin's feeling guilty for leaving her like that."

"The fish are biting," Marcel said in hopes of changing the subject. Hearing about her mother and Cricket lamenting over their latest "I got a sunburn" versus "I got robbed" scenarios was more than she cared to know at the moment.

"Roslin's putting cool compresses on her," Naomi said, "so there was a lot of noise going on."

Marcel handed her a lure from the tackle box. "Is that what drove you out here to be with me? The house was too noisy?" she asked, teasing her.

Naomi's glare and fixed expression nearly made Marcel flinch. *I guess that sounded worse than I meant for it to*, she thought.

Naomi took the lure and walked about thirty feet away from

her and prepared to cast.

"The fish are biting down here at this end," Marcel said, once again attempting to lighten the mood by indicating her part of the pier.

"I'm fine right here."

"Suit yourself," Marcel mumbled and tossed her line out again. She looked back over her shoulder to see Naomi standing there leaning against the railing, her line in the water with her hair blowing in the breeze. Marcel thought she was beautiful. *I wonder how long she'll stay mad at me? Hell, I can't even remember what I did to get her this way to begin with.*

As she slowly reeled the lure in before casting her line back out again, Marcel decided it was best to concentrate on fishing instead of women. *Most fish have more sense than some of the women I know anyway.* As she stood there leaning against the railing at the end of the pier, Marcel was surprised to hear her pocket ringing. She reached in and pulled her cell phone out. It was her mother calling. Marcel turned to see Roslin on the screened-in porch at the house waving at her.

"Why didn't you tell me her sunburn was this bad?" she demanded.

"You saw her before you left," Marcel said. "Did you think any of that would just go away overnight?"

"She was being such a jerk," Roslin said.

"Oh, yeah. That's a new trait for her."

"I feel so bad. I shouldn't have left her."

"You'll have to work that out with Cricket."

"You're no help."

"I have my own things to deal with. I caught enough fish for dinner already, though."

"I'm glad *someone's* enjoying this trip!"

Marcel got another tug on her fishing pole and nearly dropped the phone. "I've gotta go." She closed her phone and slipped it back in her pocket. Reeling the fish in, she enjoyed the fight it gave her. When she pulled it up out of the water, Marcel could tell that the trout wasn't quite big enough to keep, but catching it had at least accomplished one thing. It brought Naomi down to her end of the pier.

It wasn't until after Naomi caught her first fish that any type of meaningful conversation transpired between them. Marcel was comforted just by Naomi's presence, even if things were still tense between them. After Naomi caught the fish, Marcel helped her get it off the lure and onto the stringer. They sat down on the end of the pier next to each other and cast their lines out again.

"Remind me of something, please," Marcel said. "Why is it I'm in the dog house?"

Naomi's reluctant smile was what Marcel had been waiting for.

"Actually, you were *under* the dog house. Not in it."

That made Marcel laugh. "All because I had a girlfriend in high school?"

"I know. I know. Whatever happened before we knew each other shouldn't be held against us."

"Thank you."

"But," Naomi said, "there's something about your relationship with Cricket that isn't sitting well with me right now."

"My relationship with Cricket isn't any different now than it's ever been since I've known you."

Their fishing poles got tugs on them at the same time. Marcel's fish got away, but Naomi reeled in a nice size redfish. She took it off the lure and put it on the stringer with the others.

"Tell me," Naomi said. "Why is it we don't live together?"

"Why? Because you said it wouldn't be a good idea for you and Cricket to work together and have the same address."

After a moment, Naomi said, "Let me ask this a different way

127

then. Why is it you're still living with your mother?"

"Why?" Marcel repeated, momentarily confused. "Her house is big enough for all of us. Even more if we wanted them there."

"I can't imagine any sane person wanting to live in a house full of lesbians," Naomi said. "I only want to live with one."

Marcel didn't know what to say. She had lived with her mother ever since coming home from her last tour in Korea eight years ago. Spending her final three years in the army at Fort Sam Houston in San Antonio made it easy and economical for both of them to share the house.

"My mother never liked being alone in that big house," Marcel said.

"Your mother has Cricket there now," Naomi said softly. "She won't be alone in the house anymore."

Marcel slowly reeled in and cast the lure out again. "What exactly are you saying? That I'm too old to still be living with my mother?"

"When you could be living with your lover instead?" Naomi countered. "Yes. I guess that is what I'm saying."

Marcel was dumbfounded by the statement. It never occurred to her not to live with her mother, and the arrangement she and Naomi had of almost always spending the night together at one place or the other had seemed to be working well.

"What are you thinking?" Naomi asked. "Your silence is scaring me."

When Marcel finally found her voice, she asked. "How long have you been mulling this over?"

"Since yesterday when all that lotion-rubbing took place with you and Cricket."

Marcel slowly reeled the lure in and cast her line out again. "I've always assumed you would move in with *us*. It never occurred to me that I could be the one to move. I wonder why that is?" Marcel asked.

As the answer came rushing to the surface all at once, a little light in her head finally clicked on. "Do you know what I've been waiting for?" Marcel asked. Not giving Naomi a chance to answer, she said, "I've been waiting for Cricket and my mother to break up. Either Cricket would move on to someone else like she always does, or my mother would eventually realize she doesn't want to be in a lesbian relationship after all. That has to be it. I've been waiting for them to fall apart as a couple so that eventually you could move in with me and my mother." Marcel held her fishing pole firmly and turned to look at Naomi. "It never occurred to me that I would be the one to move. I've been waiting for *you* to be the one to move. How selfish is that?"

Naomi smiled. "I love your mother, but I don't want to live with her."

They reeled in their lures and both cast out in different directions. Marcel took a moment to think about Naomi's house and what it would be like to call it home. *Just knowing I would be there with her every day. That in itself would make it a home for us.*

"So I can move in with you?" Marcel whispered. Merely asking the question sent a chill racing through her body.

"Oh, yes."

"When?"

"As soon as our vacation is over."

Marcel leaned over and kissed her tenderly on the lips. She couldn't remember a time when she felt happier.

Chapter Eighteen

Proud of their fishing abilities, Naomi and Marcel fixed a nice dinner consisting of broiled flounder and trout. While Marcel made a rice dish and a large salad to go with it, Naomi set the table out on the deck and tried to make it look as nice as possible with what they had. Marcel was relieved to see that her mother had gotten Cricket in the bathtub and had helped her wash her hair. To Marcel's surprise, Cricket was wearing a pair of shorts and a tank top that hung loosely on her small red body. The clothes belonged to Marcel and she had given her mother permission to go through her luggage to find something for Cricket to wear. She was agreeable to anything that would get rid of that bikini.

The moon was out and bathed the deck in a soft, romantic glow. They all did what they could to help make Cricket more comfortable. Naomi had gotten a beach towel and put it on

Cricket's chair to give it some extra cushion. *That's what friends do for each other*, Marcel reminded herself, but there was still a tiny bit of resentment that went along with it, mostly because she knew that if it had been either her or Naomi who had been careless enough to have had a sunburn that bad, Cricket wouldn't have gone out of her way to make them feel any better. Cricket wasn't a mean-spirited person, but she was known to take being shallow to new depths. She was more "me" orientated than most people, and it wouldn't have occurred to her to help make someone else's life more comfortable.

"The fish sure smells good," Roslin said as she helped Cricket sit down at the table. From the look on Cricket's face, it was obvious she was enjoying all the attention.

"Feeling better?" Naomi asked her.

"I am," Cricket said. "Thanks."

"I called and talked to a pharmacist at the local drugstore," Roslin said. "She recommended a bath in cold water that had either baking soda or some kind of oatmeal treatment stuff in it. I found an old box of baking soda in the back of the fridge that smelled kind of funky, but it would do."

Cricket looked over at Roslin and smiled. Her tight red face still appeared to be incredibly painful. There was so much pride and adoration in Cricket's expression that it was hard for Marcel to be upset with her. Anyone who could love Roslin that much had to be all right no matter how annoying they were in other ways.

"So I've had a cool bath in funky-baking-soda-water," Cricket said, "and here I am."

Everyone started to eat, and Marcel was tired of the sunburn chatter. Having nothing to add to the conversation whenever it was brought up, she was just glad her mother and Cricket had already worked through their latest round of crying, apologizing and making up. As dinner progressed Marcel acknowledged the compliments on her fish preparation skills. It was nice to see there had been enough to go around.

Feeling spontaneous, Marcel said, "Naomi and I have an announcement." She had everyone's attention and noticed a flicker of surprise in Naomi's eyes. "As soon as we get back," Marcel continued, "I'll be moving in with her."

Cricket's smile was the only positive reaction she noticed between the other two. Roslin seemed to be stunned.

"For real?" Cricket said. "That's great!"

"What's so great about it?" Roslin snapped. She set her fork down and looked at Marcel. "Whose idea was this?"

When Marcel didn't answer, Roslin's gaze moved to Naomi. "She wouldn't have invited herself to move in with you. It was your idea, wasn't it?"

"This is Marcel's decision," Naomi said, not the least bit intimidated by Roslin's tone of voice, "but it was my suggestion."

Turning her attention back to Marcel, Roslin said, "You can't leave me in that big house by myself."

"Hey!" Cricket said. "You won't be by yourself. I'll be there."

"You know what I mean."

"No," Cricket insisted. "I *don't* know what you mean."

"Cricket's right, Mom. You won't be by yourself."

"If anyone will be alone there, it'll be me," Cricket said to her lover. "While you're off gambling somewhere, I'll be the one stuck taking out the trash and keeping the lawn watered."

Marcel cleared her throat loudly and asked, "Do you even know where the trashcan *goes*?"

Cricket stuck her tongue out at her.

"I've often wondered how high you two would let the trash pile up in the kitchen if I never took it out," Marcel said.

"Anyway," Cricket said over Naomi's laughter. "You won't be there by yourself," she said to Roslin.

"See?" Roslin said, pointing her fork at Marcel accusingly. "We can't leave Cricket alone there while I'm gone all the time."

"Why not?" Marcel asked. "You used to leave *me* there alone when you were out of town. I'll make sure she knows where the trashcan goes on pick-up day. How's that?"

"I'm not complaining about being alone in the house," Cricket insisted. "It's a great neighborhood and the house has an excellent security system. I've never been afraid to stay there."

"You two will have to work it out," Marcel said and turned her attention to the salad on her plate.

"Besides," Cricket said. "I wouldn't *be* there alone if you'd retire." She directed her gaze to Roslin.

"Let's not go there again," Roslin said with a wave of her hand. "I'm not retiring, so just forget about it."

"You're surrounded by unsavory characters and—"

Stopping her in mid-sentence, Roslin asked innocently, "Is that any way to talk about a United States Senator? Such a fine Southern gentleman that Senator Wainwright is." Her fluttering eyelashes made Marcel and Naomi laugh.

"You know what I mean!" Cricket said in frustration. "You were *robbed*, for crissakes! They could've killed you!"

"What happened to me and Skippy could've happened any-where," Roslin said. "Stop blaming it on the game."

"Why is it you aren't getting this?" Cricket asked in exasper-ation. While the bickering continued back and forth, Marcel and Naomi finished dinner and got up from the table. The other two were still arguing as Marcel took Naomi's hand and followed the boardwalk to the beach. They walked along the edge of the tide and enjoyed watching a crab scamper away.

"Do you think Cricket will wear her down?" Naomi asked.

"No. My mother will just tune her out like the rest of us do."

"Cricket's afraid," Naomi said, "but even I can see that she's going about this all wrong."

"Cricket likes getting her way no matter what the cost is. That's all she can see right now. Compromising isn't something she does well."

"However they choose to deal with this, it would be nice if

they would take care of it on their own time," Naomi said, "and not in front of us."

Marcel slipped her arm around Naomi's waist. The moonlight spilled across the water with a glimmering magnificence that made them both stop walking and take in the view. They stood there on the beach facing the water and Marcel felt such a warm sense of comfort and belonging.

"Can you start moving in with me as soon as we get back?" Naomi asked. She leaned against her so their heads touched.

Marcel smiled at the thought. She felt excited about the move and somewhat relieved at the prospect of not having to see her mother and Cricket on a daily basis. It made sense to her that the four of them would need more quality time alone so they could grow as couples. Until now, that had never been encouraged by any of them.

"I've spent my last night in their home," Marcel said. "It's time we made a home of our own."

Marcel woke up the next morning to Naomi kissing her neck. She turned over and saw the hint of humor around Naomi's mouth and eyes. There was contentment in her expression, and Marcel knew the day would be a good one for them.

"Don't be impatient with me when I get jealous," Naomi said. She propped her head up with her hand and searched Marcel's face with dark eyes filled with intelligence and wonder. "It doesn't happen that often, so just bear with me while it's an issue."

"It caught me by surprise, I guess," Marcel said. "You're the only one I think about that way. Making you jealous has never been something I cared about doing."

"I know. I'm not proud of these feelings. This streak of insecurity isn't like me. I don't know where it's coming from."

Marcel reached up and moved a wayward lock from Naomi's

brow. "It would be kind of cute if not for the fact it's Cricket you're jealous of. That's bordering on the ridiculous."

Naomi sat up on the side of the bed. "Maybe it's because you have such a good relationship with one of your exes. I don't see any of mine or keep in touch with them. I can't imagine even wanting to."

"Looks like between the two of us, you're the more normal one. Does that surprise you?"

Naomi's laughter was delightful to hear. She turned around and kissed Marcel lightly on the lips before heading to the bathroom.

Marcel toasted two bagels and found a small tub of cream cheese in the refrigerator. The coffee was already made. She had a mini-breakfast waiting when Naomi came into the kitchen.

"What are we doing today?" Marcel asked.

"Let's take a break from fishing," Naomi said. "Maybe we could go for a drive and see if we can get lost this time."

Roslin came in from the screened-in porch and poured two cups of coffee. "Good morning, you two," she said. "What time did you come in last night?"

"We waited to make sure the dishes were done first," Marcel said, teasing her.

Roslin pulled up a stool on Naomi's side of the kitchen counter. "I have a favor to ask you," she said to Naomi. "I called the guy I rented the Jet Skis from and he'll give me some of my money back if I can get them there this morning. Would you go with me and ride Cricket's Jet Ski back? Marcel can pick us up at the marina."

"I don't know anything about operating a Jet Ski," Naomi said.

"I'll teach you. It's easy. Will you do it?"

Naomi shrugged. "Sure. I guess I can give it a try." She

looked at Marcel with an arched brow.

"Thanks," Roslin said. "Let me know when you're ready." She picked up the two coffee cups and returned to the porch.

"Wow," Naomi said as she took a small bite of her bagel. "She's never asked me for anything before."

"Congratulations," Marcel said. "I think."

"No, this is a big deal. I hope I do a good job."

"How hard can it be?" Marcel asked. "Cricket learned to ride one. Relax. You'll do fine."

"What should I wear?"

Her teasing smile made Marcel laugh. They finished breakfast and the three of them headed to the beach for Naomi's first Jet Ski lesson.

Chapter Nineteen

It didn't take long for Naomi to get the hang of Jet Skiing, and she seemed to be having fun doing it. When they were ready to leave, Roslin came closer to the beach where Marcel was standing and watching them.

"Pick us up at the marina," Roslin said. "It'll take us about ten minutes to get there."

Marcel waved and headed back to the house to get her keys. As she came up the boardwalk to the deck, she saw Cricket waiting inside on the porch.

"Can I go with you? I'm tired of sitting around in front of the TV."

"Sure. Let's go."

Marcel waited as Cricket negotiated the steps outside in the back. She was wearing more of Marcel's clothes only because they fit her much looser than her own and didn't tug anywhere on her skin. They finally got in the car and headed for the marina.

"She's not backing down on this retirement issue," Cricket said.

"Maybe you should try another approach with her," Marcel said. "Call it something else . . . like . . . cutting back instead of retiring."

"I don't want her to cut back. I want her to quit. Besides, she won't even discuss it with me now. Maybe you could talk to her about it."

"That's the beauty of my relationship with my mother," Marcel said simply. "We don't tell each other what to do. If she wants my advice, she'll ask me for it."

Cricket was quiet for a moment then said, "Well, I'm asking for your advice now. What should I do? She won't listen to me."

"Stop nagging her about it. The only thing that'll do is have her looking for another game a lot faster."

"All right. All right. I hear you, but this sucks. I worry about her."

"She learned something with this last incident, I think," Marcel said. "I expect her to be more careful about who she plays with in the future. Senator Wainwright just got to her at a bad time. She'll be asking more questions when another game comes up."

"The more I know about that Senator Skippy, the less I like him."

That's a good way to feel about all politicians, Marcel thought.

When they got to the marina, Marcel was surprised to see it so busy already. The tour boat was pulling away from the dock with almost standing room only on both decks, and the line at the Jet Ski rental office was out to the end of the sidewalk. Marcel found a place to park and shut the car off.

"I'll stay here," Cricket said. "I don't need any more sun on me right now."

Marcel got out of the car and walked down to the Jet Ski rental. She saw the father and son team giving instructions and noticed the excitement on the faces of the customers as they tried to get the hang of riding a Jet Ski. She shook her head at the people she saw in line wearing bathing suits and skimpy tank tops and hoped they at least had up-to-date sunscreen in their possession. Walking down a ways to get a closer look at one of the fishing boats coming in, she soon lost interest when there wasn't any fish to see. She wandered back to the Jet Ski area and still found no sign of her mother or Naomi. It had certainly been longer than ten minutes. She asked a tourist for the time and waited around a while longer. Thinking she might have missed them, she walked back to the car to see if they were there, but Cricket was the only one in the car.

"Are they coming?" Cricket asked.

"No sign of them yet," Marcel said.

"They've had more than enough time to get here. It's not that far by water."

Great, Marcel thought. *I didn't need to hear that.* Earlier she had just been annoyed at the wait, but now she was beginning to worry. "Could they have run out of gas again?"

"The guy who helped us before topped off the tanks," Cricket said. "They have plenty of gas."

Marcel stood up straight and looked back toward the Jet Ski area, hoping to see some sign of them.

"Maybe Naomi is having so much fun they're taking their time and playing a little," Cricket said.

"Yeah, maybe," Marcel grumbled. "Well, I'm going back down there to wait for them."

On the return walk to the Jet Ski area, Marcel tried to keep her agitation in check. *We're on vacation. We're allowed to have fun when we can. Chill out. They'll be here soon.*

No longer able to just stand around and wait, she began to pace. Every few minutes or so she would stop and search the horizon looking for a Jet Skier with Naomi's dark curly hair. After thirty minutes of that, Marcel couldn't stand waiting anymore and decided to get in line and rent a Jet Ski of her own. She would find them, spew some choice words, wag a finger in their faces, then return to the marina with or without them.

The line was moving quickly, but not nearly as fast as Marcel wanted it to. She was getting edgy and impatient and couldn't imagine her mother being this inconsiderate even if she and Naomi were having fun skirting along the coastline. She tried to keep her fear from taking control as the line began to move again. Marcel suddenly noticed a man beside her trying to cut in.

"Marcel Robicheaux?" he whispered.

Surprised at hearing her name, she looked at him closely. He was about her height and wore a Notre Dame T-shirt, black shorts, old sneakers without socks and an Indiana Pacers cap. He seemed to be in his late thirties, and Marcel was certain she had never seen him before.

"Senator Wainwright sent me," the man said in a deep, low voice. "Can I speak with you for a moment?"

Marcel looked ahead at the dozen or so people in line in front of her and then turned to look at the line behind her. She wasn't about to lose her place. "What does the senator want?" she asked.

"I can explain that privately. Please follow me."

"Explain it to me here," she said. "I don't want to get out of line."

"This has to do with your mother and your friend. Please follow me."

Marcel felt an icy chill race through her body even as the sun beat down on her. She stepped out of line and followed the man without asking any more questions. She was too confused to do anything other than put one foot in front of the other. He led her toward the fishing boat she had seen earlier. Marcel finally stopped and forced her panic to the side.

"This way," he said. "Please."

"Where are my mother and Naomi?"

"I can tell you more once we're on board." He nodded toward the boat.

"I'm not going anywhere with you until you tell me what's going on."

"Marcel," someone said from the boat.

She looked up and saw Senator Wainwright. He waved and indicated that she should follow the man beside her.

"Where's my mother?" she asked him as soon as she got on board.

"We'll explain that to you," Senator Wainwright said.

This was a man she had known most of her adult life. He had endorsed her appointment to West Point after she graduated from high school. She didn't always agree with his politics, but she knew Senator Harlow Wainwright to be an old friend of her mother's, and for now, that was good enough for her. She didn't necessarily trust him or his judgment, but she wanted to hear what he had to say. Besides, no one else seemed to be willing to tell her anything.

Marcel wasn't sure who these people on the boat were, but they certainly weren't fishermen. Below deck there were rooms filled with computer and surveillance equipment. She had so many questions that it was difficult to find a place to begin. Suddenly, she heard the engine start up and the boat began to move.

"Where are we going?" she demanded.

"We'll get to that," Senator Wainwright said.

"Cricket's in the car waiting for me. I can't leave her there."

The man who had approached Marcel in line earlier said, "I'll go get her. Where is she?"

Marcel told him where her car was parked and he left quickly.

"Where's my mother?" Marcel asked. "I want to know now."

A man in his early thirties sitting in front of a computer said, "We're working on that."

"Working on it?" Marcel repeated. "What does that mean?"

"Let me handle this," Senator Wainwright said. "Come with me, Marcel."

She followed him through several areas crammed full of beeping and pinging equipment. On her way past, she noticed a few monitors with live video of the marina, the open water, and on one screen was a yacht in the middle of the bay. Senator Wainwright led her to a lounge that had a small bar and a nice sitting area. A few minutes later Cricket and the man with the Notre Dame T-shirt arrived.

"What's going on?" Cricket asked.

Marcel was relieved to see her.

"Senator Skippy!" Cricket said. "What a surprise. Where's Roslin and Naomi?"

"Have a seat," Senator Wainwright said. "Can I get either of you anything to drink?"

Marcel wasn't interested in pleasantries as the boat began to move again. She took a seat on a sofa and got right to the point. "Where are they?"

Cricket gingerly sat down on the other end of the sofa. "They who? What are you talking about?"

"They're together," Senator Wainwright said. "They've been picked up by someone from Miami."

"They who?" Cricket asked again.

"Naomi and my mother," Marcel told her. To Senator Wainwright she said, "Picked up where? At the marina or off the water?"

"Off the water," he said. "We decided to bring you with us when it looked like you might try to find them on your own. We couldn't risk getting anyone on the outside involved."

"What the hell is going on?" Cricket asked.

"Roslin and Naomi were picked up by a boat," he explained.

Marcel was too stunned to say anything else. She sat there staring at him, waiting for this practical joke to be over with. The fear she felt for their safety was physically devastating. She thought for a moment that she might get sick.

"What boat?" Cricket asked. "We don't know anyone here with a boat."

Senator Wainwright looked away from them and took a long sip of his drink. Slowly, in an attempt to clear up her confusion, Marcel began to gather her wits and form the questions that needed to be asked.

"My mother wouldn't have gotten on a boat knowing I was at the marina waiting for her. So when you say she was picked up by a boat, was this done against her will?"

Senator Wainwright looked at her with eyes that already reflected having had too much alcohol. He nodded.

"They were kidnapped?" Cricket asked.

Senator Wainwright shrugged. "The FBI is monitoring the situation. Perhaps I should start at the beginning."

"Yes, perhaps you should!" Cricket snapped. She reached over and touched Marcel's hand. "Picked up by a boat. Are they in any danger? And why would anyone want them? I don't think they were carrying any money." Cricket's emotions were hovering on the surface, and Marcel knew it wouldn't be long before she started to cry.

"There's an agent on board the yacht that took them," he said, "so it's not like they're out on their own."

Marcel was somewhat relieved to hear that, but it did nothing to explain why such a thing was happening in the first place. It was spring break at Key West. The place was overrun with beautiful young women out for a good time! It made no sense to snatch these two up.

143

"Let me tell you what I know," Senator Wainwright said. "Your mother and I have been looking for more sports figures to bring into our gambling circle. They have a lot of money and most are very competitive. Many of them are also bad gamblers, so that's even better." He pulled a cigar from inside his coat pocket and slowly unwrapped it from the cellophane. "Someone told me about these two basketball players who were interested in poker," he said. "One of them set the game up your mother and I played in the other night. Both basketball players and the host of the game were all eager to get into our inner gambling circle. I called your mother to see if she was interested in meeting these gentlemen for a game, and not only was she interested, but she was in Key West, of all places—a mere forty-five minutes away." He lit the cigar, careful to keep the smoke from blowing toward them.

"Okay," Cricket said. "So you get to the mansion, play cards, Roslin wins, you two leave, you get to a restaurant in South Beach and you get robbed. Right?" She sounded like a little machine gun firing off details.

His eyes were wide as he looked at her. "That's amazingly accurate, young lady."

"So where does the FBI come in?" Cricket asked. "And why are Roslin and Naomi missing?"

"Our host that evening has been of interest to the FBI for many reasons," he continued, "to include drug trafficking, smuggling, murder and money laundering. It's not just the FBI who is after him. The ATF and the IRS would also like a piece of him."

"What does he want with my mother?" Marcel asked.

"We don't really know the answer to that yet."

"How do you know for sure Roslin and Naomi are even on the yacht?" Cricket asked.

"The FBI has had it under surveillance ever since it left out of Miami yesterday. I was interested in what they had on this man, especially since he might've had something to do with robbing us the other night, so the local FBI agents let me ride along with them." Senator Wainwright took several more puffs on the cigar to make sure it was still lit. "We got them on camera intercepting your mother and her friend. The men had weapons and easily convinced them to get on board the yacht."

"Oh, no," Cricket whispered.

Marcel didn't want to think about what Naomi and her mother were having to go through right then. She just wanted them back safely.

"What's the plan?" Cricket asked in a dull, shaky voice.

"We wait," Senator Wainwright said. "Once we hear from the agent on board we'll know more about the current situation."

Marcel looked over at Cricket and felt comforted by her presence. She gave her hand a squeeze and then let go of it. Waiting was the hard part.

Chapter Twenty

Marcel and Cricket decided early that Senator Wainwright didn't know much more than they did. Nearly an hour passed before someone came into the lounge looking for them. It was the first time Marcel had seen this man. He was dressed in faded jeans and a black T-shirt. His features were pleasant and his premature gray hair made him seem older than he probably was. Marcel was surprised to see that FBI agents weren't better dressers while they were working. On television and in the movies they always wore suits.

"What do you have for us?" Senator Wainwright asked.

"Good news so far," the man said. "We received a brief report from the yacht, and it looks like the older woman is holding a poker clinic there."

Marcel slowly turned her head toward Cricket and then Senator Wainwright.

"A what?" Cricket asked.

"These people have apparently been watching your beach house for an opportunity to connect with the older one," the man said. He nodded toward Marcel. "Your mother," he clarified, as if she wouldn't know which of the two missing women the older one would be.

"Roslin," Cricket said.

The man nodded again and continued. "Right now they're on the yacht playing poker. Your mother is giving everyone on board lessons on bluffing, when to fold and how to bet."

Marcel didn't know what to say. Once again she was too stunned to even speak. Here she was worried out of her mind about her mother and Naomi's safety at the hands of gangsters all because of a card game? There had to be something else to it.

"What about Naomi?" Cricket asked. "Are both of them together?"

"According to our source," the man said, "almost everyone on the yacht is playing poker."

"They kidnapped my girlfriend for a poker lesson," Cricket said, summarizing the situation perfectly in just a few words. Her puzzled expression had to mirror Marcel's. None of this was making any sense so far.

"Cricket," Senator Wainwright said. "They seem to be safe. Let's just take it easy for a while and let these people do their job."

Marcel glanced over at him as he puffed on his cigar. He took another sip from his tumbler and said wistfully, "I kind of wish I was on that yacht now, too. A poker lesson from the infamous Roslin Robicheaux is a chance of a lifetime."

The agent escorted the three of them into another room where they were allowed to watch the surveillance tapes of Roslin and Naomi being taken aboard the yacht. There were three men with huge weapons. The video wasn't clear enough to see a lot of features on the people involved, but Marcel recognized her mother and Naomi as they climbed off their Jet Skis and into a small boat that took them to the yacht farther out into the water.

"They must've been terrified," Marcel whispered. She shoved her hands in the pockets of her shorts so no one could see them trembling. Senator Wainwright put an arm around her shoulder, careful not to spill any of his drink.

"They were smart to not put up a struggle," the agent said. "I think once this guy gets what he wants out of your mother and picks her brain about her technique and skill, he'll let both of them go. Kidnapping isn't what he's known for. He likes having a good time."

"That's not very reassuring right now," Cricket mumbled.

"I'm sorry," the agent said. "It was meant to be. According to our source on the yacht, things are going well there. That's a good sign."

As if thinking out loud, Cricket said, "This guy is loaded. Why not hire someone to teach him how to play poker?"

"He wants to learn from the best," Skippy said, "and Roslin is the best."

A few hours passed with no further word from the yacht. There were agents on the upper deck of the fishing boat to help maintain their cover, and somewhere on board there were other cameras zooming in on the yacht. While in the equipment room Marcel tried to see as much as she could without being too obvious. One screen had a satellite picture of the yacht. The amount of equipment these people had was impressive. Marcel wasn't sure how long they were there watching the monitors, but it was long enough to make her tired of standing.

Suddenly, an agent across the room said, "Here we go.

Movement on deck at the yacht."

Everyone hurried over to that particular workstation. Marcel heard Cricket say, "Ouch, ouch, ouch, ouch!" as she wound her way closer to the monitor.

"They're putting them in the smaller boat," one of the agents said.

Marcel could see her mother and Naomi on the screen now. One at a time they climbed into the smaller boat. The live video didn't provide the close-up that Marcel was hoping for. She needed to know that they were both unharmed.

"Maybe it would be better if you three waited in the other room," the agent with the Notre Dame T-shirt said. Without giving them time to protest, he took Marcel and Cricket by the arms and urged them toward the lounge area.

"Ouch, ouch, ouch, ouch!" Cricket yelled. She pulled away from him and snapped, "I'm not leaving! What? You think they'll do something to them we shouldn't see?"

"Get them out of here," someone said from across the room.

Marcel and Senator Wainwright were escorted to the lounge area and went willingly. Marcel was too numb to put up much resistance, but Cricket had to be physically removed from the room by two men who endured her kicking, shouting and a non-stop string of, "Ouch, ouch, ouch, ouch!" as they pushed her out and locked the door.

Twenty minutes later Marcel had recovered enough to begin pacing again and then pounded on the door that led to the equipment room. Cricket was crying softly on the sofa, curled up into an awkward fetal position because of her sunburn, while Senator Wainwright helped himself to another drink and kept puffing on his cigar. Finally, someone opened the door and came in with a report for them. It was the agent with the Notre Dame T-shirt.

"They're both on their way to the marina on their Jet Skis," he said. "We're heading back there now to drop you two off."

Cricket started to cry harder, and Marcel felt nothing but a huge sense of relief. Senator Wainwright jumped up to shake the agent's hand.

"You thought those hoodlums would shoot them, didn't you?" Cricket asked the agent accusingly.

"We weren't sure what would happen," the agent admitted. "I'm glad I have good news to report, though."

"Your man on board the yacht," Senator Wainwright said. "His cover is still secure?"

"Yes," the agent said. "We'll have you two back at the marina shortly. All that we ask is that no police reports are filed on this incident. We have an agent at your beach house now waiting for your return. He'll interview both women and get the information we'll need. When the time comes to bring these guys down, kidnapping will be one of the charges on a very long list of offenses."

Marcel nodded. All she wanted to do was hug her mother and Naomi again. At that particular moment, nothing else mattered to her.

The boat pulled into the marina and Cricket and Marcel got off. Marcel waved to Senator Wainwright, and she and Cricket headed toward the Jet Ski rental. It was hot and Marcel was certain that the sun beating down on Cricket's skin had to hurt.

"Why don't you go to the car and I'll wait for them?" Marcel said.

"I want to be here," Cricket said bravely, "but this sun is killing me."

"Walk back to the car as normally as possible. There's no telling who's watching us now. I'll explain everything to them when they get here."

Cricket nodded and headed for the car while Marcel focused her attention on the water near the Jet Ski rental area. She noticed the fishing boat with the agents on deck pretending to be fishing tourists as it took off again toward where the yacht was last seen. Marcel knew the queasiness in her stomach wouldn't go away until her mother and Naomi were back on land again.

She heard the buzz of Jet Skis in the distance and then saw them riding side by side toward the marina. Marcel's heart skipped a beat at the sight of them looking so safe and normal. The tears came easily then. She dabbed at them with the sleeve of her shirt, but more followed as she watched the two women who meant the most to her slow their Jet Skis and stop near a landing at the marina.

Marcel couldn't stop crying as she saw her mother and Naomi search the crowded marina looking for her. Marcel smiled and waved, trying to act as normal as she could under the circumstances. Naomi ran to her and Marcel swooped her up into a fierce hug.

"Are you okay?" Marcel asked, kissing the side of her face.

"You'll never believe what happened."

"I know all about it. Come on. Let's get out of here." She reluctantly let go of her and looked around for her mother, but didn't see her anywhere. A renewed moment of panic crept in when she couldn't find her.

"Roslin went to get her money back on the Jet Skis," Naomi said. She had a tight hold on Marcel's hand.

"For cryin' out loud," Marcel said. "She's worried about her deposit at a time like this?" She practically dragged Naomi with her to the Jet Ski rental office. By the time they got there and wove their way through the cluster of people, Roslin was already coming out again.

"My baby!" Roslin squealed when she saw them. She threw

her arms around Marcel's neck and hugged her tightly. "I'm so sorry we're late."

"Don't worry about that," Marcel whispered. Her voice was filled with so much emotion she could barely talk. "I know what happened. Let's get out of here."

Walking between them, Marcel explained how she and Cricket had been on a fishing boat with the FBI and Senator Wainwright.

"Just wait until I get a hold of Skippy again," Roslin grumbled. "I wonder how many high heels that man's ever had extracted from his butt over the years? He'll be lucky to get me into a game of Go Fish after this. I'm never playing poker with him again."

Despite the fact that Marcel was grateful to Senator Wainwright for helping keep them informed about the men on the yacht, she wouldn't be at all upset if her mother stopped associating with him. He was careless and seemed to have an alcohol problem, neither of which went together well.

By the time they reached the car, Cricket had managed to get out and meet them with her toasted arms outstretched and tears streaming down her face.

"Did those jerks hurt you?" Cricket blubbered.

"No," Roslin said. She was starting to cry, too. "But they tried to steal all my secrets!"

Marcel and Naomi got into the front seat of the car while the other two continued hugging beside it.

"Your mother is a remarkable woman," Naomi said. "The only reason we got out of that situation was because of her."

The only reason you were in that situation was because of her, Marcel thought. She reached over and held Naomi's hand. Her emotions were all jumbled up inside. Anger, hysteria, relief—she didn't know what would come tumbling out first. She started the car and cranked the air conditioner up. Finally, Roslin and Cricket got in the backseat.

"They said there would be an agent at the house who would interview both of you," Marcel said. "Let's go get that over with." She felt better knowing someone from the FBI would be with them for a while longer. Marcel's sense of safety and security had been drastically shaken.

"You know what?" Roslin said from the backseat. "I won't be leaving here with many good memories of my time on a Jet Ski. That's for sure. I've been stranded out on the ocean and hauled off at gunpoint. Those things don't make for a good time. Whose dumb ass idea was it to rent those things anyway?"

Marcel took a quick sharp breath at the attempt at levity, then joined their nervous laughter.

Chapter Twenty-one

There was a black sedan parked on the street near the driveway when they got back to the beach house. It was the first thing Marcel had seen that looked anything like her idea of what the FBI would use. She felt better as the dark-suited man got out of the car while she parked under the carport. Marcel knew she needed to find a way to get over the uneasiness she was feeling when it came to being safe there. They still had three more days of vacation left.

A short, balding man about Marcel's age introduced himself as Agent Barkley and flashed a badge attached to his official identification. Agent Barkley was ready to get down to business. He had a thin black notebook with him and asked to interview Roslin and Naomi separately. Roslin agreed to go first.

Once they were all in the house, Cricket said, "I'll be soaking in a cool baking soda bath." She padded down the hallway to her room. Marcel and Naomi went out on the screened-in porch and sat on the futon to watch the water until it was Naomi's turn to be interviewed.

After a moment, Naomi said, "Did I mention how amazing your mother was during that entire ordeal?"

"Tell me about it. I think I was so out of my mind with worry that I must've blocked out most of what they told me while it was happening."

Naomi leaned closer so their shoulders touched. "When we left here, we got up the coastline a ways, and Roslin slowed down and wanted to talk for a minute. She tried her best to convince me to move in with the three of you. She pulled out all the stops. Even offered me a rather large sum of money to help with my decision."

"She tried to bribe you?"

"It was an outrageous amount of money," Naomi clarified. The hushed tone of her voice helped relay the astonishment she still felt.

"How much did she offer you?"

"It was a lot," Naomi said, clearly uncomfortable. "I tried not to let her see how shocked and offended I was, so I reminded her that you were waiting for us and we should be going. Then before either one of us knew what was happening, a small boat with three men in it cut us off. It was like they came out of nowhere. We saw their guns and both of us stopped dead in the water on our Jet Skis. I was paralyzed with fear and couldn't have moved if I had wanted to. I'm glad Roslin didn't suggest we try to outrun them or something. I'm not sure I would've remembered how to get the thing going again."

Naomi's voice was low and controlled, as if she were choosing her words carefully and attempting to keep her emotions in check. Marcel felt anger bubbling around inside of her, and she wasn't sure how to deal with it yet.

"My mind wasn't processing things well," Naomi said. "Men

with guns . . . me on a Jet Ski . . . Roslin wanting to give me money. There were just so many things out of the ordinary going on that I wasn't working on all cylinders. But your mother," she said quietly. "She was calm and on top of it. While we're still on the Jet Skis and the men are there pointing guns at us, Roslin looked at me and said, 'Nobody mentioned anything about there being pirates out here.' If I hadn't been so scared, it might've been funny, but all I remember thinking was—these guys don't look like any pirates I ever saw."

Naomi's light laughter was strained. Marcel reached for her hand and squeezed it.

"So like two lambs being led to slaughter," Naomi said, "we did what we were told. I'd never seen any of those men before, and I couldn't imagine what they would want with us . . . other than . . . well . . . you know."

They were quiet for a moment as the connotation of what "you know" really meant. Once again Marcel could feel intense anger gurgling up inside her.

"On the boat ride to the yacht no one said anything," Naomi continued in a tired voice. "We just went along with them. I'm sure we were both in shock. I have to admit that they treated us well while we were there, though. These men dressed nicely and followed orders. There was no grabbing or pushing or shoving. They had guns and we didn't, so we did what they told us to do."

"You must've been terrified," Marcel said. Slowly she let the events of the last few days flash through her mind. It was so easy to see how none of this would've happened if it hadn't been for Senator Wainwright calling her mother for a poker game. His poor judgment in finding suitable players could've resulted in someone being seriously hurt.

"Once we got on the yacht, Roslin didn't let me out of her sight," Naomi said. "It was like aliens from outer space had plucked us up and put us on the mother ship or something. It was all so unreal. I remember her looking at the tallest man with

156

a gun—and just let me interject here that these were some very big guns. At least they looked big to me. Anyway, Roslin actually said to one of them, 'Take me to your leader.' She didn't ask who was in charge or why we were there. Just a simple, 'Take me to your leader.' Once again, if I hadn't been so afraid, it might've been funny, but no one was laughing. I was just so thankful that she was willing to do all the talking for us."

The more Marcel heard, the angrier she was getting at Senator Wainwright. He was responsible for bringing these people into their lives.

"You should've seen Roslin when they took us to where the leader was," Naomi said, interrupting Marcel's thoughts. "At first she was so mad I thought she might slap him, but he quickly turned the charm up a notch and apologized to both of us for the way we were encouraged to meet with him. Roslin calmed down a little once it looked as though no harm would come to us. The more relaxed she became, the less afraid I felt. The man in charge immediately engaged her in a conversation about poker, and it wasn't long until he said he wanted her to teach him what she knew about the game." Naomi laced her fingers through Marcel's and brought their hands up to her lips for a light kiss. "That's when the magic happened," Naomi said quietly. "Roslin was like a different person as soon as she knew what he wanted. All of a sudden, she was the one in charge. She led that guy around by the nose and taught us all a thing or two about poker. She was amazing." Naomi squeezed Marcel's hand. "I watched her read each one of those men. She studied them slowly. The only reason I even had a clue about what was going on was because I'd seen a glimpse of the real Roslin a few times. On those Hamburger Helper nights when she's feeling bad and wants to feel better. I know how she works you and Cricket so she can get what she wants. I saw all of that click into high gear—the very essence of who she is and how she functions in that kind of environment." The tone of Naomi's voice dropped to almost a whisper. "She had this low-key sensuality thing going on during the poker lessons, too. The men were mesmerized by her and hung on her every word. She's a master at manipulation and reading people. It was like watching poetry in motion."

As Marcel listened, she tried to associate the words Naomi used with the person she knew as her mother. *Reading people? A master at manipulation?*

"Anyway, I'm almost certain that she let the leader win several hands, and each time he won she would say something like 'very good bluffing' or 'that's the way to do it!' I'm sure it made sense that if he won a lot, we might be out of there sooner."

Marcel was beginning to feel queasy as she looked out across the water. *Are those men finished with us? Are they out there now wanting something else? Watching everything we do?*

"I've been thinking about this whole thing," Naomi said. "I saw Roslin in action. She's engaging, funny, charismatic and knowledgeable. Think about this for a moment. Suppose she made one of those videos where you teach people about poker. Other than the odds, I'm sure the basics are the same for all the games. The way you hold the cards, facial expressions, touching the chips, chatting up the other players. Oh! And one time when she was shuffling the cards, there were these two motions she did that made everyone at the table gasp. She fanned the cards out and picked one up and stood them all up on their side and moved them around like a little accordion, then picked them all up again and shuffled a few more times. That whole little flashy trick lasted less than two seconds, but you would've thought David Copperfield had been there and made the yacht disappear. I'm telling you, if there's a way to get that trick on tape and slow it down enough so that even ordinary, clumsy people can see how it's done so they can practice doing it, the video would be an instant hit."

As a child Marcel remembered watching her mother do card tricks. Until she went to school, she thought all mothers knew how to do things like that.

"With poker being so popular now," Naomi said, "I know there's a market for this kind of thing."

"You're probably right," Marcel said.

They both looked up at the sound of the door to the living room opening. Roslin came out.

"You're next," she said to Naomi. "Just tell him what you saw."

"I'd like to speak with him before he leaves," Marcel said.

Naomi nodded. "I'll let him know."

Chapter Twenty-two

Roslin joined Marcel on the futon where they both stared straight ahead at the water. Finally, Roslin said, "I'm sorry all of this happened."

Marcel didn't know who to be angry at anymore—Senator Wainwright for being so careless about screening poker players, or her mother for being a gambler in the first place. All Marcel knew at the moment was that she was tired of thinking about it. She was just happy to have them both back safely.

"I hear you tried to bribe my girlfriend," Marcel said.

Roslin's laughter was playful and her expression sheepish. "She's got some flappin' lips, I see." With a deep sigh she said, "I don't want to lose you."

"That'll never happen."

"I had to give you to the army for twenty-four years," Roslin said. "I'm not ready to let Naomi have you yet either."

"That's not exactly your decision."

"I realized that when she wouldn't take the money."

"How much did you offer her?"

"I'll never tell, but to me it was worth every penny."

The door to the living room opened, and Cricket came out with wet hair and a fresh set of Marcel's clean clothes on.

"How did it go?" Cricket asked Roslin. She pushed a chair closer to the futon and took her time easing down on it.

"Things went fine," Roslin said. "He had pictures of everyone on the yacht for me to identify. He probably knows more about what happened than any of us do."

"What else will it take, Roslin?" Cricket asked.

Marcel looked at her and thought she saw the beginning of a tan across Cricket's forehead where the painful red had previously been. On closer inspection, Marcel also noticed other areas that were starting to tan as well.

"What are you talking about?" Roslin asked.

"That's twice in less than twenty-four hours that you've had a gun pulled on you."

"This probably isn't a good time, Cricket," Marcel said.

"According to both of you, there's never a good time."

"I refuse to have this discussion," Roslin said. "Blame the people, not the game."

"If it weren't for the game, you wouldn't have gotten mixed up with these people in the first place," Cricket said.

Marcel decided to leave them alone. When the bickering started she usually made herself scarce and found something else to do. Fishing sounded good right about then, but she wanted to talk with the agent before he left. To keep them from getting too far into a heated discussion, she brought up the idea Naomi had mentioned earlier.

"Do either of you know if there's a book out called *Poker for Dummies*?"

"There's a *Dummies* book out for everything nowadays,"

Roslin said.

"I think someone should write a *Lesbian Sex for Dummies* book," Cricket said. "Young lesbians would buy it, and I bet straight men would buy it too if it had pictures."

"Eww!" Roslin said with a crinkled nose.

"We could've used one when we were kids, right, Marcel?" Cricket said.

Marcel was just glad Naomi wasn't there to hear that statement. *I'd be under the doghouse again . . .*

"I could've used a book like that a few years ago myself," Roslin said with a laugh.

"What about instructional DVDs?" Marcel asked.

"For lesbian sex?" Cricket said. "You go, girl!"

"No!" Marcel said. "For poker." She turned to her mother and decided to ignore Cricket altogether. "Someone was just willing to kidnap you to get poker information. It sounds like there might be a market for what you know about the subject."

"Hmm," Cricket said.

"I'm not giving away my secrets," Roslin said.

"You did that already," Cricket said. "They had guns and you told them how to win."

Roslin started to laugh. "I just barely skimmed the surface. I still have my secrets."

"So there's more?" Marcel asked.

"Of course there's more. The things I told those hoodlums any amateur poker player would know."

"Let's just suppose for a moment," Marcel said, "that your average amateur poker player does indeed know all of those things already. What about the people who watch this game on TV and wish they could do what the big boys do in the tournaments? I think poker is bigger now than it's ever been. People are hungry for all kinds of things that can help their game."

"Sorry," Roslin said. "I'm not selling my secrets."

"I'm not talking about your secrets," Marcel insisted. "Keep those. I'm talking about the basics to start out with. Then later perhaps get into the intermediate aspects of what makes a good poker player."

"Save your secrets for the advanced video," Cricket said.

"There you go trying to give away my secrets again!" Roslin said.

"You won't be giving them away," Cricket said. "You'll be selling them."

"If I tell everyone else how to do it, I'll never win another pot."

"Oh, I disagree," Marcel said. "Too many other factors play into winning or losing. The psychological aspects of the game and the patience it takes to wait out the bad hands—those are things you can't really teach someone. There's a certain amount of instinct that goes along with it, too. You have all of that. I've seen you work a table. You can smell it in the air."

Roslin's light laughter made Marcel smile.

"I say keep your secrets," Marcel said, "but share with the world how they can be better when those Friday night poker games at a friend's house come along."

"Why would I want to draw attention to myself that way?" Roslin asked. "I prefer staying out of the limelight. If I start selling videos, the next thing you know, the tax man is looking for me with his hand out. And you know how I feel about paying taxes."

"Yes, we know," Marcel and Cricket said at the same time.

Great idea, Naomi, Marcel thought, *but she's not going for it.*

Naomi came out on the porch when she was finished with her interview, and Marcel went in to have a word with Agent Barkley. He was sitting at the kitchen counter with his notebook open waiting for her.

"How can I help you, Ms. Robicheaux?"

163

Marcel sat down on a stool across from him at the counter. "What's the possibility that we'll see those people again?"

"We believe Mr. Lozano got most of what he wanted already," Agent Barkley said.

"What else do you think he wants?"

"More high stakes poker games. He has a lot of money, and he enjoys a good game. He also likes having such events at his home where he feels safe. Each time he leaves the security of his compound, he runs the risk of being arrested by a number of agencies."

"Then my mother isn't much safer now than she was on a Jet Ski minding her own business. Is that correct?"

"We expect Mr. Lozano to be in touch with your mother when he's ready to play poker again. We expect him to also contact Senator Wainwright for the same reason."

"What will happen if neither of them wants to have anything else to do with him?"

"That's hard to say."

"Why can't you just arrest him now?" Marcel asked. "You know where he is, and he's wanted on all sorts of things, to include kidnapping."

"We're closer to doing that now than we've ever been," Agent Barkley said. "This gambling fever is relatively new for him. We're interested in seeing where else it'll lead. Your mother was very helpful. If Mr. Lozano contacts her or Senator Wainwright, they've both been instructed to let us know."

"I don't think my mother is interested in playing cards with either one of them again."

He smiled. "She did mention that. The fact that both women were released unharmed tells us a lot. Mr. Lozano has great respect for your mother's skill as a gambler. He wants to be thought of as a viable opponent in her circle of players. Having three of his men pick her up and escort her to his yacht is just how he does things. The harm that such an act can cause just

164

wouldn't occur to him."

Marcel didn't like the sound of that at all.

"You had the yacht under surveillance while they took my mother and Naomi at gunpoint," she said. "Why didn't you try to do something then? There's no way anyone could've known what they wanted them for."

"We had an agent on board the yacht," he said. "He was ready to take action and call us in if things had started to go bad."

"In my eyes," Marcel said, "the minute three men pointed guns at my mother, things had started to go bad."

"I understand how you feel."

The sincerity in his voice made Marcel actually believe him.

"Is there a way we can get some sort of protection from this man?" she asked.

"Senator Wainwright has already made those arrangements," he said. "The senator feels responsible for what happened to your mother and Ms. Shapiro."

"He should," Marcel said pointedly.

"As long as you're in Key West, someone will be watching your house."

That made her feel better. "Thank you," she said. "Is there anything else you need from us?"

"Nothing at this time. If anyone contacts your mother again, call this number." He slid a business card across the counter. Marcel slipped it into her pocket.

"That's all the questions I have," she said. "Thanks for your time."

He closed his notebook and tucked his pen into a pocket inside his coat. "Try to enjoy the rest of your vacation, Ms. Robicheaux."

Marcel looked at him and groaned.

Chapter Twenty-three

Sitting on the end of the pier holding her fishing pole, Marcel couldn't help but wonder who, if anyone, was keeping an eye on them. It wouldn't have surprised her at all if that had been nothing more than something Agent Barkley had told her just to make her feel better. At the moment she would believe almost anything about these people.

She heard footsteps on the pier and turned to see her mother ambling toward her with pursed lips. It made Marcel wonder what else could possibly go wrong. Roslin sat down beside her, their feet dangling off the end of the pier about twenty feet above the water. There was a cool breeze that made this the perfect place to be.

"Catch anything yet?" Roslin asked.

"No, not yet."

"That's why they call it fishing instead of catching, you

know."

"I've had a few bites. What's up?"

"Cricket and I are going home if we can get our flight changed."

Marcel was a little surprised but not disappointed. Being alone with Naomi at the beach house would be a nice change for them.

"Cricket's miserable now that she can't even go outside," Roslin said. "I guess we could buy her a long-sleeved shirt and sweat pants or something, but she's talking like she would rather go home."

"And you?" Marcel asked.

"Me?" Roslin laughed. "After getting mugged and then kidnapped, I think I've seen about all I care to see of Florida for a while. Never did get to make my stick-a-ritas."

Marcel got a tug on her line, but the fish fell off just as she pulled it up out of the water.

"Is this a place you'll ever want to come back to?" Marcel asked. She cast her line out again and slowly began to reel it in.

"This place, as in the beach house?" Roslin asked. "Or Key West in general?"

"Both, I guess."

Roslin shrugged. "I've been to more exotic places than this. I was never kidnapped in Maui or Tahiti, though."

"What kind of plans do you have for the beach house?" Marcel asked.

"I'll unload it in a poker game the first chance I get."

"What if I wanted to buy it from you?"

The question hung out there in the air before Roslin said, "Are you serious? Why would you want it?"

Marcel looked out at the beautiful blue water and couldn't imagine why anyone *wouldn't* want it.

"This place is way overdue for a storm to hit," Roslin said. "I usually try to get rid of it each year at about this time before hurricane season comes along."

"Does that mean if I wait a few months, I'll get it cheaper?"

They shared a laugh, and Roslin leaned back on her elbows and swung her feet.

"How much would you sell it for?" Marcel asked.

"I can't sell it to you."

Marcel felt such a huge wave of disappointment. She had been visualizing spending quality time there with Naomi and liked the idea of having a place where they could invite friends and make some nice, fun memories of their own. "I'm willing to pay you what it's worth," Marcel said.

"You're my baby. What's mine is yours. If you want this place then I'll give it to you."

"I don't want you to give it to me. I want to buy it. I know what these pieces of property mean to you when it comes to gambling. Games where having the deed to some property in the pot makes a few gamblers all itchy to win and get their hands on it. Things like that make them careless."

Roslin smiled. "This place in particular has made the rounds. That's for sure. The Florida Shuffle. I was able to trade it to a sheik when I got in the hole in Moscow once. I was making a run with a full house—jacks over nines. I was all in. The sheik ended up with four fives and cleaned me out. My ticket home was paid for already, but I'd been hoping to connect with a game in Geneva the next evening. The sheik was happy to buy the Key West house, and he gave me an excellent price. I had enough money to go to Geneva, win there, and come home with a nice chunk of change. That guy kept the place for several years before Skippy ended up with it somehow. I've lost it at least three times since then."

"How much did the sheik pay you for it?" Marcel asked.

"He got it for a steal even then. I wanted about five hundred thousand to go to Geneva with, so I cut him a deal on it."

"Then cut me a deal, too."

"Free is about the best deal you can get anywhere, my baby," Roslin said with a laugh. "We've both worked hard to have nice things. When I'm gone, I know I'll be able to leave you a big house, an impressive art collection, choice pieces of real estate on three continents and a work ethic that would make any parent proud. If it's mine, it's yours. Giving you this little sliver of paradise would be my pleasure. I'll take care of the paperwork when I get back."

"I'm paying you something for it," Marcel insisted. "You wouldn't have kept it all this time if it wasn't useful to you in some way."

"You can pay the taxes on it," Roslin said. "How about that? They're coming due soon. And just wait until you have to buy insurance for it. That'll knock your hat in the creek and save me a bundle at the same time."

Marcel had just finished cleaning the day's catch and carrying the two big redfish up the back steps to the kitchen when she found Cricket and Roslin all packed and ready to leave for the airport.

"All I'm getting is a busy signal for the airline," Roslin said. "We'll give you a call if we can't get our flight changed once we get there because you'll have to go to the airport and pick us up again."

"I'm sorry to see you both leaving," Naomi said.

Cricket seemed to be getting around better, but was still moving like a crispy robot. Naomi picked up Cricket's two pieces of luggage and offered to carry them down the back stairs for her. *Yeah*, Marcel thought. *We're sorry to see you go, but let me help you get your stuff in the car before you change your mind.*

"Call me if you have second thoughts about that thing we discussed earlier," Roslin said to Marcel.

Marcel nodded.

"What thing did you two discuss?" Cricket asked.

Marcel opened the back door and wasn't about to clue Cricket in on anything. She would find out about ownership of the beach house changing hands soon enough.

They all went down the back steps single file. Naomi helped get their luggage in Roslin's rental car.

"Let us know what happens with your flight," Naomi said. "There's been too much weirdness going on to assume everything's okay."

Marcel and Naomi watched them get in the car and drive away. Marcel imagined that she might miss spending more time with her mother, but it was a huge relief seeing the back of Cricket's head as they drove down the driveway on their way to the airport.

Naomi and Marcel went fishing again and finally heard from Roslin about two hours later. They had gotten their flight changed and would be leaving within the hour. On the way back to the house from the pier, Marcel suggested she and Naomi move into the other bedroom. Once they got back to the house, they both noticed a much different feeling there—as if only positive energy had taken over every room.

Marcel was excited at the prospect of owning this place. The key to keeping it in good shape would be using it more often. She could picture in her mind having Carmen, Reba and Juanito there with good food and hours of laughter. *Vacations should be fun, and this place has some serious potential to be just that.*

"I'm so irritated with myself," Naomi said as they worked together to put clean linens on the bed in the master bedroom.

"About what?" Marcel asked. She tucked the top sheet in with a military crease on her side of the bed.

"For being so glad they're gone," Naomi said.

Marcel's laughter reflected her opinion of the situation. "I'm sure they're just as happy to be on their way home again."

Naomi suggested a shower and then a nap, but before they got very far with that idea, Marcel's phone rang.

"Ms. Robicheaux?" a man's voice said before she even got the cell phone up to her ear.

"Yes?"

"This is Mickey Valencia. I work in Senator Wainwright's office."

"How did you get this number?"

There was a slight pause before Mr. Valencia said, "I work in Senator Wainwright's office," as if that were all the explanation he needed to answer her question. "The Senator has been trying to get in touch with your mother. He'd like to speak with her if that's possible."

"Tell the Senator that Ms. Robicheaux will contact him at another time. I'll be sure to give her the message."

"Marcel," Senator Wainwright said. He was on the phone now. With a grudging nod, Marcel vowed to screen her calls better in the future.

"Good afternoon, Senator Wainwright," she said. "My mother isn't here. She left to go back to San Antonio."

"Oh," he said, the disappointment apparent in his voice. "I'm sure the chances of her accepting a phone call from me are fewer than slim anyway."

Marcel was relieved at his grasp of the situation and allowed her silence to confirm what he obviously already knew.

"Would you and your friends allow me to take you to dinner this evening as a way of making up for all that's happened?"

"That's not necessary," Marcel said.

"Please. I insist. It's the least I can do. We'll find a nice place away from the tourists. Key West has several fine establishments. My driver and I'll be along to pick you up at seven. Thank you for agreeing to see me, Marcel."

Her phone went dead, and she held it away from her ear and

then stared at it with a confused, puzzled expression.

"Looks like we're having dinner with Senator Wainwright," she said simply.

"What!" Naomi said. "Without your mother? He's her friend."

Marcel slipped her cell phone into the pocket of her shorts. "He had a little desperation thing going on there," she said. "He probably has a good idea that my mom has cut him off where poker is concerned. I'm sure he wants us on his side."

"I don't have anything to wear to dinner with a senator. All I brought was shorts and one set of work clothes."

Marcel laughed. "Well, I'm sure your work clothes look a lot fancier than the ones I brought. Besides, from what I've seen around here, the clothes police don't issue many citations. He's all puckered up to kiss our butts. He couldn't care less what we wear."

"No way to get out of it, I guess."

"He didn't give me a chance to say that much."

"Then maybe we can call the shots and pick the restaurant," Naomi said. "Some place nice and gay friendly."

"He's so self-absorbed, he probably wouldn't even notice."

Chapter Twenty-four

Marcel kept watching out the window in the kitchen while Naomi played a game of pool by herself. They were ready for their dinner engagement and both had found something appropriate to wear. Marcel had on khaki pants, a yellow polo shirt and brown loafers, while Naomi looked striking in a white silk blouse, black slacks and white sandals.

"Holy cow," Marcel said. "Wait until you see the limo that just pulled up!"

"Do you think the neighbors are watching?" Naomi asked as she put her pool stick away and grabbed her purse. "Maybe we'll get a little respect around here."

Marcel held the back door open for her and then locked it behind them on their way out. "If they see us crawling in that thing they'll probably think we're a couple of hookers."

Carefully negotiating the steps, Naomi said, "You have such a positive outlook on everything, darling. My goodness! Look at the size of that limo!"

The limousine driver got out and opened the door for them with a pleasant, "Good evening, ladies."

Naomi got in and reached for Marcel's hand and tugged her in as well. The faint scent of men's cologne offered an ambience Marcel didn't experience often or particularly care for, but the temperature inside was pleasantly cool and refreshing. They sat in the seat across from Senator Wainwright and directly behind the driver. A finely dressed Hispanic man sat across from Naomi. Marcel assumed he was the aide who had called her earlier.

"Ladies," Senator Wainwright said with a smile. He held a drink that looked deceptively like a watery iced tea. "I appreciate you taking time away from your vacation to spend an evening with me."

"Where's the other one?" the man asked the senator.

"She went home already," Senator Wainwright whispered out of the side of his mouth.

"You told me the older one would be here."

"You!" Naomi said, pointing at the other man. "It's *you*!"

Marcel jumped, startled by her outburst. Alarmed, she asked, "What's the matter?" The doors to the limousine locked automatically as the driver pulled out onto the road.

"That's the man from the yacht," Naomi said. "The one who wanted to learn poker!"

Marcel looked at him and wondered what he was doing there. He was dressed in a dark blue suit with a light blue shirt and tie. He reminded Marcel of a younger Al Pacino, which didn't make him any more likeable under the circumstances. Everything suddenly felt out of sync. She chewed on her lower lip and stole a look at Naomi.

Speaking quietly, the man said, "Senator Wainwright has generously allowed me this opportunity to—"

"Stop the car," Naomi said, interrupting him. "Driver! Stop

the car!"

When the limousine driver didn't even attempt to slow down, much less stop, Marcel put her hand on Naomi's arm to keep her from trying to get out of the moving vehicle. As panic welled in her throat and threatened to overcome her, Marcel tried desperately to think of a way to get things under control.

"I apologize for the circumstances of our first meeting, Ms. Shapiro," the man said.

Naomi yanked her arm out of Marcel's grasp, but at least she wasn't still trying to get out of the limo. Marcel glanced at the men and attempted to reel in her temper. She drilled the senator with a look that made her pupils feel like they were smoking around the edges. "How dare you put us in this kind of situation."

Senator Wainwright had a flicker of fear in his eyes as he looked away from her. He took a sip of his drink and let his friend do all the talking.

"Ms. Robicheaux," the man said. "My name is Salvador Lozano, and I'm a great admirer of your mother's talent. I was led to believe she would be here this evening." He gave Senator Wainwright a piercing look without moving his head then returned his focus back to Marcel. "My purpose now is to apologize for what happened earlier today. I hope you and your friend will see how sincere I am in my quest to—"

"Your men held guns on us," Naomi said. The intensity in her lowered voice sent a shiver down Marcel's spine. "You kept me and Roslin on your boat against our will. There's only one place I'd like to see you, Mr. Lozano."

He flinched at her words then slightly adjusted his tie before glancing out the tinted window. A cold knot formed in Marcel's stomach. While Naomi suddenly appeared to be fearless and confrontational, Marcel found it nearly impossible to steady her own erratic pulse. Her mind became a crazy mixture of hope and fear as she tried to sort through their options.

"Please stop the vehicle," Naomi said over her shoulder to the driver. Once again, he didn't slow down or even acknowledge that he heard her.

With Naomi showing no signs of relenting, Marcel realized that one of them needed to try to maintain a neutral, conciliatory tone even as fear twisted around her heart. *We're in a limousine with at least one ruthless person*, she thought while looking at Lozano, *along with a drunken wimp beside him. Why didn't I just say no earlier when this fool called? I could've saved us all a lot of trouble.*

With her stomach still clenched tightly, Marcel took her time trying to size up the two men and the position she and Naomi were in. She noticed that all of the color had drained from Skippy's face, which told her they weren't the only ones upset about what was happening. At this point Marcel understood that directly antagonizing Lozano wouldn't be in anyone's best interest, and keeping things as normal as possible for the time being while they were more or less trapped in the limousine made the most sense to her. Folding her hands in an uncharacteristic pose of tranquility, Marcel settled back and tried to swallow the lump that lingered in her throat. After a moment, she found the courage to break the uncomfortable silence.

"I have some issues with the way you interrupted my friend's first Jet Ski lesson, Mr. Lozano," Marcel said. "I'm sure you can understand that."

Without giving Lozano a chance to say anything, Senator Wainwright said, "Let's try to have a pleasant evening, shall we? I've been wondering, Marcel. What are your views on the Patriot Act these days? As a retired military officer I'd be interested in your opinion."

Is he for real? Marcel thought. *He wants to discuss politics now?*

"Don't do this, Marcel," Naomi said under her breath. "I want out of this limousine."

Marcel reached for Naomi's hand, but she yanked it away. That made Marcel even angrier at Skippy.

"You have to have an opinion," the senator prodded.

"Take us back to the beach house," Marcel said, her mood veering sharply to anger.

"Dinner, Marcel. A simple dinner."

Marcel could see the impatience growing on Salvador Lozano's face. Finally, he said, "Are you a gambler, Ms. Robicheaux?"

"No," she replied.

His expression revealed his disappointment. "Would it be possible for you to speak to your mother on my behalf?"

Looking at him closely, Marcel's instincts told her that he hadn't become such a powerful man by being an imbecile. *He must really be hooked by the gambling bug. It's certainly ruined a lot of people in addition to making them extremely careless.*

"What would you suggest I say to her?"

"Send her my apologies for the way I handled things this morning," Lozano said. "I didn't know what else to do. She's not an easy woman to keep track of."

Senator Wainwright laughed nervously and took another sip of his drink.

"My mother is usually careful about choosing who she plays with," Marcel said. "She likes the challenge of a good game, but she would never consider subjecting herself or others to danger." She looked at Lozano and then Senator Wainwright. "I imagine you've both played your last hand of poker with her."

"I certainly hope you're wrong about that," Skippy said with a nervous laugh.

"So do I," Lozano agreed.

Keeping her eyes fixed on both of them, Marcel stated very simply, "We don't want to have dinner with either of you. Please take us back to the beach house."

After a moment Lozano bent his head slightly forward. "My yacht is very—"

"Your *yacht?*" Naomi repeated incredulously. "Is that where we're going?"

Marcel gave the men a laser beam stare and slowly said again, "Take us back to the beach house."

After giving them a fiery look, Lozano nodded with a taut jerk of his head. He said something in Spanish to the driver who immediately pulled the limousine over and turned it around.

Just having the driver park near the carport at the beach house made Marcel feel better. She took the keys from her pocket only to have Naomi snatch them from her hand before scrambling out of the limousine as soon as the doors were unlocked. The driver opened Marcel's door and stood there waiting for her, but she wasn't quite ready to get out yet. As if seeing Senator Wainwright for the first time, she stared at him until he looked away from her.

Finally, Marcel asked, "Did you really think we would get on that yacht with you?" Her question was directed at Skippy, but neither of them answered or would even look at her. Marcel's voice faded to a hushed jumble of words and her anger continued to reverberate through the backseat. She raised her chin with a cool stare in Skippy's direction and got out.

Once inside the beach house, Marcel locked the door behind her and leaned against it while listening for footsteps on the stairs. It wasn't long before she heard the limousine drive away. She waited a bit to make sure they were really gone before going to search for Naomi, eventually finding her in the bedroom packing.

"I want out of here tonight," Naomi said without preamble. She threw clothes, toiletries and souvenirs in her suitcase with absolutely no hesitation. Marcel couldn't blame her for feeling that way, but she was surprised at the malice she heard in her lover's voice. Not sure what to do next, Marcel attempted to try to collect her thoughts. Her fears were running rampant as she walked over to the bedroom window and gazed out at the beach.

Leaving this place wouldn't be as easy for her. She wasn't ready to go yet. *Those assholes are practically chasing us off. If we leave now, it's almost like they've won.*

With mounting resentment toward Skippy and Lozano, Marcel reluctantly concluded that their vacation was over. Being ready for it didn't matter. They were both packed and in the car twenty minutes later.

The tension between them increased with frightening intensity the rest of their short time in Key West. They hadn't spoken in the rental car during the drive to the airport, when they arranged an earlier flight back, or while they waited to board the aircraft to go home. To Marcel it felt as though Naomi was blaming her for the limousine episode, but she didn't want to argue about it or even take the time to defend herself. It had already been an exhausting, emotional day. Fighting with her lover just added one more thing to an already long list of troubling incidents.

Once they got on the plane and Marcel was settled in her seat by the window, she buckled her seat belt just as her cell phone rang. It was her mother.

"You'll never guess what we're doing," Roslin said breathlessly. Without waiting for an answer, she said, "We're on our way to Manhattan for the rest of our vacation! I can't remember the last time I was at the condo there!"

She sounds so happy, Marcel thought. *At least someone's having a good time.*

"Anyway," Roslin said, "we'll be back Sunday night. I didn't want you to get worried. Enjoy the beach!"

Manhattan. I'm too tired to even think about it. All I want to do is go home.

Before turning her cell phone off, Marcel called Carmen and told her when their flight would be arriving.

"Cricket told me what happened there," Carmen said. "I'm sorry Key West was a bust."

Marcel didn't bother telling her about the latest fiasco with

Skippy. "Coming back early wasn't my idea," she said, "but we'll be there anyway. Thanks."

Attempting to get comfortable in the land-of-no-leg-room, she found Naomi's silence now less irritating than it had been earlier. They were both tired, and Marcel eventually dozed off on the flight back. She didn't wake up again until they landed. They still weren't speaking and only exchanged a few words from the time they got off the plane until collecting their luggage at the baggage claim area.

"Are you coming home with me?" Naomi asked Marcel when Carmen's truck pulled up to the curb to get them.

Still sleepy, along with being upset at having their vacation cut short, Marcel muttered a grouchy, "I don't know yet."

Naomi heaved one of her suitcases up into the back of the truck and said to Carmen, "Please take me home first."

Even while it was happening and they rode through the late-night San Antonio traffic in strained silence, Marcel let her anger and frustration with Skippy get in the way of everything else. At the moment, all she wanted to do was go home. She didn't have enough energy to deal with more than one bad mood at a time.

When Carmen finally parked behind Naomi's car in her driveway and the three of them got out to help sort the luggage, Marcel stood beside the truck and watched them get all of Naomi's things into the house. It wasn't that she didn't want to help—Naomi just made sure there wasn't anything left for Marcel to carry in. With her frustration building and a brief sense of longing trying to tug her in several directions, Marcel got back into the truck and waited for Carmen. Biting her lip, she looked away as the lights came on in the house. Going on vacation had been a lousy idea.

Marcel went home to her mother's huge, empty house and was grateful that Carmen didn't ask any questions on the way. It was late and Marcel went right to her bedroom as soon as Carmen left. It was hard to believe there had recently been honest discussions about moving in with Naomi. At the time it had sounded like a good idea, but now things between them looked a lot bleaker.

She took off her clothes and pulled on a worn, baggy T-shirt before crawling into bed. *Maybe it's time you really moved out on your own*, she thought as she fluffed up her pillow a few times. *Mom and Cricket will be back here on Sunday night. Do you still want to deal with any of that again?*

While tossing and turning, she decided to have her things out of the house by Sunday afternoon. She could stay at the shop while figuring it all out. That would give her two days to rest, emotionally regroup and start contemplating what she wanted to do next. *You're too old to still be living with your mother anyway*, Marcel thought before attempting to fall asleep. *We all need our own space.*

Chapter Twenty-five

Marcel's first official day back at the shop was Monday morning, and it was just as bad as she thought it would be. All the furniture pieces Carmen had finished while they had been away now needed her attention. Getting them crated and shipped out would take most of the day, but she was glad to have the distraction.

The aroma of freshly brewing coffee filled the shop by the time Carmen and Reba arrived. Seeing them together always made Marcel aware of what two people in love should actually look like.

"I thought I'd come along and explain what the messages are," Reba said. Her short gray hair went well with her blue flowery blouse and dark blue slacks. "I know what it's like to have someone else tinkering with your things."

Marcel glanced at the stack of papers beside the cash register.

She hadn't even noticed them the day before. "You're so nice and organized, the shop probably groaned when it saw me come in," Marcel said. With a playful wink, she added, "You can tinker with my things any time. So how was business while I was gone?"

With a slight blush at the compliment, Reba said, "I thought it was busy."

"We moved some of the older pieces in here from the Fort Worth trip to keep it from looking so empty," Carmen said.

"And we *sold* some of them!" Reba said. She poured two cups of coffee and fixed Carmen's the way she liked it. "But then I always get a little nervous each time a customer comes in. Whenever they'd ask me a question about a certain piece of furniture, I'd have to go to the back and get my little expert."

Carmen blew on her coffee and smiled at her lover. "I think you did that mostly because you missed me."

"That goes without saying, dear." Reba looked directly at Marcel and asked, "How was your vacation?"

Marcel glanced over at Carmen. Apparently she hadn't told anyone about the problems they'd had in Key West. *Good friends don't gossip*, she reminded herself.

"Key West is a place I would recommend everyone see at least once," Marcel said. "It's beautiful and very gay friendly."

Carmen nodded and let Marcel's description stand on its own. "Maybe some day we'll get there," she said to Reba.

"When might that be?" Reba asked. "We're not getting any younger, you know."

A few hours later Marcel heard the shop's door ding open and she saw her mother standing there staring at her.

"Good morning," Marcel said pleasantly. "How was Manhattan?"

Roslin let the door slowly close behind her. "You really did it."

Marcel didn't say anything. A heavy mother-daughter discussion wasn't something she had time for at the moment. She had furniture to get out, mail to read and bills to pay.

"You packed up your things while I was gone," Roslin said accusingly.

She let her mother talk, knowing very well that Roslin didn't want to hear what anyone else had to say. Marcel's silence seemed to infuriate her even more.

"Aren't you going to ask me how the rest of my vacation was?" Roslin snapped.

"How was Manhattan?" Marcel asked for the second time.

"How do you *think* it was? Once she recovered from the sunburn, all that little friend of yours wanted to do was shop and . . . and . . . get all romantical and stuff."

Marcel didn't want to get into that.

"If she doesn't shut up about me retiring I'm not sure what I'll do next," Roslin said. "I'm so tired of hearing about it I could hurl."

"Just tell her," Marcel said calmly. She flipped through her Rolodex and found the number for the shipping company. They didn't open until mid-morning.

"I've done that so many times already even *I'm* tired of hearing me say it," Roslin grumbled.

Marcel dialed and went through a series of selections before she reached the number she wanted. After finally getting a live person on the phone, she was put on hold.

"You need to be very specific with Cricket," Marcel said. "She doesn't respond to anything else."

"I'm thinking about something more drastic than that."

Roslin made her way to the workshop area in the back to see Carmen and Reba while Marcel finished making arrangements for shipping the furniture. Later as she returned to sorting the mail, her mother came back to the front of the shop.

"So is this where I have to come to see you every day now?"

Roslin asked in a clipped, snippy tone of voice. "You used to have coffee with me every morning."

Marcel raised her head and stared at her mother for a moment. "It's my first day back to work. I wasn't sure what you had going on today."

"My daughter left home! That's what I have going on."

"Your forty-eight-year-old daughter finally moved out," Marcel said. "Don't you think it's about time?"

Roslin sat down on one of the stools at the counter. "Nothing I say will get you back, will it?"

Marcel hated playing this little pouting game with her, but she knew from experience that if she waited long enough, Roslin's mood would eventually improve.

"Then could you maybe come by for breakfast every morning on your way to work?" Roslin asked. "At least I'd get to see you that way."

Marcel didn't want her mother to know that she wasn't living at Naomi's house as they had previously discussed. Now instead of waking up with the woman she loved, Marcel was getting out of a single bed to the hum of a refrigerator in her office. Her hesitation at the suggestion of "breakfast at Mom's house" spurred Roslin to continue.

"When you lived there with me we spent a few minutes each morning catching up on things," she said. They looked at each for a moment. "A cup of coffee on your way here every morning," Roslin said, making a motion with her hand. When she didn't receive a response, she said, "Some toast."

Marcel held the look, but her mother was encouraged and didn't give up.

"Dry toast," Roslin said in a softer tone. "No butter," she added meekly.

Her persistence eventually made them both laugh.

"Just a short visit in the mornings you're not running late," Roslin said. The pleading look on her mother's face almost made

Marcel feel ashamed of herself for being so difficult.

"You can usually find me here all day, you know," Marcel said.

"It's not the same as having you home."

A customer came in and Marcel devoted her attention to answering his questions about a trunk that Carmen had restored. She opened it up and showed it to him. His interest was genuine, but he decided to think about it and not do anything hasty. After the man left, Roslin leaned over and crossed her arms on the counter.

"What happened with Skippy after Cricket and I came back?" Roslin asked.

Marcel took a deep breath. "What a weenie that guy is. I don't like you associating with him."

"He's in some kind of trouble," Roslin said. "You know he's the reason that Lozano guy took us on the yacht, right?"

"Skippy is? How do you know that?"

"I spoke with Skippy this morning and he let it slip. Besides, he's the only one who knew where I was."

"We met him and Lozano after you and Cricket left, by the way."

Roslin's expression changed to a hardened, angry mask with piercing blue slits for eyes. "Skippy and Lozano? You met them where?"

Marcel explained how she had gotten a call from Senator Wainwright with a dinner invitation that he insisted they accept. "Good old Skippy pulled up in a stretch limo as long as the pier and had Lozano with him," Marcel said. "There were some tense moments for a while until we insisted they take us back to the beach house."

Roslin yanked her cell phone out of her purse and excused herself. She went outside to make a call while Marcel returned her attention to the stack of mail near the cash register. Occasionally she would look up to see her mother standing outside on the sidewalk either waving a hand around or jabbing her finger in the air to emphasize a point while she continued talking on the phone. Finally, she came back into the shop and sat down again.

"He's in trouble, all right," Roslin said. "Skippy owes this Lozano guy a lot of money."

Marcel wasn't the least bit interested in Senator Wainwright's finances, but she was curious about why he would share such a thing with her mother.

"What does any of that have to do with you?" Marcel asked. "I don't get it. He drinks and gambles too much. That's no secret. Write him off as bad news."

Roslin averted her eyes, but kept a steady rhythm with her fingernails on the counter.

"Mom?"

"That slime ball," Roslin whispered.

"Which slime ball?"

"Skippy! On the phone just now he admitted to trading some of his debt to this guy for info about where we were staying in Key West. If Naomi and I hadn't left on the Jet Skis when we did, Lozano and his goons would've shown up at the beach house looking for me."

Marcel felt an eerie chill race through her body.

"Apparently some federal agency knows about the money Skippy owes Lozano," Roslin said. "Both of those bastards put my baby in danger. That's just totally unacceptable." With a curt nod, she stood up. "I'll be back later. I have some calls to make."

Chapter Twenty-six

Marcel helped supervise getting the furniture pieces crated and on their way to Mexico. It felt good to see them loaded on the truck. Now there was more room to walk around in the workshop area.

Just before closing time, Roslin came back to the shop looking tired and upset. They both said good-bye to Carmen who promised to be back again the next day to start all over again. After the front door closed, Roslin pointed to the sign on the door. "May I?"

Marcel nodded and watched her turn the sign over to indicate they were closed.

"I've been on the phone with Skippy most of the day," Roslin said as she walked to the counter and climbed on the same stool she had occupied earlier. "He's been drinking a lot, and he gets chatty when he's looped. He's gotten himself in a real pickle."

Marcel still wasn't at all concerned about Senator Wainwright's problems, and she was irked that her mother had been in contact with him again.

"You can't be any more upset with him than I am," Roslin said, seeming to read Marcel's mind, "but you don't understand the situation. I owe him."

"You owe him what?" Marcel asked with a note of caution. "Money?"

Roslin laughed. "No. Never money. I don't leave a game owing anyone anything. If I don't have the funds to play, then I'm out. Period." She shrugged and then mumbled, "I might not have much more than bus fare to get me back to the airport, but I never owe gambling debts."

"Then what do you owe him?"

Reluctant to answer, Roslin finally said, "A short, important list of favors."

Favors, Marcel thought. *That doesn't sound good.*

"I'm pretty sure Skippy's the reason the IRS has left me alone all these years. A close friend of Skippy's is in charge of it."

"How could he do anything to help you with that?" Marcel asked. "The IRS doesn't look the other way for anyone. What else do you think he's done for you?"

"Investments. Perks from lobbyists. Free meals at expensive restaurants. Airline tickets. The usual senatorial stuff."

Marcel tried to hide her disappointment at how easily her mother just rattled off these things. "What does he get from you in return?" she asked.

Roslin looked at her with a tired expression. "The chance to lose his money to some of the finest card players in the world. I'm invited to these games," she said. "Some of these people allow me to bring Skippy along. He's such a bad gambler that they don't mind him being there." She stretched her arms out on the counter. "I always thought he had money. He's been in politics a hundred years. What politician doesn't have money? It just

189

goes to show, Marcel. All that glitters isn't gold. Some of that glittering stuff is downright ugly."

Marcel shook her head.

"But he's racked up a lot of gambling debts," Roslin said. "Now he's mixed up with this Lozano guy. Let me ask you something. When you were on that fishing boat with Skippy when Naomi and I were gone, what made you think those people were with the FBI?"

"Skippy told me it was the FBI."

"You never saw any kind of identification?" Roslin asked. "A badge? Some sort of ID card?"

"No," Marcel said. "On the boat they were all running around in Key West clothes—shorts and T-shirts. Pretending to be tourists. No one had a badge that I could see."

Roslin slowly sat up straighter. "They weren't FBI agents. It was an IRS Criminal Investigation Unit. Skippy's working with them to try to catch Lozano for tax evasion."

"The IRS?" Marcel said incredulously. "The guys I saw on the boat had guns! Since when does anyone in the IRS carry a gun?"

"I'm just telling you what Skippy told me today." Roslin sounded very tired. "He owes Lozano a lot of money, and Lozano was willing to erase Skippy's debt if he could get me to a poker game."

Marcel tilted her head a little hoping to be able to hear her mother better since what Roslin was saying so far wasn't making any sense. "I've never heard of gangsters forgetting about money someone owes them. But then again, I don't know any real gangsters either."

"That's what Skippy told me," Roslin said with quiet emphasis. "Salvador Lozano has his hands in so many things and is so big in southern Florida that the IRS wants him really bad. Apparently Lozano contacted Skippy about six months ago and they've been playing poker ever since. Skippy kept mentioning my name so much that Lozano insisted on meeting me. We went to Miami where Lozano saw me play cards that night just like Skippy had promised. When we finally left, Skippy thought his old debts had been forgiven just because he had talked me into going to Lozano's place." With a shrug she added, "But apparently Lozano wanted a few more things from him."

Roslin sat on the stool with a glazed look in her eyes before she continued. "Skippy told him where we were staying in Key West, so Lozano made plans to arrange to have me on his yacht for a few hours."

"You're saying Skippy knew about the yacht and the plan to—"

"Skippy told him where we were staying," Roslin said again. "By volunteering that information, his complete debt to Lozano was supposed to have been forgotten."

All Marcel could think of to say was, "That weenie." Her thoughts flashed back to the call from Senator Wainwright's aide and the conversation that transpired where she and Naomi had been left with no real choice but to see him that night.

"Anyway," Roslin said in a voice that seemed to come from a long way off. "Skippy claims he got angry at Lozano about the first poker night in Miami not being enough for him. That had been the deal between them—Skippy gets me there and Lozano forgives the debt. It just so happens that the IRS Criminal Investigation Unit has been checking into Skippy's gambling habits for a while now. According to Skippy, the night we got robbed, the IRS approached him about setting up Lozano."

Confused, Marcel asked, "Why did Skippy lead me to believe we were on a fishing boat with the FBI?"

"I guess because it's more prestigious than being on a fishing boat with the IRS. Can't get any lower than the IRS, in my opinion." Her words were loaded with ridicule as she sat there staring ahead. "Would you have felt safer on a fishing boat full of IRS guys? Or FBI guys?"

"It wasn't my safety I was worried about," Marcel said. "The guys on the boat never mentioned what organization they were with, but they had some state-of-the-art equipment in their possession." She heard her mother sniff and suddenly noticed that she was crying. "What's the matter?"

"There's more," Roslin said, her eyes filled with tears. "Skippy thinks I'll be investigated now."

"Investigated by who?"

"The IRS."

"He told you that?"

"He hinted at it."

"Do you think he knows something about it?"

"Right now he'd sell his mother if it would get him out of this Lozano and IRS thing. He can't afford a gambling scandal." Roslin wiped tears away with the back of her hand and said, "Elections are coming up."

"So you think he's sold you out?" Marcel asked. Her dislike for Senator Wainwright had suddenly reached new heights.

"I can't be certain about anything, but like I said—he hinted at it. He's running scared."

Marcel waited for her to say more, but her mother seemed to be lost in thought. Finally, Marcel said, "What happens now?"

"Let the IRS investigate. I'm not giving them my money, Marcel."

"Tax evaders go to jail, Mom."

"I know," Roslin said, suddenly starting to cry in earnest. "But those bastards aren't getting one red cent of my money. It's *my* money. They didn't do a *damn* thing to earn it!"

They'd had this same conversation for years, and so far, Marcel hadn't found a way to reason with her.

"I've been thinking about a solution," Roslin said through her tears. She took a long, labored breath that had a hiccup toward the end. "I need to relocate. I'm tired of worrying about this. I'd be able to stay in Paris with your grandparents for a while. I can use that as my home base."

"For how long?"

"Forever, I guess. If you're gonna make an omelet, you gotta break a few eggs. I'm just gonna move there."

Marcel didn't know what to say.

"I can make a good living in Europe. The place is crawling with bad poker players."

"What about us?" Marcel asked. "Your family? What about Cricket?"

Roslin put her hands over her face and began to sob.

"How much do you think you owe the IRS?"

"Don't even think about it," Roslin growled through her tears. "Not *one* red cent, Marcel. Do you hear me?"

Marcel held out her palms as if weighing something. Indicating her right palm she said, "You either go to jail for tax evasion or," she flopped her left palm open and said, "lose your family." Alternating her palms she repeated, "Go to jail—lose your family. Go to jail—lose your family." Marcel put her elbows on the counter. "Find out how much you owe, liquidate your assets and pay the damn taxes on it."

"Not one red cent, Marcel. Those bastards aren't getting my money."

Never had they been this far apart on an issue. "So relocating is your solution," Marcel said. "When do you plan on doing this Paris move?"

"Tomorrow," Roslin said bravely. With one big sniff, she appeared to be ready to get on with her plans.

Marcel felt queasiness in the pit of her stomach. *Tomorrow? She's leaving tomorrow?*

"I can't wait much longer than that," Roslin said. "If they freeze my bank account here, I'll really be pissed. I need that money for my initial traveling expenses. Once I get to Paris I can make arrangements for the rest of it." Watching her mother collect her purse and keys, Marcel felt as though someone had punched her in the stomach. She didn't know what to say.

"You and the girls will come and see me there, won't you?" Roslin asked. Her voice broke, but she tried valiantly to regain her composure.

"It would be easier for us to just visit you here in jail, you know."

Roslin's crooked smile eased some of the tension. "How did I ever raise such a mouthy kid?"

Marcel was entering sales into the computer when her cell phone rang. Hoping it was Naomi, she was disappointed to hear Cricket's voice.

"Where are you?" Cricket asked.

"Still at work."

"I need to speak with you and Naomi."

"I'm busy. Sorry." Eventually Marcel needed to let everyone know that Naomi wasn't around anymore, but that was too painful to even think about, much less actually do yet.

"This is important," Cricket said. "I need your advice on something."

"You'll probably have to speak with us separately then."

"I'm coming over there," Cricket said.

Great, Marcel thought.

A few minutes later she unlocked the door to the Antique Villa and found a tanned, emotionally-charged Cricket who looked as though she had been crying for a while already.

"I've got a lot to think about and very little time to do it in," Cricket said as she came in. They both took stools at the counter across from each other. "I'm sure you know what's happening with your mom," Cricket said. "I either go with her or I lose her forever."

Marcel sat motionless for a moment letting that sink in. "You're thinking about going to Paris with her?"

Cricket looked at her with a frightened innocence Marcel had never seen before. She had an almost uncontrollable urge to hug her right then. How had things gotten this far so quickly?

"I *have* to go with her," Cricket said as she began to cry again. "She's the love of my life. It's what I have to do, right?"

"That's a decision you'll have to make on your own."

"Maybe I just need to have someone else tell me this is the right thing to do."

"The right thing to do," Marcel said, "is for her to pay her frickin' taxes!"

"We all know that's not gonna happen, Marcel. She's determined to leave tomorrow. She's made up her mind about that already, so I don't have much of a choice. I have to go with her."

"What about your job?" Marcel asked. "You've got over twenty years at—"

"I'll take a leave of absence. I'm calling my boss right after I see Naomi later."

Just the mention of Naomi's name gave Marcel's heart an extra thump. "A leave of absence for how long?" she asked.

"I don't know."

Shifting uncomfortably on the stool, Marcel took a quick breath in utter astonishment. Not only was she about to lose her mother, but her best friend as well. "I can see my grandparents welcoming my mother there to live. She was married to their son. But you can't go to Paris and stay with them as her lover. They're old. They don't understand such things. Have you thought about that?"

"I haven't thought about anything but losing her," Cricket said, holding her head in her hands. "That's why I'm here."

"If you go with her," Marcel said, "it'll only encourage her to keep fighting the IRS. She can't run away forever, and I can't have my mother being a fugitive from the law."

"Well," Cricket said, "she's making reservations to leave the country, and she refuses to pay any taxes. So it's pretty clear to me what our choices are. Besides, I'm almost sure Skippy was bluffing about turning her in, but she's so paranoid about every-thing now she's quick to think the worst."

"Nothing about that guy would surprise me," Marcel said.

"So what should I do, Marcel?"

"You'll be giving up your retirement and life as you know it."

"What else?" Cricket asked in a dry monotone.

"You don't speak French," Marcel reminded her.

"What else?"

"How will you make a living over there?"

"She'll keep gambling and I'll take care of her."

As irritating as Marcel usually found Cricket to be, the thought of having them live in Paris was crushing her inside. This was her family. Just because she didn't want to share the same house with them any longer didn't mean they wouldn't be terribly missed. Suddenly, Marcel felt totally overwhelmed.

"Then it sounds like you have all the answers," she said, her voice dropping in volume. "You don't need my opinion."

Cricket sighed. "I guess you're right." She climbed off the stool and pushed herself away from the counter. "I have a lot to do. I'm not even sure where my passport is. I haven't used it since we went to Peru a year ago. Will you come by the house in the morning on your way to work and say good-bye to us?"

The question was like a little stab in her heart. Marcel offered a slight nod, and with marked sadness, she watched Cricket leave.

Chapter Twenty-seven

Almost overnight, Marcel became an expert on the IRS Criminal Investigation Unit by going online and downloading information. Established in 1919, she knew it had been responsible for the downfall of Public Enemy Number One Al Capone, the New York godfather John Gotti and Chicago crime boss Rocco Infelise. *Soon they'll be able to add that notorious gambler Roslin Robicheaux's name to this list*, Marcel thought with a roll of her eyes. Reading on, she also learned that the IRS Criminal Investigation Unit had solved the Lindbergh kidnapping, so at one time they had been a force to be feared and reckoned with for anyone waging crimes against the United States.

It also didn't take her long to see that all information she came across regarding tax evasion strongly suggested that the tax evader seek legal counsel. The most disheartening thing she uncovered was how all property obtained by illegal means such as gambling could be seized and used to settle the tax debt.

"The two Monet paintings," she said aloud in her office at the shop. "The El Greco and the Van Gogh." Marcel read over that particular section again several times and felt her heart sink deeper each time. "The Key West beach house," she mumbled, almost in shock. "The villa in Tuscany, the Vancouver condo." Looking up from the papers she held, Marcel thought, *the government could take all of it, and she could still owe them money.*

The next morning Marcel arrived at her mother's house to find it a mess and both women crying and bustling around with suitcases, shoes and clothes strewn about everywhere.

"You just missed Naomi," Cricket said. "How late did you work last night?"

"If those bastards have frozen my bank account, I don't know what I'll do!" Roslin wailed. "I only have enough money stashed around here to get us through a few months."

Marcel was grateful to be out of the spotlight, but she was sorry to have missed seeing Naomi.

"Marcel," Roslin said through her tears. "Did you hear that my Cricket wants to go with me?"

Marcel nodded. "I heard."

"She loves me, you know."

"Yeah, I know."

Roslin held her arms open. "We might not be able to come back," she said with a sniff.

Marcel gave her a hug. "Yeah, I know," she said again. She hated seeing her mother cry this way. Always at a loss as to how to comfort her when the tears were driven by fear and anxiety, she just held her for a moment.

"When can you two come and see us?" Roslin asked.

Marcel shrugged, uncertain if she and Naomi would ever do any traveling together again. That made her even sadder than seeing these two leave.

"The earliest will be June when Naomi gets out of school," Cricket said.

Roslin squeezed her tightly and continued to cry. "Those bastards," she whispered. "I can't have a crisis today. My schedule is full!"

"When does your flight leave?" Marcel asked.

"Before noon," Roslin said. "We'll be at the bank the moment it opens, and then we're leaving for the airport immediately afterward." She turned her attention back to packing.

"She didn't sleep last night," Cricket said, nodding gloomily. Marcel wondered how much sleep either of them had gotten. "I've never known anyone to hate an organization the way she hates the IRS. It's almost scary."

Marcel knew she didn't have to agree with her mother in order to admire her spunk and conviction. "It'll be up to you to help her forget about that."

Cricket looked exhausted. "If they freeze her bank account, I'm not sure what she'll do. That's kind of freaking me out right now. I'll feel a lot better once we're on our way to Paris."

Marcel called Carmen to let her know she wouldn't be at the shop until later. If there was a problem at the bank when it opened, Marcel wanted to be there to keep her mother from causing too big of a scene. There was a good chance the IRS had finally moved in on her after forty-five years of ignoring the problem. Marcel would do what she could to make it easier on all of them.

Roslin had Marcel doing all sorts of things before they were even close to being ready to leave for the bank. "You picked a really lousy time to move out," Roslin told her. "We need someone here to watch our stuff."

Marcel refrained from informing them both that their "stuff" wasn't her responsibility. She kept alternating between feeling angry at the IRS and angry at her mother for suddenly having to leave the country, but then she decided none of that negativity was helping anyone.

"All those cars parked in the garage need to be driven," Roslin said. "Maybe I should get rid of some of them."

Roslin's gambling relationship with a local car dealer had netted her several new cars over the years. At the moment there were four in the garage. She drove them a few times a week when she was in town.

"Yeah, mine needs to be driven, too," Cricket said. "I love that car."

Reality is setting in, Marcel thought. *For all of us.*

"Make it look like a lot of people are always here," Roslin said. "The car keys are on a hook by the back door."

"Or you could park some at the shop to make it look like you have customers," Cricket said with a smirk.

Ignoring her, Marcel said, "I'll take care of things here." She made up her mind to move back into the house later that evening. She needed a place to stay, and her mother's house needed someone living in it.

Sitting on one of her suitcases to try to get it closed, Roslin asked Marcel in French, "*Pouves-vouz m'aider?*"

"*Bien sûr. Avec plasir,*" Marcel answered.

"Oh, don't start that already!" Cricket grumbled. "In English, please."

"You better get used to it," Marcel said. "That's your future."

They had gone to Cricket's bank first and gotten her finances taken care of. Marcel drove and was surprised at the lack of conversation taking place in her car. All three of them seemed to be lost in thought. Occasionally Marcel noticed her mother dabbing at her eyes with a tissue.

As they headed down the street toward Roslin's bank, nervous tension filled the vehicle even though nothing was being said. Marcel pulled into the bank's parking lot and waited a moment before turning off the car.

"I'm going in with you," Cricket said, breaking the uneasy silence. She was in the backseat fidgeting.

"I think we should all go in," Marcel said. In the rearview mirror, her eyes met Cricket's. "If there's a problem, you stick with me and stay quiet. Let me handle it."

"There won't be a problem," Roslin said with enough confidence for all of them. "There can't be. It's my money and I'm here to fetch it."

Let's hope so, Marcel thought as they got out of the car. *The last thing I want to do right now is send these two on their way with any of my money.*

Roslin and Cricket practically danced a jig all the way to the car after Roslin closed her account. Once they all got in the car, her mother cackled outrageously and said, "Step on it, Marcel, before they change their minds!"

"Get our butts to the airport!" Cricket said with a gleeful giggle. "I am just so happy to be out of there."

Marcel had a mountain of mixed emotions inside. She didn't want her mother living in Paris for the rest of their lives, but she also didn't like the idea of her being wanted by the IRS either. She drove without comment. Her opinion didn't seem to matter to anyone anyway.

"When we get there just drop us off," Roslin said once they were closer to the airport. "Don't go in with us."

Marcel was disappointed to hear her say that. A quick hug at the curb would be hard enough, but she thought a clinging, crying scene at the ID check station would make things seem more real for her. A big dose of reality was what she needed more than anything else, but apparently that wasn't on her mother's agenda.

Marcel pulled up to the airline drop-off point and helped them unload their luggage. Cricket grabbed her first and hugged Marcel so tightly that they were both surprised by the emotion they felt. Her mother wouldn't look directly at Marcel, but it was obvious she was crying.

"I'll call you when we get there," Roslin said in a hoarse, tired voice.

Marcel nodded and got in her car and drove away.

The fact that they arrived in Paris without incident was like a tiny miracle and made Marcel wonder if Roslin and Cricket had left the country without really needing to. Roslin wasn't so much upset that things had gone smoothly, but surprised that she hadn't incurred more interest with her international travel under the circumstances.

"If that Skippy misled me about this IRS stuff," Roslin said on the phone several days later, "I'll find someone to kick his ass for me."

"Just be grateful things went as planned," Marcel said.

"I miss you," Roslin said in a voice filled with emotion. "You're moving the cars, right?"

Marcel answered with an impersonal nod. "Every evening after work." She didn't mention that she was living there at the house again. There was too much room for one person, and she missed the laughter and togetherness she remembered sharing with them, but revealing her current personal situation wasn't something Marcel was very good at, so she left many things unsaid to a lot of people.

In the beginning, phone calls from her mother had been almost unbearably emotional. The first three days they were gone, Roslin called and cried the entire time Marcel was on the phone with her. Now the calls consisted of questions about how she and Naomi were doing and reminders of chores at the house that needed to be done—water the plants, check the mail, put different cars in the driveway every day, monitor the phone messages. Marcel assured her that things were being taken care of, but she dodged all queries about Naomi. It was too painful to think about. Naomi hadn't called to see how Marcel was doing, and Marcel wasn't sure how to go about fixing things with her now that so much time had passed.

In addition to keeping the house up, Marcel worked hard at the Antique Villa every day and stayed busy enough there that it was possible to occasionally forget about the people in her life. Working long hours served her best. Marcel did miss Naomi terribly, and had periods of depression over the way things had ended up for them. One evening she thought a change might be on the way when she heard a knock on the front door of her mother's house. Marcel looked through the peephole hoping to see Naomi standing there, but instead she saw two men in dark suits.

"Who is it?" she asked. *This can't be good*, she thought. *Lozano's men after Mom again?*

Each man held up a badge with his identification. "IRS Criminal Investigation," one of them said in a deep, rumbling voice.

Feeling jittery and uncertain, Marcel slowly unlocked the door.

"Ms. Robicheaux?" the same man asked. They were both younger than any of the agents she had seen in Key West—late twenties, dark hair, about Marcel's height. Nondescriptive and clean-cut, both could have easily been thought of as belonging to some religious cult that depended on recruiting door-to-door for its followers.

"Yes," she said, opening the door wider.

"I'm Special Agent White, and this is Special Agent Mick." They came into the foyer, but Marcel didn't invite them in any further.

Agent White seemed to be the one in charge. He put his badge away and said, "We'd like to ask you some questions in reference to your tax liability."

Marcel arched a brow. "Oh, really?" She knew she didn't have a tax liability.

"Under the Fifth Amendment, of course, we can't compel you to answer any questions or give us any information if that will incriminate you."

Marcel took a deep breath to calm herself down. Closing her eyes, she gently rubbed her right temple that was beginning to throb.

"I'm also advising you that anything you say or any documents you submit can be used against you."

Agent Mick slipped his hands in his pockets and looked around the foyer as if he were a potential client interested in buying the place.

"You may also call an attorney before responding if you so choose," Agent White added.

My tax liability, Marcel thought wearily.

"Do you waive your rights to an attorney?" Agent White asked.

"No," Marcel said.

"Then let's go downtown."

Chapter Twenty-eight

Marcel placed a call to Carmen and let her know two IRS Criminal Investigation agents were taking her in for questioning. She also asked that Carmen get in touch with her cousin, Laverne Romero, who was a tax attorney. Laverne had also handled a few things for the Antique Villa in the past, so they occasionally had a working relationship with her.

"If she's not out on her motorcycle with my uncle," Carmen said.

Marcel gave Carmen the address where the agents were taking her, but didn't offer the two men any other information about her current situation. She wanted to know what they had on her or her mother and she was willing to put up with these two for a while longer if it meant she might eventually get some helpful information on her mother's tax status.

"You boys don't punch a time clock, do you?" Laverne asked

the two agents when she and Carmen walked into the conference room where they were keeping Marcel. "Laverne Romero," she said, sticking her hand out and forcing each agent to respond.

Marcel was glad to see them both. Laverne looked enough like Carmen to be her sister, with short black hair, square shoulders, medium height and a stocky build, but their fathers were actually cousins. Other than their appearance and brusque self-confidence, they were nothing alike. "I need a word with my client, please."

"Five minutes," Agent White said. He and Agent Mick got up from the table and left the room.

"Do you have something to write on?" Marcel quietly asked.

Laverne opened her briefcase and slid a pen and tablet across the table. Marcel wrote: *I'm pretty sure they think I'm my mother. They mentioned my tax liability earlier, but I've always paid my taxes on time. I don't have a tax liability that I'm aware of. I'd like to know what—if anything—they have on me and my mother. That's my reason for being here now.*

She slid the tablet across the table for Carmen and Laverne to read. Laverne nodded then wrote: *Carmen briefed me on your mother's tax situation on the way over. Let's see how much they know about her before we make it clear who you are.*

They were talking about business at the Antique Villa when the agents returned. This time the men had a stenographer with them, a young brunette who glanced at her watch before sitting down. Agent White placed a small voice-activated cassette recorder on the edge of the table. Marcel watched as Laverne put the tablet back into her briefcase then took out a small cassette recorder of her own and set it on the table.

"What is it you think my client has done, gentlemen?" Laverne asked.

"We have it on good authority that Ms. Robicheaux has spent several years evading taxes," Agent White said.

"Ms. Robicheaux?" Laverne asked Marcel. "Do you have a

206

response to that?"

Marcel looked at the two agents across from her and asked, "Would your 'good authority' happen to be Senator Harlow Wainwright?"

Surprised by her question, Agent White replied, "I'm not at liberty to say."

Laverne opened her briefcase and tore off a sheet of paper from the tablet. She slid the paper and a pen over to Marcel and said, "Write your name and social security number down, please." To the agents Laverne said, "In order to get something . . . you'll need to give something, gentlemen."

Agent White's cocky smile was as egotistical as it was irritating. "We aren't here to make any deals, Ms. Romero. Taxes need to be paid and your client needs to pay them."

"Not this client," Laverne said. She reached for the piece of paper Marcel had written her information on and handed the paper to Agent White. "Run this name through your computer and see what you find on her. A retired army colonel who served this country honorably and with distinction."

"Who is this?" Agent White asked, holding the paper between his fingers.

Laverne nodded toward Marcel. "My client."

"Roslin Robicheaux?" he asked.

"Marcel Robicheaux," Laverne said.

Agent White let the paper fall from his fingers and float to the table.

"That's the daughter," Agent Mick whispered to his partner.

"I *know* that's the daughter!" White snapped. To Marcel he said, "You misrepresented yourself."

"Not at all," Marcel said. "You came to my mother's house and asked for Ms. Robicheaux. That happens to be me."

There was a sudden burst of laughter at the end of the table. The stenographer put her hand over her mouth to stifle any further noise.

"Are we finished here?" Laverne asked the two men.

"Not yet," Agent White said. His face was so red Marcel thought he might actually have a heart attack. "Where's your mother?"

"In Europe," Marcel said.

"Where in Europe?"

"I don't know."

"You'll have to do better than that."

"When she calls me," Marcel said, "I don't ask where she is, and she doesn't discuss her plans with me. She's traveling around Europe. That's all I know."

"Are you charging my client with something?"

"Not right now," Agent White said, "but get your affairs in order, Ms. Robicheaux. If I find out you've helped your mother evade paying her taxes in any way, you'll be arrested and prosecuted. Is that clear?"

Laverne stood up and snapped her briefcase closed. "We're finished here."

On the way to Carmen's truck, Laverne had a good chuckle at Agent White's expense. "That was interesting," she said. "IRS intimidation is all part of the game. Those two weren't very good at it either. Not all agents are that inexperienced, Marcel. If they get a chance to show cause, they *will* prosecute."

"I don't know where my mother is now," Marcel insisted, climbing into the roomy backseat of Carmen's pickup. "She went to Paris initially, but she's on a private gambling circuit now. She could be calling me from a different country every day."

"Let's go to my office and plan some strategy," Laverne said. "These guys can play hardball when they want to."

"She gets to charge more if we meet in her office," Carmen said to Marcel with a playful grin.

All the way over to Laverne Romero's office Marcel kept

thinking of ways to get her mother out of this situation, but nothing was coming to her. She was tired of dealing with it, tired of moving cars every day and tired of being alone.

Laverne's office had two beautiful paintings on the wall—one of the River Walk and the other of the Alamo. There were pictures of her husband and three children on one entire shelf of a bookcase, as well as a picture of Laverne on a huge motorcycle, her smile radiant for the camera. Marcel could feel a dark mood coming over her that even a warm, cheerful office couldn't penetrate. She missed her mother and Naomi, and even had to admit that she missed Cricket, too. Life had been so simple a few weeks ago. She was finding it hard to remember when things hadn't been complicated.

"I'm glad you're here," Marcel said to Carmen. They sat down across from Laverne's huge executive desk. Laverne started out by telling Marcel that the IRS could try to find evidence against her as an accessory. Hearing that made her heart sink.

"They have several ways to get what they want," Laverne said.

"Is there any way to find out how much my mother owes in back taxes?" Marcel asked.

"Not from an IRS standpoint," Laverne said. "The fact is, all income is taxable—income earned through legal as well as illegal means. Does your mother have any idea how much money she's won over the last six years?"

"That's where I'm confused," Marcel said. "Her winnings aren't common knowledge. How does the IRS know what she owes and when she owes it?"

"Good question," Laverne said. "Compliance with the tax laws relies heavily on self-assessments of what tax is owed. In other words, it's up to the taxpayer to provide that information and give full disclosure. When people make deliberate decisions to not comply with the law, they have to face the consequences."

"That would be your mother," Carmen said to Marcel. "Send her to jail or take away her birthday. She doesn't care. The IRS isn't getting—"

"One red cent of her money," Marcel finished for her. "Yeah, I know."

"It's actually a good thing I helped you set up the paperwork for your business a few years ago," Laverne said to both of them. "As part of the eventual criminal investigation into Roslin's finances, the IRS makes effective use of the forfeiture statutes. That means they can deprive people of their illegally obtained cash and assets. It would be easy for them to try to close the Antique Villa and seize it for Roslin's tax debt if there had been any indication that she had provided some of the funds to get you started in the business."

Marcel sighed and then rested her head in her hands.

"However," Laverne added, "the paper trail for the shop's funding won't lead them anywhere in Roslin's direction, but that'll give you some idea about what they're looking for and how they operate. I can't stress strongly enough, Marcel, how serious this could get if they find out you've helped your mother evade paying her taxes. They will incarcerate you. As I said before, not all agents are as green and inexperienced as the two we dealt with earlier this evening. Those two learned a lot today."

Carmen reached over and gave Marcel a friendly pat on the back. "So what do we do now?" she asked her cousin.

"If they don't charge Marcel with anything soon," Laverne said, "then she's probably off their radar. That's the alligator closest to the boat right now. I'm sure you're not their focus anyway. There's also a good chance that Roslin's name has come up because of her acquaintance with Senator Wainwright and not as a result of any evidence they have on your mother. His gambling friends might all be investigated as a result of this."

"You know," Carmen said, "that really sucks. Guilt by association. I'm getting flashbacks of the old army."

Laverne jotted a note down on a pad. "You really don't know where your mother is?"

"No," Marcel said. "She started out in Paris, but didn't stay there long. She's played on several gambling circuits over the years, so she has connections and good friends throughout Europe. These are very rich people who enjoy poker. Some will travel a long way to gamble and meet each other again. My mother could be anywhere, and she's using cash to get where she needs to be. That's how she's always done it."

Laverne nodded. "They can't do anything to her if they can't find her."

Chapter Twenty-nine

Marcel's time spent with Carmen and Laverne hadn't done much in terms of making her feel any better, but it was nice to know she hadn't been charged with anything yet. It also looked like her mother had made the right decision by leaving the country. Pouring herself a glass of wine later that evening, Marcel tried to unwind enough to sleep. She missed Naomi and thought about calling her, but a glance at her watch changed her mind. It was after ten already.

Even those weeks before she retired from the army when her boss's wife had been grabbing Marcel's butt every chance she got, there at least had been hope for a way out of a difficult situation. Eventually, the general would either retire or be transferred and take his pretty young wife with him, which was exactly what Marcel wanted to happen. Every problem had a solution, but with her mother and the IRS standoff, things weren't anywhere near that easy to solve. The government had a way of always winning. Marcel had worked for them long enough to know that.

Taking her glass and dragging herself up the stairs, that dark cloud continued following her everywhere she went. She crawled on her bed on top of the covers and let the tears roll down her cheeks. She wasn't accustomed to feeling so lost and alone. *Where's my old friend Fireball when I need him? He always made things better.* She fell asleep and tossed and turned all night. Nothing came easily anymore.

She was at the shop the next day when her mother called. It had occurred to Marcel that all the phones could be tapped, but she decided she had nothing to hide from the IRS. More than likely, her mother had her hands full putting up with Cricket, so there was no need to add to that burden intentionally by bringing up what all had happened the night before.

"Are you winning?" Marcel asked. It was especially good hearing her mother's voice today.

"I am! If I were any better, I'd be twins! Cricket is bringing me luck. How's business? And how's that beautiful girlfriend of yours?"

"Business is great," Marcel said, feeling an acute sense of loss and pain with the girlfriend reference. She cleared her throat and spoke a little louder. "I have something to ask you. Remember the other day when you mentioned that Senator Wainwright had a friend in the IRS?"

"Yes. Maxwell Christy. Pretty good poker player," Roslin said with a laugh.

"How often did you play cards with him?"

"At least once a month for a few years. His wife didn't like him being gone so much, so we mostly played in the DC area— Maryland and Virginia. Pretty good poker player," she said again.

213

"How good was he?"

"A master at bluffing," Roslin said. "He talked constantly, and I mean constantly. It was almost like he couldn't go any length of time without hearing his own voice. He knew a lot of people . . . important people. He had interesting stories on presidents and the chief of this and the chief of that. He could be a real distraction sometimes, and he liked working that to his advantage."

Marcel mentally tucked that information away then asked, "Have you heard from Senator Wainwright?"

"Nah. He's probably at home working on some damage control. Has anything about him been on the news yet?"

"No," Marcel said.

"Then whatever he's doing at home is working. The bastard. Putting my baby in danger that way. Oh, don't get me started."

"Tell Cricket I miss her," Marcel said. She was no longer surprised at how much she meant that.

"We miss you, too," Roslin said quietly.

After she hung up with her mother, Marcel went online to try to find some information on Maxwell Christy. She eventually learned that he was still in charge of the IRS. She found a phone number for his office in Washington and spoke with three different people who insisted they could help her with whatever problem she had. Each person had the phone number of the San Antonio regional office to give her as their way of helping.

Okay, she thought. *This isn't working.* Using her cell phone, she located the number Senator Wainwright's aide had used to call her in Key West. Finally getting the aide on the phone, she told him it was urgent that she speak with the senator. Skippy called her back about twenty minutes later.

Marcel arrived in Washington DC, without luggage, so meeting Senator Wainwright's limousine at the airport was convenient for both of them. The limousine driver got out and opened the back door for her where she found Skippy inside signing a stack of papers on top of his briefcase. It was a show of importance for her benefit, and she let him think she was impressed with his attempt to appear busy and congressional.

"Marcel," he said, not bothering to look at her. "Our appointment with Maxwell Christy is in thirty minutes. May I ask what's so urgent that you have to see him?"

"It's a personal matter," she said. "You don't even have to stay for the meeting if you have other things to do. Just get me in there."

"This isn't a good time for me to be seen with him."

"I understand that," Marcel said sincerely.

If he was under investigation for any type of income tax matters, Maxwell Christy's office wasn't a place Skippy should be going in and out of.

He looked at her over the rim of his reading glasses then went back to signing papers. *He wants me to know this is a big favor he's doing for me,* she mused. *That's fine with me. Once we get there, he'll probably just dump me off at the curb and be on his way.*

Marcel knew Senator Wainwright to be a natural politician, which to her wasn't much of a compliment. He enjoyed the attention his political office gave him, and he used it to his advantage whenever possible. Luckily, this time Marcel needed his influence and statesmanship to open a few doors for her. Since he had spent a lifetime using people to get what he wanted, she didn't mind using him for this one favor. After all, she hadn't forgotten that little episode in Key West where she and Naomi had been nearly scared speechless after coming face to face with Lozano in the back of a limousine. Their relationship still hadn't recovered from that. In Marcel's eyes, Skippy owed her this much. He must've thought so too since there had been just a brief complaint about the inconvenience of getting her in to see his old friend.

They took an elevator all the way to the top floor in silence. When they stepped off the elevator, several people in the hallway spoke to the senator and addressed him by name. *He's certainly not a stranger here*, Marcel thought as they walked by a few large potted plants that had been used effectively to brighten the place up and camouflage entrances to cubicle areas. It looked like every other federal building Marcel had ever been in.

"Right this way, Senator," an impeccably dressed older woman said as she left her desk and lightly knocked on the door behind her. "Mr. Christy," she announced. "Senator Wainwright and Ms. Robicheaux are here to see you."

Maxwell Christy was a tall man in his early sixties. He had thick gray hair and a boyish grin that Marcel was certain had helped get him where he was today. He came around the side of his desk offering a handshake.

"Skippy! Good to see you again." He looked at Marcel with a big smile. "Colonel Robicheaux. This is indeed a pleasure. Your mother has told me many wonderful things about you over the years. I appreciate your service to our country."

Marcel shook his hand and suddenly felt better about being there. His rich Southern accent was a rarity for someone who had spent so much time in the Washington area, but for Marcel, it added warmth and sincerity to his words and actions.

Skippy held up his pager, and in a rude gesture of self-importance said, "Excuse me for a minute. I need to call my office." He went back out the door and closed it behind him.

"Please have a seat, Colonel," Mr. Christy said. "What can I do for you? I have to admit that your mother has always been one of my favorite people."

Marcel wasn't sure how much time he had for her, so she got right to the point. "I'm here to see if you can help me clarify a few things."

"Just a delightful woman," he said—more to himself than to

her. "Such an excellent poker player, too. How is she? It's been a while since I've seen her."

"She's fine," Marcel said. "It's the poker aspect that I'd like to discuss with you. There's been some interest recently in her finances and a perceived tax debt centered around gambling."

"Really? Poker, bingo, lotto, a trip to the race track," he said. An easy smile played at the corners of his mouth. "All forms of entertainment for some, and a way of life for others. Who is interested in her finances? Have agents been to see Roslin?"

"They have, but she's out of town and unavailable right now."

He nodded. "Special agents begin their investigations assuming that the taxpayer has committed a tax crime. They view their job as a mere matter of developing the evidence." He leaned back in his chair. "I can assure you, Colonel Robicheaux, that your mother's gambling activities are in no way associated with the likes of an illegal gambling operation, which is where the focus should be. Internet gambling issues are another high priority these days. Poker is pure entertainment for Roslin, just as it is for many of us. There's no harm in that. Her situation is especially unique in the fact that she has you." He reached for a pen on his desk and scribbled something down. "Is your mother still in San Antonio?" he asked. "I remember how excited she was when you retired. I'll give that field office a call this afternoon and ask a few questions."

Marcel remembered her mother saying how much Maxwell Christy liked to hear himself talk. She let him do as much of that as he wanted without interruption.

"I've always admired how you've supported your mother all these years," he continued. "A second lieutenant fresh out of West Point doesn't make much money. That couldn't have been easy for either of you."

Marcel sat there attempting to contain her shock at such a statement. *Where would he get the idea that I've ever supported my mother? Had that been the case, we would've been in the poor house a long time ago!*

Christy set his pen down. "Roslin still dabbles in the game?"

Shifting uneasily in her chair, Marcel said, "She does."

He reached for a business card in a gold holder on his desk and handed it to her. "Have her get in touch with me the next time she's in town. I'll set up a game for us."

Marcel stood and walked with him to the door. The entire meeting had lasted no more than three minutes, but for Marcel those few minutes had been worth the expense of traveling there.

"I'd really appreciate it if you'd make that call," she said, indicating the note on his desk. "My mother's been upset about all of this."

"I'll take care of it right away," he said, flashing that boyish grin. "Let me walk you out."

Once they were in the main office area, Maxwell Christy asked his secretary where Senator Wainwright had gone. There were a few other people waiting to see this man already.

"He mentioned being needed back at his office," the woman said.

What a weenie, Marcel thought. *He really did leave me here!*

"Have my driver take Colonel Robicheaux anywhere she needs to go," Christy said graciously. He shook Marcel's hand again and said, "It's a pleasure to finally meet you. Please send my regards to your mother."

Carmen picked up Marcel at the airport later that afternoon and drove to the Antique Villa. Reba was there working and was happy to see them when they arrived.

"You *know* how nervous I get when we have a lot of customers," Reba said.

"That's funny," Carmen replied, teasing her. "We get nervous when there *aren't* a lot of customers."

Gathering up her things to leave, Reba said to Marcel, "Your mother called. We had a nice little chat. She said she would call back later."

Carmen walked her lover out to her car and came back in with a troubled expression. "How long have you been living at your mother's house?"

"About two weeks now."

"When was the last time you spoke with Naomi?"

Marcel turned away without offering a reply.

"Why didn't you tell me there was a problem?"

"It's not something I want to talk about, okay?"

"I'm not one to tell anybody what to do, Marcel, but—"

"And I appreciate that," Marcel said.

"*But*," Carmen said a bit louder, "you need to take care of things."

"I'm afraid a little vacation pissiness has snowballed out of control already."

"Have you called her?"

Marcel didn't answer.

"Not even a stinkin' phone call? What's the matter with you?"

"I've got a few things on my mind."

"What can be more important than the woman you love?"

They looked at each other as the words hung in the air between them. Finally, Marcel turned away and said, "Nothing. You're right. I guess I thought . . . maybe . . . she would've missed me a little by now."

"I'm sure she does."

"Yeah, well, I'm not so sure about that."

"She does," Carmen said.

"How do you know? What have you heard?"

"Be the bigger person. Call her first."

"What makes you think she even wants to hear from me? She thinks I set us up for dinner with a gangster."

"Stop being so hardheaded for once," Carmen said. "She was

mad and afraid. Anything a person says under those circumstances shouldn't be held against them forever."

"She wasn't the only one who was afraid. Besides, the phone lines go both ways. She knows how to find me."

Surprised at the sudden emotion the conversation inspired, Marcel's eyes welled up with tears. *Great*, she thought. *I can't do this at work.*

"Hardheaded," Carmen mumbled on the way to her workshop.

Marcel was the first to admit that being without Naomi these past two weeks had been extremely hard. It was getting more difficult to tuck the loneliness away each night. She wasn't sleeping well, and every time the phone rang, she wanted the caller to be Naomi. Wandering around in that big house in the evenings made her miss the way things used to be for all of them. Marcel didn't function well without order in her life.

To get her mind off Naomi and how screwed up things in general seemed to be, she called Laverne Romero to see if there was a way to find out information on Roslin's tax status. If Maxwell Christy had made that phone call as promised, then she hoped that at least one thing had been resolved. Laverne called her back about ten minutes later with the information.

"Agent White has been instructed to drop any investigation on you and your mother," Laverne said. "He didn't sound happy about it either."

Marcel felt a fresh sting of tears in her eyes. No one was going to jail. "Agent White's happiness isn't a concern of mine."

"I have a suggestion, Marcel. Since gambling is considered a small business, why not set your mother up that way? For under a hundred bucks, she could be a business owner, and you could make everything she does in the future legal."

Marcel inclined her head with a heavy sigh. "Oh, if only it were that simple. It's the 'paying taxes' part that she's adamantly against."

"Hire an accountant to handle your mother's finances and pay the taxes for her."

Marcel threw her head back and roared with laughter. "She would never go for that!"

"Then don't tell her about it."

Once Marcel got past the deviousness of the idea, she warmed up to it a little more.

"Will she get homesick enough to want to come back from Europe?" Laverne asked.

"That's probably happened already," Marcel said.

"You've set up one business," Laverne said. "You know what's involved and how easy it is. Lay the groundwork for her. She'll have to sign some papers to get it up and running, but that will certainly beat the alternative."

"She wouldn't go for it."

"Jail isn't a nice place, Marcel. Whoever Roslin's friends are in the IRS . . . well . . . they won't be there forever. Now's the time to get her on the right track whether she agrees with it or not. Does she think anyone *likes* paying taxes? It actually hurts me each time I have to write that check."

"I've tried everything," Marcel said. "From insinuating she's a bad American to giving her a menu of what jail food consists of."

"Just consider doing it all for her once you get the business set up. As far as I know, there aren't any poker games in jail. Remind her of that a few times."

"There's not a doubt in my mind that poker would find its way to jail if my mother were to ever be locked up."

During the drive home that evening, Marcel mulled over Laverne's suggestion of setting up a business for her mother. *Maybe it's time for me to be a bitch about this. It doesn't just involve her any longer. This IRS tax issue has screwed up a lot of things.*

221

The next day, before reason kicked in and she changed her mind, Marcel went to the local post office and rented a box. From there she did some research and made a few phone calls to city hall to get the specifics on how to register a small business. There were papers Roslin would need to sign, so that was initially discouraging, but Marcel decided that this was something she would have to convince her mother to do. In addition, Marcel called her accountant and told her what she needed done, and within a matter of hours, Roslin's new business was close to being completely set up. Now all Marcel had to do was talk her mother into coming home and letting someone else keep track of her finances.

Later when she told Carmen what she planned on doing, Carmen asked what the name of the business would be.

"Not One Red Cent," Marcel said. "I've given it some thought, and that's what keeps popping up."

"Well, she can't find fault with the name," Carmen said. "I've heard her say it often enough. She might eventually go along with this idea if she's truly ready to come home. Get her back here and plan a few field trips to the county jail. That might help readjust her attitude."

"I'm counting on Cricket's help with this, too," Marcel said. "Getting Mom home will be the easy part. Convincing her to do the right thing and sign a few papers to get this new business off the ground once she's here will be the hard part."

"Don't hold your breath, my friend."

Marcel felt a strange numbed comfort in all of this. The next time her mother called, Marcel told her she needed to speak with Cricket. *There's a good chance Cricket is the key to getting them back here and starting this business. If at least one of them is ready to come home, that's a major step in the right direction.*

Chapter Thirty

Cricket called later that evening. Marcel had worked late and had just gotten home.

"Are you starting up my car every day?" was the first thing she said.

Marcel sat down on the sofa and slipped off her shoes. "I'm taking care of the cars, okay? Are either of you ready to come home yet?"

"Whoever thought I'd get tired of living in a hotel and traveling all the time?"

"Is that a yes or a no? Are you ready to come home?"

It was so quiet on the other end of the phone that Marcel wondered if they had been disconnected.

"Cricket?"

"I . . . uh . . . I miss my students," she said. "I don't necessarily miss getting up early every day, but I wonder how they're doing without me. It's weird what I miss—my friends . . . work . . . home . . . Mexican food . . . even you."

Marcel smiled. "What if I told you the IRS problem was solved? Would you both be ready to come back anytime soon?"

"Are you serious, Marcel? Don't bullshit me."

"I'm serious. I even had a tax attorney verify it today."

"Ohmigod!" Cricket squealed. "That's wonderful! What happened?"

"That's not important. I have some questions for you, though."

"Oh, Marcel, this is great news! Just knowing I can go home where everyone speaks English is such a relief! I never know what's going on anymore. It's been very frustrating over here. I'm picking up a few words, but everyone talks too fast for me. I feel like I just fell off a cabbage truck or something."

Marcel waited for her to finish. As an afterthought, Cricket asked her about the questions she had.

"Does my mother ever tell you how much money she's won?"

"I know *when* she wins," Cricket said, "but not how much. She never discusses that kind of thing with me."

Marcel sighed. "If you both come back, we'll need to know that information each time she's in a poker game."

"Why?"

This isn't going to work, Marcel thought. *We can't run my mother's business if the only sign of income is whether it's a steak or Hamburger Helper night at the house.*

"Why, Marcel?" Cricket asked with a suspicious edge to her voice. "Why do we need to know anything about her winnings?"

"We just will."

"I don't like the sound of that one bit. What's going on?"

"That's the catch, Cricket. If you want to come home, you'll need to find a way to know what her income is after each game."

"Did you strike a deal with those bastards?"

Marcel noticed how Cricket had picked up Roslin's favorite

word to describe the IRS. "I haven't made a deal with anyone," she said, "but I'm tired of this. Things have to change. I found a way to get you back here, now it's up to you to make sure you can stay once you're home."

"Oh, hell. You're no help! I can't believe you got my hopes up for nothing!"

"I'm sorry, but that's the way it'll have to be."

With a heavy sigh, Cricket said, "Let me see what I can do. Damn you, Marcel. I was getting all excited and everything."

"I can't do it all, Cricket. You need to do your part, too. Not only that, but Mom will have to sign some papers in order to set up a business. Once that happens, someone else can take care of the details for her."

"Are you kidding me?" Cricket snapped.

"Do I sound like I'm kidding you? There have to be some changes, Cricket. Are you happy with the way things are?"

There was silence on the other end of the phone before Marcel heard her whisper, "No."

A few hours later when Marcel was getting ready for bed, her mother called. It was good to hear her voice.

"Is something going on there I should know about?" Roslin asked. "Cricket hasn't been the same since she talked to you earlier."

"I called in a favor from Skippy," Marcel said. "He got me in to see Maxwell Christy."

She heard her mother gasp. "You saw Maxie?"

"Senator Wainwright made a phone call for me, and I flew to Washington to get a few things straightened out."

"You saw Maxie," Roslin mumbled.

To get her mother's mind off the fact that she had paid a visit to the head of the IRS, Marcel said, "He spoke very highly of you. He even mentioned you giving him a call the next time you're in the DC area."

"What did you say to this man?" Roslin asked in a stiff, staccato tone of voice. Suddenly Marcel didn't feel like a retired army colonel or a successful forty-eight-year-old business owner. She was a child again, being asked a stern question by her mother. "Did you go there to talk about *me*?"

Not knowing exactly what to say next, Marcel let several seconds pass before even attempting to speak. "Uh . . . two agents came to the house and took me in for questioning a few nights ago."

This time Roslin's gasp was loud enough to make Marcel jump.

"Did those bastards hurt you?"

For some reason, that made Marcel laugh. "No, they didn't hurt me, but they managed to scare the crap out of me. Look, Mom, I didn't mean to step on any toes with my call to Senator Wainwright or my visit with Maxwell Christy, but at the time both things seemed necessary and right. The bottom line is—Mr. Christy doesn't believe you're any good at what you do, and there's no way you could make enough money at gambling to warrant an IRS investigation."

"What!"

"That's basically what he told me."

"That arrogant, egotistical bastard."

She didn't dare tell her mother that Christy also thought Marcel had been supporting her all these years. At this point, there was no telling what kind of response that would've provoked out of her.

"He may be all of those things," Marcel said, "but he also placed some phone calls and made it possible for you and Cricket to come back if you want to. It's official. There won't be an investigation."

After a moment, she heard her mother sniff.

"I do miss you," Roslin said with softness in her voice.

As a new and unexpected warmth surged through her, Marcel said quietly, "Then please come home. You don't have to be there any longer."

The next morning was Saturday. Marcel arrived early at work to find Carmen there already. The rich aroma of fresh coffee met her as soon as she opened the door. "Well?" Carmen said.

"Well what?"

Marcel hadn't had a chance to let Carmen know about the latest developments with Cricket and Roslin. They had both been too busy with other things to talk much lately.

"Did you call Naomi yet?"

"Oh," Marcel said, taking the cup of coffee she handed to her. "That."

"Yeah. Oh, that. There was a lesbian and gay teachers' support group meeting at our house last night."

"Was Naomi there?" Marcel asked. A slew of questions flashed in her head. *How did she look? Did she ask about me? Was she happy? Sad?*

"We had a few new people there," Carmen said. "Two female teachers—science and P.E.—both very nice and friendly women."

Marcel blew on her steaming coffee. "Glad to see there's more interest in the group."

"Call her," Carmen said. "This is going beyond hardheadedness with you. I don't get it. You're branching out into flaming butt-hole territory now."

"Well, gee thanks."

Carmen picked up her coffee cup. "Other people are taking notice."

"Taking notice about what?"

"Call her." With coffee cup in hand, Carmen went to her workshop, leaving Marcel feeling empty, alone and uncertain.

It was a busy morning, which was exactly what Marcel had

227

needed to take her mind off things. The shop had a steady stream of customers with several sales that resulted in them having to bring other pieces of furniture up front into the showroom area to fill in space. Just before lunch, Cricket called.

"She's made about seven hundred thousand dollars since we got here," Cricket said. "Can you believe that? Who the hell plays with that kind of money?"

"How do you know that's an accurate amount?"

"I remembered how she answers questions after . . . after . . . after we make love. I can ask her all sorts of things then."

Being reminded that her mother frequently had sex with Cricket wasn't something Marcel wanted to hear about, but if that was a reliable way to get information from her, then Marcel would just have to get over it.

"We've been talking about coming home," Cricket said, "but she wants to spend some time at the villa in Tuscany first. She's been talking about getting the villa ready for you and Naomi to visit us."

Marcel felt a twinge in her stomach at the mention of Naomi's name. "I'm not sure that can happen."

"Well, *make* it happen," Cricket said. "Your mother's counting on it."

"I've got a business to run and . . . and—"

"There's plenty of time to plan for it," Cricket said. "That's all she talks about now—the four of us in Tuscany."

Marcel tried to swallow the lump in her throat, but it seemed to be growing larger by the second. "Uh . . . it looks like Naomi and I have broken up."

There was silence on the other end of the phone. Finally, Cricket said quietly, "What did you say?"

Marcel held the receiver for a long time without anything else being said. After a moment Cricket asked softly, "When did this happen?"

Marcel cleared her throat. "When we got back from Key

West."

"I . . . I don't know what to say. Hearing this makes my heart hurt, Marcel."

"I can't talk about it," Marcel said as her voice broke. She cleared her throat again. "I need to go."

"Wait," Cricket said. "Please."

"I can't."

"We're coming home. I'll get us on the first flight out of here."

"Cricket—"

She hung up. Marcel stood there stunned, attempting to blink back more tears.

"Call her," Carmen's voice boomed from the doorway.

Startled at the sudden gruff sound behind her, Marcel juggled the phone that miraculously landed in her outstretched hand.

"You scared the crap out of me!"

As she set the phone down on the counter, Marcel heard Carmen say again, "Call her."

Chapter Thirty-one

Marcel waited until the latest batch of customers was gone then glanced at her watch. She couldn't decide if she should wait until she got home to call Naomi or do it right then. Still hearing Carmen's words in her head, she picked up the phone, slowly rubbing her thumb over the key pad. Naomi's number was on speed dial. *Call her at home or on her cell? You're stalling, Robicheaux. Just get on with it!* She pushed a button, and after the second ring Naomi answered.

There was a slight pause before she said, "Marcel?"

Not knowing for certain if her voice would even work right then, Marcel gripped the phone tightly and was surprised at the tears that formed in the corners of her eyes. *Don't cry now*, she told herself. *Please.*

"Hello?" Naomi said.

Feeling drained, hollow and weary, Marcel leaned her elbows

on the counter. "Uh . . . hi. It's me. Marcel."

There was another pause before Naomi said, "The shop's name came up on my caller ID. How are you?"

Marcel shrugged and located a box of tissues under the counter. "I'm okay. Actually, I've been better, I guess."

More silence. Marcel wanted to get this over with before it became obvious that she was so upset—especially since from the tone of Naomi's voice, she didn't seem to be bothered by any of this at all. Finally, Marcel said, "Uh . . . I was . . . wondering if you were . . . free for dinner this evening."

"I have plans tonight."

Marcel reached for another tissue. She hadn't seen that coming. "Oh, okay. Uh . . . then how about breakfast in the morning?"

"Sure. The usual place? About nine?"

"That'll be fine," Marcel said as normally as she could muster. "See you then."

The line went dead in her ear. She switched the phone off and set it down.

She's got plans tonight. What kind of plans could she have? Carmen mentioned new lesbians showing up at the support group meeting last night. Great. She's got plans already. She put her head in her hands and closed her eyes. Allowing her subconscious thoughts to surface, she felt a momentary sense of panic as her mind jumped around from one scenario to the next. *She hasn't called,* Marcel reminded herself, *and she didn't sound very glad to hear from me. Maybe she's moved on to someone else already. Why did I wait so long to call? But it's only been two weeks! She's supposed to love me!*

"You look like something the cat dragged in," Carmen said.

Standing up straighter, Marcel tossed the wadded tissues into the trashcan behind the counter. "I called and she has plans tonight. There. Are you happy now?"

"Well, whoop-de-do. Did you expect her to just hang around

231

waiting for you to get off your arse and call?"

"Well . . . yeah. I guess I did."

Carmen laughed.

"Why is it *I'm* the one who had to call? Why hasn't she called me?"

"How long have you been in the relationship business? This can't be your first rodeo, cowgirl. If you wanna keep her, you better start acting like you care."

"I do care. Maybe I care too much."

"There's no such thing as caring too much."

"My girlfriend has plans tonight. She said it just like that, too. 'I have plans tonight.'"

"So? That could mean anything—washing her car, painting her kitchen."

"Or going out with new friends."

Carmen nodded. "Or going out with new friends."

"I'll make myself nuts worrying about this the rest of the day," Marcel grumbled. "At least she promised to meet me for breakfast in the morning."

"She's actually having dinner at our house tonight," Carmen said. "Some project she's working on with Reba and Juanito for the support group."

Marcel kept her features deceptively composed, but inside she was both relieved and furious at the same time. She refused to give Carmen the satisfaction of seeing any of that, though.

"You can join us for dinner if you like," Carmen said. "We'll have plenty of food. It'll be fun."

Marcel picked up a stack of receipts for the day and shuffled through them. "You could've told me about her plans earlier."

"I know. Dinner at our house?"

"I'll just wait and meet her for breakfast."

Carmen turned to go back to the workshop area, but before she left, Marcel heard her mumble, "Damn hardheaded woman."

Marcel got home late and was tired from a long day. The house seemed to be even bigger and emptier recently without Cricket or her mother there. The prospect of living alone still wasn't that appealing to her. Marcel didn't like admitting how lonely she was.

She had given the Rice brothers a call earlier in the day to ask if they had any furniture for her. The Antique Villa was low on inventory again. Jeff Rice called her back with news about having several nice pieces they were sure she would like. Marcel made arrangements with him to pick it up then jotted down a note to remind herself to see if Juanito would ride up to Fort Worth with her one day during the week.

She heard a knock on the door and glanced at the clock on the mantel. It was nine thirty already. As she got up from the sofa and slipped her shoes back on, Marcel wondered if Agent White had found something else to harass her about. Looking through the peephole, she saw Naomi standing on the porch. Marcel fumbled with the locks and threw the door open.

"Hi," she said, her voice sounding a little higher and more excited than she had expected. "Come in."

"Carmen said she had invited you over for dinner this evening."

"Uh . . . that's true." *After about ten minutes of stringing me along*, she thought. Marcel closed and locked the door again. "I haven't been home but a few minutes."

Naomi looked great, and Marcel could feel an unusual giddiness sweeping through her from just having her there. *It seems like forever since I've seen her.*

"I know we're meeting for breakfast in the morning," Naomi said, "but I'd like to talk for a few minutes now if you have time. I was glad to see your light on when I drove by."

"Can I get you something to drink?"

They were still standing in the foyer. Neither had progressed too much farther than just inside the door. Then in one forward motion, Naomi was in her arms kissing her with a deep-seated hunger that took Marcel's breath away. She returned the kiss with reckless abandon and felt the hot rush of desire race through her body. Shocked at her own eager response to the wildness of the kiss, Marcel drank in the sweetness of such soul-searching passion. Finally raising her mouth from Marcel's, Naomi gazed into her eyes.

"You waited over two weeks to call me?" she whispered, her breath warm against Marcel's ear.

"I was afraid to call."

Naomi buried her face against Marcel's throat. "So was I."

Marcel leaned back against the door and closed her eyes. "What the hell happened? We've never done anything like this before."

Kissing the side of Marcel's face, Naomi briefly found her lips again, reclaiming them with a slow firmness that demanded a response. Marcel slipped her hand under Naomi's silk blouse where just touching her skin made Marcel's heart do a little somersault.

Naomi pressed her body against Marcel's and uttered a low, throaty moan. Taut beneath the thin fabric of her bra, her nipples begged to be touched. Weak with desire, Marcel could feel the air around them electrified with heat and passion.

"Take me upstairs," Naomi said in a broken whisper. "We'll talk tomorrow."

They continued kissing in the bedroom as they scrambled out of their clothes, Marcel felt such peace and satisfaction at having Naomi in her arms again. She didn't know whether it had been the stress of vacationing with Cricket and Roslin or the two incidents with Salvador Lozano that had sparked so much discontent

234

between them, but Marcel did know this much—Naomi was the missing piece in her life, and she would never again take that for granted.

Gently pushing Naomi back on the bed and gazing down at her soft, beautiful body, Marcel silently promised herself and her lover that nothing would ever come between them again. The brief separation had forced her to see their life together with complete clarity. Her newly awakened sense of life, love and passion brought her a tremendous amount of comfort. Life was too unpredictable even on a good day, and treating each moment as the gift it actually was suddenly became her focus.

Naomi reached up and touched Marcel's hair. The love in her eyes made Marcel's body almost vibrate with longing. A vaguely sensuous light passed between them, and with a pulse-pounding certainty, Marcel knew they were both feeling the same way. She kissed Naomi with slow, dazzling determination and wrapped her arms around her. Working her way down Naomi's body, Marcel took charge with quiet assurance. She could feel a thumping heartbeat against her ear just before Naomi wove her fingers through Marcel's hair and encouraged her to explore. Caressing her with lips, tongue and nose, Marcel heard another low groan escape from her lover's lips and used it as an invitation while passion continued inching through her veins.

Naomi's utterances of "ohhh" were all the encouragement Marcel needed. Naomi's nipples were like smooth pebbles against her palm. Moving slowly downward, she continued her search and easily found a very wet, throbbing reception. Marcel took her time teasing her with a darting tongue and a playful chin. Naomi increased her grip on Marcel's hair and quickly used that to her advantage, eventually exploding in a downpour of fiery sensations.

After a while, Marcel nuzzled the inside of Naomi's thigh with her wet nose and kissed the soft flesh. They both eventually succumbed to the numbed sleep of a satisfied lover.

Marcel woke up the next morning and slid her foot across the bed looking for Naomi's bare leg under the covers. *Whew*, she thought while moving closer to her. *Last night wasn't a dream.* She took Naomi into her arms and breathed in the sweet, early-morning scent of her. Marcel's lips found their way instinctively to hers, and their first kiss of the day was slow and searching.

The deeply delicious sensation of Naomi's sleepy touch made Marcel's body wiggle to meet her. She moved her lips over Naomi's, devouring their softness. The involuntary tremors of arousal had already begun before either of them was fully awake. Naomi left warm kisses around Marcel's mouth and along her jaw, eventually leaving a tantalizing kiss at the hollow of her neck. Marcel's body radiated with pleasure, the very center of her soul racing with heat and longing.

As she turned Naomi over onto her back, Marcel's lips grazed her earlobe. She heard another moan that encouraged her own passion, but it was Naomi's shivering response that Marcel had been waiting for. Their bodies were in exquisite harmony, and together they entered into a feeling of love and desire. For Marcel, nothing had ever felt so right.

Later that morning, Marcel got the coffee going. She had taken a shower while Naomi slept after an amazing bout of love-making. For Marcel it was good to know that Naomi had missed her just as much during their brief separation and mutual streak of stubbornness.

A few minutes later strong arms engulfed her and ample soft breasts settled easily against her back. Smelling of lavender soap from her shower, Naomi tugged on Marcel's T-shirt and kissed her bare shoulder.

"Do we have to go out?" Naomi whispered.

The throatiness of her voice sent chills down Marcel's spine.

"Uh . . . no," Marcel said. "We can stay in. I can make French toast or something." She closed her eyes while Naomi turned her around and kissed the corners of her mouth. "I'm French, you know," she added breathlessly. "French toast is easy for us."

"French toast will be fine."

"Or," Marcel said as a determined hand eased up under her T-shirt and cupped her breast. "We have . . . a lot . . . of . . . Hamburger Helper . . . if . . . "

Naomi's mouth covered Marcel's and drew her into a kiss that sent a jolt surging through her body. *Two weeks without her,* Marcel thought as the T-shirt was pulled over her head. She wrapped herself around Naomi's soft, naked body where they were able to take the time to explore and arouse each other. *Two weeks without her,* Marcel thought again. *What was I thinking?*

Breakfast was the last thing on anyone's mind.

Publications from
BELLA BOOKS, INC.
The best in contemporary lesbian fiction

P.O. Box 10543, Tallahassee, FL 32302
Phone: 800-729-4992
www.bellabooks.com

THE EDUCATION OF ELLIE by Jackie Calhoun. When Ellie sees her childhood friend for the first time in thirty years she is tempted to resume their long lost friendship. But with the years come a lot of baggage and the two women struggle with who they are now while fighting the painful memories of their first parting. Will they be able to move past their history to start again?   978-1-59493-092-8 $13.95

DATE NIGHT CLUB by Saxon Bennett. *Date Night Club* is a dark romantic comedy about the pitfalls of dating in your thirties . . .   978-1-59493-094-2 $13.95

PLEASE FORGIVE ME by Megan Carter. Laurel Becker is on the verge of losing the two most important things in her life—her current lover, Elaine Alexander, and the Lavender Page bookstore. Will Elaine and Laurel manage to work through their misunderstandings and rebuild their life together?   978-1-59493-091-1 $13.95

WHISKEY AND OAK LEAVES by Jaime Clevenger. Meg meets June, a single woman running a horse ranch in the California Sierra foothills. The two become quick friends and it isn't long before Meg is looking for more than just a friendship. But June has no interest in developing a deeper relationship with Meg. She is, after all, not the least bit interested in women . . . or is she? Neither of these two women is prepared for what lies ahead . . .   978-1-59493-093-5 $13.95

SUMTER POINT by KG MacGregor. As Audie surrenders her heart to Beth, she begins to distance herself from the reckless habits of her youth. Just as they're ready to meet in the middle, their future is thrown into doubt by a duty Beth can't ignore. It all comes to a head on the river at Sumter Point.   978-1-59493-089-8 $13.95

THE TARGET by Gerri Hill. Sara Michaels is the daughter of a prominent senator who has been receiving death threats against his family. In an effort to protect Sara, the FBI recruits homicide detective Jaime Hutchinson to secretly provide the protection they are so certain Sara will need. Will Sara finally figure out who is behind the death threats? And will Jaime realize the truth—and be able to save Sara before it's too late?   978-1-59493-082-9 $13.95

REALITY BYTES by Jane Frances. In this sequel to Reunion, follow the lives of four friends in a romantic tale that spans the globe and proves that you can cross the whole of cyberspace only to find love a few suburbs away . . .   978-1-59493-079-9 $13.95

MURDER CAME SECOND by Jessica Thomas. Broadway's bad-boy genius, Paul Carlucci, has chosen Hamlet for his latest production. To the delight of some and despair of others, he has selected Provincetown's amphitheatre for his opening gala. But suddenly Alex Peres realizes that the wrong people are falling down. And the moaning is all to realistic. Someone must not be shooting blanks . . .

978-1-59493-081-2 $13.95

SKIN DEEP by Kenna White. Jordan Griffin has been given a new assignment: Track down and interview one-time nationally renowned broadcast journalist Reece McAllister. Much to her surprise, Jordan comes away with far more than just a story . . .

978-1-59493-78-2 $13.95

FINDERS KEEPERS by Karin Kallmaker. *Finders Keepers*, the quest for the perfect mate in the 21st Century, joins Karin Kallmaker's *Just Like That* and her other incomparable novels about lesbian love, lust and laughter.   1-59493-072-4 $13.95

OUT OF THE FIRE by Beth Moore. Author Ann Covington feels at the top of the world when told her book is being made into a movie. Then in walks Casey Duncan the actress who is playing the lead in her movie. Will Casey turn Ann's world upside down? 1-59493-088-0 $13.95

STAKE THROUGH THE HEART: NEW EXPLOITS OF TWILIGHT LESBIANS by Karin Kallmaker, Julia Watts, Barbara Johnson and Therese Szymanski. The playful quartet that penned the acclaimed *Once Upon A Dyke* are dimming the lights for journeys into worlds of breathless seduction.   1-59493-071-6 $15.95

THE HOUSE ON SANDSTONE by KG MacGregor. Carly Griffin returns home to Leland and finds that her old high school friend Justine is awakening more than just old memories.   1-59493-076-7 $13.95

WILD NIGHTS: MOSTLY TRUE STORIES OF WOMEN LOVING WOMEN edited by Therese Szymanski. 264 pp. 23 new stories from today's hottest erotic writers are sure to give you your wildest night ever!   1-59493-069-4 $15.95

COYOTE SKY by Gerri Hill. 248 pp. Sheriff Lee Foxx is trying to cope with the realization that she has fallen in love for the first time. And fallen for author Kate Winters, who is technically unavailable. Will Lee fight to keep Kate in Coyote?

1-59493-065-1 $13.95

VOICES OF THE HEART by Frankie J. Jones. 264 pp. A series of events force Erin to swear off love as she tries to break away from the woman of her dreams. Will Erin ever find the key to her future happiness?   1-59493-068-6 $13.95

SHELTER FROM THE STORM by Peggy J. Herring. 296 pp. A story about family and getting reacquainted with one's past that shows that sometimes you don't appreciate what you have until you almost lose it.   1-59493-064-3 $13.95

WRITING MY LOVE by Claire McNab. 192 pp. Romance writer Vonny Smith believes she will be able to woo her editor Diana through her writing.

1-59493-063-5 $13.95

PAID IN FULL by Ann Roberts. 200 pp. Ari Adams will need to choose between the debts of the past and the promise of a happy future.   1-59493-059-7 $13.95

ROMANCING THE ZONE by Kenna White. 272 pp. Liz's world begins to crumble when a secret from her past returns to Ashton.   1-59493-060-0 $13.95

SIGN ON THE LINE by Jaime Clevenger. 204 pp. Alexis Getty, a flirtatious delivery driver is committed to finding the rightful owner of a mysterious package.
1-59493-052-X $13.95

END OF WATCH by Clare Baxter. 256 pp. LAPD Lieutenant L.A Franco Frank follows the lone clue down the unlit steps of memory to a final, unthinkable resolution.
1-59493-064-4 $13.95

BEHIND THE PINE CURTAIN by Gerri Hill. 280 pp. Jacqueline returns home after her father's death and comes face-to-face with her first crush.
1-59493-057-0 $13.95

18TH & CASTRO by Karin Kallmaker. 200 pp. First-time couplings and couples who know how to mix lust and love make 18th & Castro the hottest address in the city by the bay.
1-59493-066-X $13.95

JUST THIS ONCE by KG MacGregor. 200 pp. Mindful of the obligations back home that she must honor, Wynne Connelly struggles to resist the fascination and allure that a particular woman she meets on her business trip represents.
1-59493-087-2 $13.95

ANTICIPATION by Terri Breneman. 240 pp. Two women struggle to remain professional as they work together to find a serial killer.
1-59493-055-4 $13.95

OBSESSION by Jackie Calhoun. 240 pp. Lindsey's life is turned upside down when Sarah comes into the family nursery in search of perennials.
1-59493-058-9 $13.95

BENEATH THE WILLOW by Kenna White. 240 pp. A torch that still burns brightly even after twenty-five years threatens to consume two childhood friends.
1-59493-053-8 $13.95

SISTER LOST, SISTER FOUND by Jeanne G'Fellers. 224 pp. The highly anticipated sequel to *No Sister of Mine.*
1-59493-056-2 $13.95

THE WEEKEND VISITOR by Jessica Thomas. 240 pp. In this latest Alex Peres mystery, Alex is asked to investigate an assault on a local woman but finds that her client may have more secrets than she lets on.
1-59493-054-6 $13.95

THE KILLING ROOM by Gerri Hill. 392 pp. How can two women forget and go their separate ways?
1-59493-050-3 $12.95

PASSIONATE KISSES by Megan Carter. 240 pp. Will two old friends run from love?
1-59493-051-1 $12.95

ALWAYS AND FOREVER by Lyn Denison. 224 pp. The girl next door turns Shannon's world upside down.
1-59493-049-X $12.95

BACK TALK by Saxon Bennett. 200 pp. Can a talk show host find love after heartbreak?
1-59493-028-7 $12.95

THE PERFECT VALENTINE: EROTIC LESBIAN VALENTINE STORIES edited by Barbara Johnson and Therese Szymanski—from Bella After Dark. 328 pp. Stories from the hottest writers around.
1-59493-061-9 $14.95

MURDER AT RANDOM by Claire McNab. 200 pp. The Sixth Denise Cleever Thriller. Denise realizes the fate of thousands is in her hands.
1-59493-047-3 $12.95

THE TIDES OF PASSION by Diana Tremain Braund. 240 pp. Will Susan be able to hold it all together and find the one woman who touches her soul?

1-59493-048-1 $12.95

JUST LIKE THAT by Karin Kallmaker. 240 pp. Disliking each other—and everything they stand for—even before they meet, Toni and Syrah find feelings can change, just like that. 1-59493-025-2 $12.95

WHEN FIRST WE PRACTICE by Therese Szymanski. 200 pp. Brett and Allie are once again caught in the middle of murder and intrigue.

1-59493-045-7 $12.95

REUNION by Jane Frances. 240 pp. Cathy Braithwaite seems to have it all: good looks, money and a thriving accounting practice . . . 1-59493-046-5 $12.95

BELL, BOOK & DYKE: NEW EXPLOITS OF MAGICAL LESBIANS by Kallmaker, Watts, Johnson and Szymanski. 360 pp. Reluctant witches, tempting spells and skyclad beauties—delve into the mysteries of love, lust and power in this quartet of novellas. 1-59493-023-6 $14.95

ARTIST'S DREAM by Gerri Hill. 320 pp. When Cassie meets Luke Winston, she can no longer deny her attraction to women . . . 1-59493-042-2 $12.95

NO EVIDENCE by Nancy Sanra. 240 pp. Private investigator Tally McGinnis once again returns to the horror-filled world of a serial killer.

1-59493-043-04 $12.95

WHEN LOVE FINDS A HOME by Megan Carter. 280 pp. What will it take for Anna and Rona to find their way back to each other again?

1-59493-041-4 $12.95

MEMORIES TO DIE FOR by Adrian Gold. 240 pp. Rachel attempts to avoid her attraction to the charms of Anna Sigurdson . . . 1-59493-038-4 $12.95

SILENT HEART by Claire McNab. 280 pp. Exotic lesbian romance.

1-59493-044-9 $12.95

MIDNIGHT RAIN by Peggy J. Herring. 240 pp. Bridget McBee is determined to find the woman who saved her life. 1-59493-021-X $12.95

THE MISSING PAGE A Brenda Strange Mystery by Patty G. Henderson. 240 pp. Brenda investigates her client's murder . . . 1-59493-004-X $12.95

WHISPERS ON THE WIND by Frankie J. Jones. 240 pp. Dixon thinks she and her best friend, Elizabeth Colter, would make the perfect couple . . .

1-59493-037-6 $12.95

CALL OF THE DARK: EROTIC LESBIAN TALES OF THE SUPERNATURAL edited by Therese Szymanski—from Bella After Dark. 320 pp.

1-59493-040-6 $14.95

A TIME TO CAST AWAY A Helen Black Mystery by Pat Welch. 240 pp. Helen stops by Alice's apartment—only to find the woman dead . . . 1-59493-036-8 $12.95

DESERT OF THE HEART by Jane Rule. 224 pp. The book that launched the most popular lesbian movie of all time is back. 1-1-59493-035-X $12.95

THE NEXT WORLD by Ursula Steck. 240 pp. Anna's friend Mido is threatened and eventually disappears . . . 1-59493-024-4 $12.95

CALL SHOTGUN by Jaime Clevenger. 240 pp. Kelly gets pulled back into the world of private investigation . . . 1-59493-016-3 $12.95

52 PICKUP by Bonnie J. Morris and E.B. Casey. 240 pp. 52 hot, romantic tales—one for every Saturday night of the year. 1-59493-026-0 $12.95

GOLD FEVER by Lyn Denison. 240 pp. Kate's first love, Ashley, returns to their home town, where Kate now lives . . . 1-1-59493-039-2 $12.95

RISKY INVESTMENT by Beth Moore. 240 pp. Lynn's best friend and roommate needs her to pretend Chris is his fiancé. But nothing is ever easy.
1-59493-019-8 $12.95

HUNTER'S WAY by Gerri Hill. 240 pp. Homicide detective Tori Hunter is forced to team up with the hot-tempered Samantha Kennedy. 1-59493-018-X $12.95

CAR POOL by Karin Kallmaker. 240 pp. Soft shoulders, merging traffic and slippery when wet . . . Anthea and Shay find love in the car pool.
1-59493-013-9 $12.95

NO SISTER OF MINE by Jeanne G'Fellers. 240 pp. Telepathic women fight to coexist with a patriarchal society that wishes their eradication. 1-59493-017-1 $12.95

ON THE WINGS OF LOVE by Megan Carter. 240 pp. Stacie's reporting career is on the rocks. She has to interview bestselling author Cheryl, or else!
1-59493-027-9 $12.95

WICKED GOOD TIME by Diana Tremain Braund. 224 pp. Does Christina need Miki as a protector . . . or want her as a lover? 1-59493-031-7 $12.95

THOSE WHO WAIT by Peggy J. Herring. 240 pp. Two brilliant sisters—in love with the same woman! 1-59493-032-5 $12.95

ABBY'S PASSION by Jackie Calhoun. 240 pp. Abby's bipolar sister helps turn her world upside down, so she must decide what's most important. 1-59493-014-7 $12.95

PICTURE PERFECT by Jane Vollbrecht. 240 pp. Kate is reintroduced to Casey, the daughter of an old friend. Can they withstand Kate's career?
1-59493-015-5 $12.95

PAPERBACK ROMANCE by Karin Kallmaker. 240 pp. Carolyn falls for tall, dark and . . . female . . . in this classic lesbian romance. 1-59493-033-3 $12.95

DAWN OF CHANGE by Gerri Hill. 240 pp. Susan ran away to find peace in remote Kings Canyon—then she met Shawn . . . 1-59493-011-2 $12.95

DOWN THE RABBIT HOLE by Lynne Jamneck. 240 pp. Is a killer holding a grudge against FBI Agent Samantha Skellar? 1-59493-012-0 $12.95

SEASONS OF THE HEART by Jackie Calhoun. 240 pp. Overwhelmed, Sara saw only one way out—leaving . . . 1-59493-030-9 $12.95

TURNING THE TABLES by Jessica Thomas. 240 pp. The 2nd Alex Peres Mystery. *From ghosties and ghoulies and long leggity beasties . . .* 1-59493-009-0 $12.95